JONATHAN CHATEAU

# The Sprawling

HALF WING PRESS

First published by Half Wing Press 2021

This novel is entirely a work of fiction. The names, characters and incidents portrayed in it are the work of the author's imagination. Any resemblance to actual persons, living or dead, events or localities is entirely coincidental.

Jonathan Chateau has no responsibility for the persistence or accuracy of URLs for external or third-party Internet Websites referred to in this publication and does not guarantee that any content on such Websites is, or will remain, accurate or appropriate.

Designations used by companies to distinguish their products are often claimed as trademarks. All brand names and product names used in this book and on its cover are trade names, service marks, trademarks and registered trademarks of their respective owners. The publishers and the book are not associated with any product or vendor mentioned in this book. None of the companies referenced within the book have endorsed the book.

First edition

ISBN: 978-0-9988504-9-8

Editing by Serena Fisher
Cover art by Jonathan Chateau

This book was professionally typeset on Reedsy.
Find out more at reedsy.com

*Thank you to the following people who helped me survive 2020:*
*Mom, Serena, Manny & Tony.*

*And to Sage... whoever you are.*
*Wherever you are.*
*Thanks for taking my call.*

"Viewed narrowly, all life is universal hunger and an expression of energy associated with it."

— Mary Ritter Beard

"Be yourself, don't take anything from anyone, and never let them take you alive."
— Gerard Way

# Contents

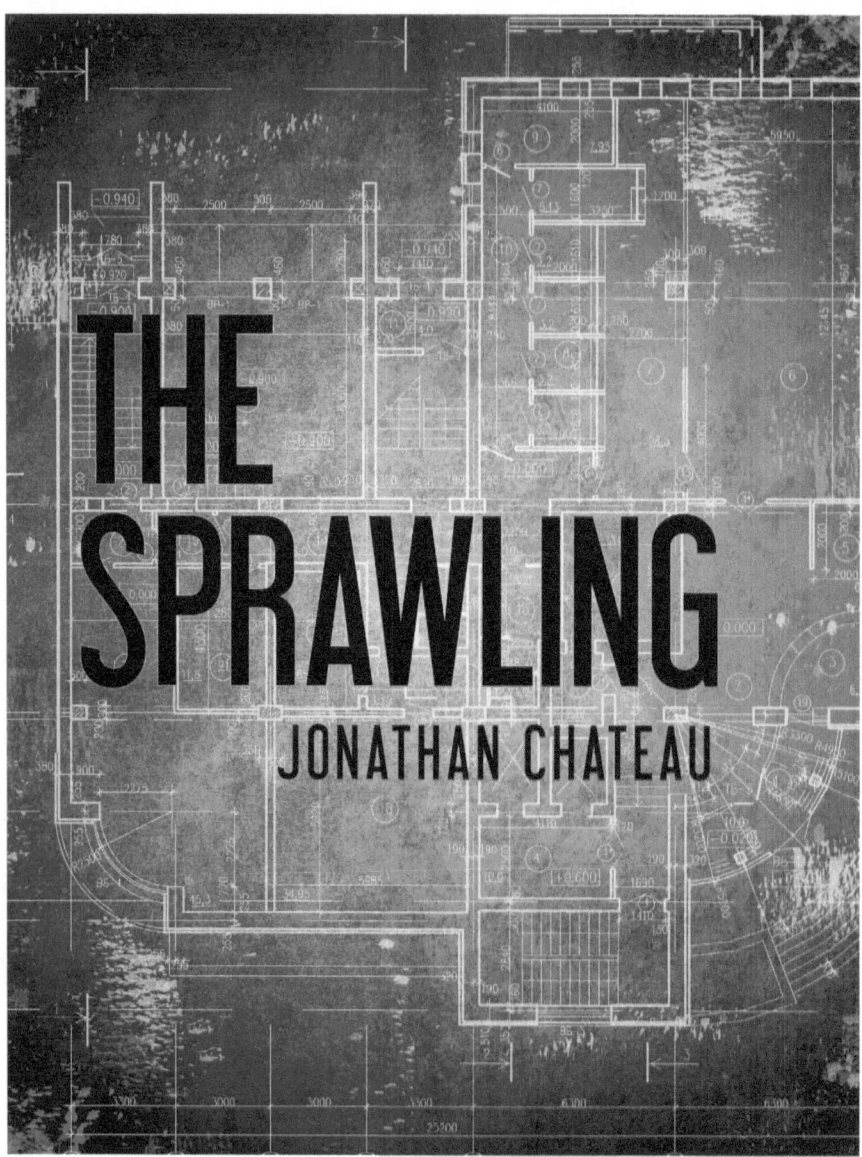

# THE SPRAWLING

## JONATHAN CHATEAU

## Books by Jonathan Chateau

The Sprawling

The Death Wish Game

Nightmares in Analog

Energy Drink

The Saltwater Marathon

Video is Dead

**The Travis Rail Series**

Faith Against the Wolves (Book 1)

Faith Against the Angels (Book 2)

**NEVER MISS A BOOK!**

Join **Jonathan Chateau's** mailing list for updates on new releases, giveaways and free book promotions on Amazon & Audible.

(Only a few emails sent out per year. You can unsubscribe at any time.)

Click or visit the link below to sign up!

-» CLICK HERE TO SIGN UP «-

Or visit JChateau.com to join the list.

# Chapter 1 – Only On Paper

The job opening for SiDug Tech looks like it might be the best job Zander has ever had.

At least on paper.

The position offers him:

A new boss—Mr. Gudu—who, so far, seems respectable and laissez-faire.

A flexible work schedule—Zander can work however much he wants and whenever he wants.

The ability to work from home.

And double the hourly rate of what local and national IT firms are paying.

When Zander arrives at SiDug headquarters in downtown Tampa to touch base with Mr. Gudu, he is immediately impressed by the grandiose building before him. It is a brand-new office with dark slate windows, buttressed with slabs of marble that run vertically along its columns. Attached to the building is a parking garage with ample parking—something of a commodity within the city. At first glance, it is clear to Zander that no expense was spared in erecting this fourteen-story office structure in the middle of a rather unkempt area of the city's slowly gentrifying warehouse district. It stands close to Ybor City—a renowned entertainment district where the promise of a good time, sponsored in part by booze and sweaty nightclubs, ultimately leads to twenty-something-year-olds puking into gutters that habitually flood at the first sign of lightning.

Still, beyond those party-going streets, tucked amongst the unloved and dilapidated buildings that surround it, this rather ambitious, yet somewhat menacing, skyscraper stands out like a well-polished onyx monolith. The tower is emblazoned with bold blood-red letters, proudly bearing the name SiDug Tech, and is crowned with an ominous spire that disappears into the louring September sky above.

Zander rolls the name around in his head: *SiDug*

He is not even sure how to pronounce it.

*See-Dug?*

*Sy-Dug?*

*Sih-Dug?*

*Whatever. It could be called Shit-Dug, for all I care,* he thinks. *They had me at 'hello' with my salary.*

His position will be composed mostly of tier-one tech assignments. Printer drivers. Windows updates. Software installations. Virus removal. Basic issues that can be handled remotely via the magic of the internet, or in rare cases, over the phone.

Zander walks through the enormous glass doors and enters the main entrance hallway. He is struck with two marked scents: one is floral, soapy, almost April-fresh. The other is barely detectable, yet present.

The smell of rot—

"Mr. Lyle!" A very exuberant Mr. Gudu bursts into the hallway from out of thin air, arms extended as if he wants to hug Zander. Voice booming through the mostly empty space, bounding off the walls with the ferocity of a racquetball. "It is great to see you. So excited to have you on our team!" He closes the distance, greeting Zander in a hurried, almost purposely distracting manner as if trying to prevent Zander from studying his surroundings too much.

"Glad to be here," Zander replies as they shake hands. Mr. Gudu's grip is uncomfortably firm, to the point of almost squeezing too hard, but Zander does his best to hide his discomfort. "And you can just call me Zander, by the way."

"Right. Right. Well... welcome aboard, *Zander*," Mr. Gudu says as he breaks away from the awkward greeting. Appearance-wise, he looks like a fifty-something Clark Kent. A square head, an impeccably manicured, pomade fresh hairdo, and the physique of a bodybuilder.

Mr. Gudu guides Zander to his office. Maybe just *an* office, as it lacks any sort of personality. No pictures of kids and significant others. No reminders plastered everywhere. No trinkets or collectables of any kind.

Not even a nameplate.

The office is something out of a car dealership or an interrogation room. Sparse. Economical. Two basic leather office chairs. The lifeless stock desk found everywhere. Lukewarm gray walls. A safe, yet banal, Berber brown carpet. Not a lick of character.

Continuing to distract Zander from eyeing his surroundings, Mr. Gudu starts the conversation off lamenting about topics such as the last Star Wars film, how rock music isn't what it used to be in the nineties and early two-thousands, and where he thinks the NASDAQ is headed next quarter.

Zander takes this all in, going along with his new boss's ramblings like the agreeable employee dance partner he is pretending to be.

*Talk about whatever you want,* Zander thinks. *So long as I'm getting paid for this.*

Mr. Gudu halts his monologue. Inserting an uneasy laugh, he remarks, "I did mention that I've already put you on payroll, right?"

Buried within the avalanche of Mr. Gudu's emails, voicemails, and texts, Zander assumes so, and nods appropriately.

"Ok, good." Mr. Gudu shakes his head, bemused with his own antics. "I tend to multitask myself into oblivion. I get a lot of stuff done, but not all of it to completion. Just want to make sure you know that you're getting compensated—starting today."

Zander nods again. At first, there is a feeling of relief knowing he will not get screwed over financially. He had one IT firm do that in the past by paying him with bounced checks.

However, this sense of relief is promptly washed away by an unnerving question:

*Did this guy just read my mind—*

"But before you get too excited about working for us," Mr. Gudu dives in again, breaking Zander's thought train, "I must reiterate that you'll need to need to complete the one-week training course."

Zander recalls seeing something like that mentioned within one of Mr. Gudu's communications.

"Will that be an issue?" Mr. Gudu asks.

"Of course not."

"Great. Because we need reliable people. Not flakes. Nor do we sympathize with *that* entitled work ethic that seems to be prevalent this century. I don't know how this world even functions with such an apathetic labor force. No love for their work, you know?" Mr. Gudu clears his throat suddenly, as if to shift gears conversationally. "Anyway, I'm not worried with you. You have a significant work history. Given your experience, you'll breeze through this position in no time. Obviously, I know all of this, because I've reviewed your Indeed profile... you've no doubt checked us out as well."

Zander had not.

SiDug Tech was one of many places he shot-gunned his resume to. Even once he locked in an interview with Mr. Gudu, he had not bothered to thoroughly research them. In his experience, there had been too many other companies he had interviewed with that went nowhere. His rationale was *Why waste time researching a company unless it was going to land me a job?*

But Zander plays along with, "Oh, definitely," not letting on that he never really bothered to check out Mr. Gudu and his mega-tech firm. SiDug was just one of many prospects. One of many online applications, emails, and random websites he'd gone fishing in just to land a new job. "I know that SiDug Tech is leaps ahead of the other IT companies in the Bay area. Renowned for delivering great customer service," Zander throws this line out and winces inside.

*Customer service*—the millennial buzzword that all managers love to hear.

Mr. Gudu bites and confirms, "Indeed. SiDug Tech is all about ensuring our customers get the best technical help possible. I'm sure you read the rave reviews from our clients reinforcing that?"

"I did," Zander lies. "So many great reviews. And I can't wait to contribute."

"Neither can we," Mr. Gudu adds with a wide grin.

The conversation moves along, but Zander counts at least three more times that the topics of punctuality and reliability come up. It's sprinkled in between other discussions regarding video games, high-end coffee machines, and a lengthy digression into Mr. Gudu's fervent love of all things sushi.

"There's something about the raw nature of it," Mr. Gudu explains with an expression that lights up his face like a kid bearing down on his presents Christmas morning. "The texture. The way the meat seems to liquify in your mouth. It's truly an exhilarating experience."

To Zander, Mr. Gudu makes it sound like eating raw fish is better than sex.

"I'm sure you've already noticed this about me, but once you get me talking–especially about myself–I'm like a boulder barreling downhill," Mr. Gudu admits with a thwap of his massive hand on the desk.

"It's totally cool," Zander says while musing *You can talk about fish, football, or the weather for all I care. I'm just happy to be getting paid good money.* "I've been told I'm a skilled listener by many of my former help-desk clients."

*A good listener? No, you're not,* a stray voice inside Zander's head chimes in. *That's why Vicky left you the first time for that piece-of-shit 'best friend' of yours. Because you don't listen! Why would you? You're a selfish ass. Be real with yourself for once!*

*She was right to leave you!*

Zander stiffens. His body goes cold. He tries to shake off the discomfort brought on by the painful truth his subconscious is throwing at him.

"Zander?" Apparently, the break in his demeanor unfortunately gets noticed by Mr. Gudu, who asks with a tone that is a little less game-show and a little more talk-show, "You ok, there?"

"Oh... oh, I'm fine." He places his palm against his temple, feigning a headache. "Just feel a migraine coming on. That's all."

"Hmm. That reminds me," Mr. Gudu presses a pensive finger against his lips, tapping it as he thinks, "Did I mention our twenty percent matching 401K during the interview? Or our healthcare package?"

"Actually, no."

"One hundred percent coverage."

"Seriously?"

"Yes. As in, not a penny out of your pocket. You and your significant other will have fully covered medical, dental, and vision. As well as free fitness memberships and monthly massage privileges at several of our partnering spas." There's a smarmy grin on Mr. Gudu's face as he prods, "Judging by that look on your face, you're thinking that this is too good to be true?"

"Kinda. Yeah."

"Well, then let me ask you this: why do you think the CEOs of our competitors all have luxury boats and sprawling mansions that hug the interior of Tampa Bay?" He pauses. Then presses, "You know what I'm talking about, Zander. You've worked for them."

"Course I have. Many of them."

"Right. And those guys can afford those frills because they pay lousy and skimp on benefits. So, it's not that SiDug is too good to be true. It's that our competitors are too selfish to be viable." Mr. Gudu folds his hands neatly as he leans in. "We actually care about our people. We recognize our employees are the source, the energy, the fuel that keeps SiDug growing and becoming the powerhouse that it is today."

Mr. Gudu's voice seems to trail off as Zander thinks *Vicky is gonna freak when I tell her how much I'm making.*

He thinks about how he and Vicky could get the hell out of that armpit of an apartment, the one overloaded with termites since the all-wood South Tampa dump was built in the seventies and never renovated. Nor was it ever treated for those subterranean nightmares. The only thing the landlord prioritized was raising the rent every year.

He thinks about the engagement ring he has been eyeing at this posh jewelry store in the mall—one adorned with a diamond the size of a peanut. With his old jobs, he'd be looking at over nine months' salary to afford that one.

Not now.

Not with this new position at SiDug.

He could afford that ring in two months, tops.

"Well, I'm grateful you chose me and super excited to be a part of the company," Zander declares, grinning ear-to-ear at the possibilities. "When do I officially start?"

"I've got a group beginning their training on..." Mr. Gudu swivels in his chair to check his computer, "Monday. That work?"

"That works."

"Excellent! And the crew you will train with are good people like yourself. Eager. Hungry. Committed. You'll all be taking over the spots from the old team."

"The old team–"

"Promoted." Mr. Gudu responds without so much as a flinch. "You were going to ask what happened to them, right?"

"Y-yeah."

"They worked tier-one for less than a year, and boom! We moved them on up. They're all permanently working from home, or from Fiji, or wherever they want, making six figures."

Zander flinches at that last part.

"Yes, Zander. Six figures." With a wink he adds, "And they're making that in under forty hours a week. Talk about some serious work-life balance, huh?"

For just a moment, every hair on Zander's body speaks to him. Screaming again that this is all too good to be true. But Zander argues internally. Pushing away the sudden emotions with logic:

*Could twice the pay seem so implausible? Tech companies were blowing up financially all the time.*

And Mr. Gudu was right–the CEO's of these firms were buying themselves yachts, small islands, and whatever the hell they could *because* they could.

Because they cut corners.

Because they paid their employees like crap.

As if sensing the vacillation of Zander's emotions, the suave-haired Mr. Gudu spins his monitor around, displaying multiple professional and human resource websites. Scrolls through them. Rattles on about the company's reputation. Reassures him with ardent reviews of SiDug on Indeed, Glassdoor, and all the other relevant hiring sites.

"Just look for yourself, Zander. I know you did the research. Our employees' reviews speak for themselves. We have a turnover rate that's close to zero. Our IT positions are as coveted as Apple, Facebook, and Google. Let me ask you something," Mr. Gudu leans forward, brow furrowing upwards, voice lowered as if about to tell a secret, "have you ever lost your keys?"

The question catches Zander by surprise.

Mr. Gudu raises an eyebrow, awaiting his response.

"Yeah," Zander replies with a shrug. "Of course. Who hasn't?"

"Ok, and once you found them... what did you do?"

Zander mulls it over, not sure what the right answer is, or at least what answer Mr. Gudu is looking for. "I don't know. I stopped looking?"

"Exactly! Once you found your keys, you stopped looking. Then," Mr. Gudu closes the gap between them and asks, "why continue to look elsewhere for your future? Your future is with SiDug. I've already hired you. Why the sudden reservation? You're not taking a position with that mom & pop outfit in Ybor City, are you?"

"What?" Zander recoils. "No, sir. Not at all."

"Then you're still interested?"

"Of course!"

"Perfect!" Mr. Gudu extends his hand. Zander shakes it but is rewarded with that unnecessarily uncomfortable squeeze. Mr. Gudu continues to shake it for just a beat longer. "All you have to do is give me your word that you'll work hard during the training and give it your all. Do whatever it takes to get the training finished."

"I promise you, Mr. Gudu," Zander responds, "I'll be there bright and early this Monday."

Zander couldn't have been more ecstatic to share the news with Vicky. He hadn't initially told her he'd gotten the job. Not until he talked a little further with Mr. Gudu to make sure this wasn't some kind of scam. Indeed, today's meeting assured him that this was the opportunity of a lifetime.

All the talk about sushi inspires Zander to take Vicky out to the most expensive sushi bar they can find. They dine on sashimi, pound sake, and talk of moving plans–finding peace away from the flying insects that spawn at night. At one point, their celebrating seizes the reluctant attention of their server, who asks that Zander calm down.

She tells him he's freaking out other guests.

*Freaking out,* he thinks. *We're celebrating here! What's wrong with this lady?*

The server then says something that strikes him as completely odd. "I don't know where you're hiding your cell phone, but could you take your invisible conversation outside?"

Zander and Vicky share a baffled look. Resigned to lowering his voice, he leans close to her, commenting, barely audible, that the server is just jealous and that soon he'll be making enough to move them to a better neighborhood where:

"We'll find a better sushi bar!"

Moments later they're kicked out, snickering and exulting over how they got banned from a sushi place for being, as they saw it, *too happy.*

*Whatever,* he thinks. *One more place to never return to in this old life. Monday starts the reboot!*

This is going to be the best job opportunity ever for Zander.

But only on paper.

# Chapter 2–The First Monday

**M**r. Gudu has the hands of a giant.

"Zander!" He exclaims as he greets Zander with a welcoming smile and that token bone-crunching handshake of his. "Good to see you!"

"Same," Zander says as he thinks, *Though I wish you'd stop crushing my hand.* "Monday couldn't come quickly enough. I was so eager to start, I had a rough time falling asleep."

"Well, I'm glad to hear that you're excited... and thanks for coming on time."

"Of course." *You only told me a million times!*

"I've already had several people no-show," Mr. Gudu admits with a shake of his head, in a *tsk-tsk* manner. "And two fine candidates cannot get here on time. They called in, informing me that traffic was bad and that they'd be late." With a dismissive wave, he continues, "But I told them don't bother. I only want committed folks working for us. Folks like yourself. You're going to fit right in." This is followed by several hearty slaps to Zander's back. "By the way, love the tie."

Zander had chosen a cornflower blue tie. Subtle chic, yet professional. Most of the time he just sported polos in past positions.

However, this is week one.

This is training.

Once he was working from home, he could default to polos, hoodies, or his birthday suit. For now, it was professional attire all the way.

"Thanks," Zander says. "My girlfriend has this thing about the color blue—"

"Tell me later." Mr. Gudu cuts him off as he gestures towards the hallway. "I want to introduce you to your coworkers. Save the stories for then. Deal?"

Zander nods.

Over the weekend, Zander had mentioned to Vicky that there was a certain unease he got when he interacted with Mr. Gudu. It was almost as if his words, his gestures, they were all communicating something fake. Like there was another layer, an energy underneath all that showmanship crap that was Mr. Gudu's true intent.

Zander's body communicated this disquietude by giving him goosebumps, sending a prickly sensation all over his skin.

Vicky told him to brush it off.

To go with it.

"It's not like you'll be working in that office anyway. You'll rarely have to see him," she had reminded Zander. "So, suck it up, babe. Deal with his weird bullshit, do the training, and then you'll be working from home making the best money you've ever made."

*His weird bullshit.* Zander ruminated on that phrase. *What is it about his weird bull—*

As if reading his thoughts, Mr. Gudu blurts out, "Mr. Lyle. Follow me. I want you to meet the rest of the crew."

Zander hadn't realized that he had stopped walking. Trailed behind Mr. Gudu to the point of staring off into space. "Oh. Sorry. I... I uh—"

"Didn't get enough sleep." Mr. Gudu gives Zander that head coach style pat on the back. "It's alright. Just keep up with me, ok?"

"Yeah, sure."

Mr. Gudu marches through a series of narrow hallways decorated by someone with a very sterile sense of staging. Varying shades of a sanitarium inspired taupe cover the walls. Brushed aluminum sconces hung like inverted waffle cones placed every six feet cast clean white circles onto a slate-gray tiled floor. Between the fixtures are polished platinum picture frames. Most of them are oddly... empty. One of them catches Zander's eye as he passes, and he stops short. There's a silver nameplate affixed just below the frame:

EMPLOYEE OF THE MONTH

Above that is a picture of a man with his back to the camera. Arms are up at his side as if he's holding something.

"Mr. Lyle?"

Zander turns and sees Mr. Gudu at the end of the hall, glaring at him.

"Are you with me, son?" he asks, one eyebrow raised.

Zander nods. Gives the odd picture a second glance to find that the man is facing him with eyes as black as oil stains, mouth slung open, dangling a snakelike tongue the color of charcoal. He's holding a certificate with only one word on it:

FEED

Mr. Gudu is right behind him. "I need you to keep up with me."

Zander whirls around. Mr. Gudu is standing there, arms folded. "We've got a lot of ground to cover today," he tells Zander. "If you want a tour, we can schedule that later. Ok?"

Zander shakes the image. Forces a smile. "Sure. Sounds good."

"Alright then," Mr. Gudu confirms as he takes off, "this way." His steps quicken and the scent of his cologne wafts into Zander's nose masking an underlying odor of...

*Raw meat?* Zander wonders as he brushes aside the stench.

Yet there is no ignoring it.

It is there.

Clinging in the air like a microwaved lunch experiment gone horribly wrong. In fact, as Zander weaves through the hallways, he notices people busily zigzagging from one office to the next with hurried steps, stacks of papers in hands. Some nod as they pass. Some stare with an ominous yet conspicuous look. Some greet with empty gazes. A cold sensation wrenches inside him−

"You ok?"

Zander shakes his head. "Just..."

*Just what?*

"Just thought I might have left the toaster on." A nervous, light chuckle follows.

Mr. Gudu rests his hands on his hips. "Are you ready for this, Mr. Lyle?"

Zander's stomach lurches. He does not want to blow this gig. Vicky would be so upset–but he would be *more* upset at himself. "Yes... I'm... sorry..."

Mr. Gudu narrows his eyes. Then turns abruptly, continuing on.

They reach an elevator, then Mr. Gudu leads Zander into the second-floor office. Inside is an expansive room inhabited by a labyrinth of cubicles populated by employees with poor posture. They sit hunched forward at their desks, typing with maddening speed, yapping incoherently into their headsets.

Mr. Gudu charges along the outer perimeter of the cubicles. As Zander follows, he eyes his new boss. The man takes great strides, shoulders back. He moves with the precision of a well-calibrated machine. Everything about the man is perfect: his crisp white shirt is wrinkle-free, fitted, tailored, and tucked with military exactitude into his coal black slacks. The glimmer of the LED bulbs above reflects off every angle of his polished ebony shoes.

*Military,* Zander thinks. *Dude must've been in the military.*

They round a corner into a large conference room. It's windowless. Sparse aside from a long oval table. Seated at it are six other employees. *The new hire team,* Zander surmises. They've all got name tags. Behind them is a whiteboard with the following words written in red marker:

*The World is your Oyster.*

*Let SiDug be the sword,*

*To get you that pearl.*

Mr. Gudu gestures for Zander to take an open seat next to an older gentleman wearing a badge that displays the name Bishop. The man has hardly any hair on the crown of his balding head, but what few gray strands he has are carefully combed over. He is in his mid-to-late sixties, not quite the septuagenarian yet, boasting a stocky physique that even the late Jack LaLanne would approve of. Along his bulky forearms are a random series of faded traditional American tattoos. Nautical symbols. Sugar skulls. Voluptuous mermaids.

*Great,* Zander thinks. *Popeye is training with us. Hope he knows how to turn on a PC.*

Mr. Gudu closes the door behind him. Opens his arms as he heartily exclaims, "Welcome to SiDug! You've all been carefully screened and selected."

Zander glances over at Bishop briefly. *Guess Popeye knows where the ON button is, after all.*

Mr. Gudu continues, "Trust me when I say that we were bombarded with candidates, but we are very selective in our approach. You all have either the professional qualifications, technical background, or both to have been chosen."

Everyone trades looks with one another. Approving nods and timid smiles are exchanged by some employees. Zander doesn't bother looking at the others, though he feels Bishop eyeing him.

"Now before I rattle on about the training," Mr. Gudu proceeds, "I'd like you guys to take a moment to get the introductions out of the way. Your training is only a week long, so don't get too attached." He laughs uneasily and informs them, "This will be the only time you guys actually work together in person."

One employee, a frumpy, tall drink of water wearing a nametag that reads *Wayne*, belts out, "Not a problem." He has a puffy, unkempt pompadour that swirls across the crown of his head like a haphazard dollop of soft serve ice cream. There are residual food stains on his wrinkled shirt from whatever he scarfed down for breakfast. "Not about to make friends here. Last person I got attached to took half my savings and my bulldog!" This is followed by a nervous laugh that no one joins in on.

"Anyway," Mr. Gudu remarks as he takes out his cell phone and sets a timer, "hate to be this formal, but we are on a tight schedule. I'll give you all about fifteen minutes to go around and introduce yourselves. In the meantime, I'm going to make a fresh pot of coffee." He surveys the room. "Anyone want a cup?"

Most say no.

Wayne holds up a finger. "I'd love one."

Mr. Gudu stares Wayne down for a beat. Then he exits the room, throwing his hand in the air, adding, "Carry on. Be back shortly."

The introductions go quickly.

A young woman named Kate goes first. Brunette. Barely eighteen. Freckles all over her face. She wears prescription glasses two sizes too big for her petite nose. She tells everyone she's an introvert and is grateful for this opportunity. She admits that she's an avid movie buff, loves cats, and left the retail industry selling trendy home décor for a career in IT.

Mike is next. African-American. Big guy. He'd give Mr. Gudu a run for his money. Built like an ex-NFL superstar, but is a former construction worker that wanted to try something different. Something that required more brains than brawn. Although he'd always had more of a knack for working with his hands, he figured why not try working with computers? Construction had been taking a toll on his body and his health. The stress on his joints. The long, grueling hours. The crooked contractors and bounced checks. It was too much. He longed for stability and purpose in his life.

And this job with SiDug seemed to promise that.

Bishop is next in line. Doesn't volunteer much in the way of his background other than he's been on his own for a long time and is ready to help people, and he believes that this position offers him the chance to do that. He's tinkered with computers since the early eighties. His first PC was an old Commodore 64. He pauses midway through his intro, as if to say something else, but turns to–

Kyle. Looks like he's straight out of high school. Just turned twenty-one with a face full of zits and a fresh set of braces. Claims he's been hunched in front of a computer and an Xbox since he was in diapers. He hides most of his face under a hoodie. What little of his wrists and neck are exposed reveals an extensive network of tattoos. He clutches an energy drink as if his life-force depends upon it. He seems equally uneasy and reluctant to talk, and this interaction is further cut short by–

"Wayne Sulkie." When Wayne opens his mouth, he reveals a set of rotten teeth that only a meth loving mother would adore. "Yep, yep. Let's get it out of the way. My last name sucks. I know, I know." Insert cringe-worthy laugh. "But while the jerks in grade school gave me hell, those dudes eat crow now. Because *now*, I make the money they wish they could." He sticks a thumb against his chest as he makes his point. "This man right here always makes it happen."

Mike leans back in his chair and chuckles, bemused. "Are you for real, dude?"

"Affirmative," Wayne replies with an animated nod. "I always get what I want. My father always told me to make something of myself, and that's exactly what I plan on doing!"

"How's that working out?" Kate asks, as she leans forward and covers the growing smile on her face.

"Well... now that I'm with SiDug... it's working out pretty spiffy."

"That's amazing, Wayne," Kate retorts, rolling her eyes but making it completely obvious. "Please. Tell us more about yourself and how amazing you are."

"Gladly! I—"

"I was being sarcastic. Besides, I'm sure our fifteen minutes are almost up." Kate and the others look to Zander.

"Right." Zander quickly mulls over what he wants to say. Then informs the group, "Well, I've actually been doing IT for a bit. I'm technically a tier-two help desk agent, but I was totally fine coming back in at tier-one, given the opportunity with this company." Zander's eyes search the floor, not wanting to be on the spot like this, but with a sigh he carries on, "IT was a career change as well. I used to bartend. Late nights. Too many drunks. But the one thing it brought me was a beautiful woman. My best friend."

"Aww." Wayne makes a face as if someone in the room passed gas. He trades glances with the others, but everyone ignores him. "That sounds... sweet."

Zander shoots him a look, then continues. "I almost left IT after working for a firm that treated its employees like second-class citizens. Expendable. Condescending as hell. Then I found SiDug. So... here I am."

"Well, it's great to meet all of you," Bishop declares. "Truth be told, I had a rough time sleeping last night. I was so excited to get to work this morning."

"Yeah," Kyle lowers his head, hiding his face under his hoodie even more so as he agrees. "Well, I slept like crap too."

"Same," Zander adds flatly.

"Good," Bishop says as he shakes his head. "Glad we're all excited to be here then–"

"I didn't say I was excited." Kyle perks up as if his name was called and tells them, "Had me a panic attack. This job got me shook."

Mike points at the energy drink. "Maybe you ought to cut down on that Monster garbage."

"It ain't Monster. It's RECRÜT."

Mike throws his arms up in surrender. "Ok, whatever it is."

"And it ain't the drink, dude. I could pound ten of these and they wouldn't make me feel the way I did last night." Kyle surveys the corners of the room as if looking for something. Cameras. A false window. Something. Then he turns back to the group and confesses, "It's this... strange feeling, man. I can't shake it. Like this job offer is too perfect. Like they're going to knock us out and take our kidneys or sell us as sex slaves or something." He puts his hands to his head as if to suppress it from splitting open. "I mean, last night... I had nightmares about–"

"Whoa, whoa, whoa, kid!" Wayne holds up a hand to halt the onslaught. "Calm down. You're creeping me out."

"It's just first job jitters," Kate says in Kyle's defense. "Cut him some slack."

"I've never had first job jitters like that. Sex slaves? Kidneys?" Wayne scoffs. "I'm with Mike. That's all those artificial ingredients in that drink of yours. You're going to wreck your kidneys if you keep drinking those."

On some level, Zander relates. A coil of anxiety springs inside him. On paper, everything sounds good. But he can't shake it.

"It's not the drink! And I ain't crazy, alright?!" Spittle flies from Kyle's mouth as he exclaims, "I-I know something is wrong about this place, and while I can't put my finger on it, I'm not sure I'm going to stick around to find out."

"But nothing's happened, man," Mike reassures him, his tone calm. "We just got here."

"Yeah. Yeah. Nothing's happened... yet!" Kyle trembles. The empty soda can rattles unnervingly in his hand.

"Well, if you feel that strongly," Wayne advises as he points to the door. "Just leave—"

"Will you guys shut up?" Kate turns to Kyle and asks, "You want me to grab you a bottled water or something?"

Kyle shakes in his chair. Rapidly taps his foot and nods his head. He responds, "Nah. I think I'm going to bounce."

"Look, Mr. Gudu is coming right back," Bishop says. "Maybe you can just talk with him before we start the training. I mean, I get it. You're a young guy. First actual job. It's a lot—"

Kyle bolts up out of his chair, and it goes flying backwards. "You guys don't get it! It ain't my age. Something has been eating me up all night, and it ain't the taurine and caffeine, bro." And with that, he flings the empty can against the wall and makes for the door. "I gotta go. I'm sorry if I seem crazy, ok, but whatever."

Kyle gets to the door. Gives it a violent crank. Pauses. He jiggles it furiously several more times. Hearing the others get out of their seats, he desperately shakes the doorknob, but nothing happens.

"What?" Bishop asks. "You ok?"

Kyle spins around to face the group, putting his back flat against the door. He stares at everyone, all of them eyeing him as if he were a rat trying to escape a maze that somehow ended up backed into a corner. He faces the door, once more jiggling the handle with the strength of an insane man on his last inkling of sanity.

"Hey, calm down," Mike tells him.

Kyle spins back around, facing them and demands, "Calm down?" His skin is the color of bleached bone. "I can't calm down!"

"Why not?" Mike asks.

"Because the door's locked, that's why." Another burst of spittle flies from Kyle's mouth as he announces, "He fucking locked us in here!"

And that's when the lights go out.

# Chapter 3–Conference Room Blues

The employees are only sitting in the dark for a mere moment, about to turn on the lights from their cell phones, when one of the LED strips above comes on, barely illuminating the room.

"What the hell's going on?" There's venom in Wayne's voice as he directs his question at Kyle. "Did you lock us in here?"

"Yeah, you figured me out. I magically locked the door from where I was sitting!"

"Kyle, stop playing," Mike interjects. "This ain't funny."

"I'm not playing. Look," Kyle jiggles the handle to make the point. "It. Is. Locked!" He gestures with his hand as if modeling the door's hardware. "And look... no keyhole. So, no. I didn't lock us in here, ok?"

Wayne huffs, frustrated. He approaches the door. "Move." He presses his face into the thin opening along the doorframe like a dog trying to push his way into the next room using his nose. His voice is muffled as he shouts into the crack, "Mr. Gudu! Hey! Mr. Gudu?" He pauses as if awaiting an answer. "Hey, the door's locked!"

No response.

"Hello? Is anyone–" Bishop lays a hand on Wayne's shoulder and Wayne jumps. "The heck?"

Bishop tells him calmly, "He's obviously not responding."

"Well, I had to try." Wayne shakes Bishop loose. "I'll just call Mr. Gudu." He pulls out his cell phone, goes to dial, then sighs with frustration. "Of course. No signal. That's what I get for signing up for a budget plan!" He glances to the others. "Anyone else got signal?"

The others check.

"Nope," Mike says.

Then Kate, "Me either."

"I got a burner phone," Kyle admits. "I got shit for service."

"Burner phone?" Wayne laughs incredulously. "What... are you a drug dealer or something?"

Kyle says nothing. Tries the door again as if something could have possibly changed in the last few minutes, but unfortunately it is still locked.

"I'll take that as a yes." Wayne turns to Bishop. "How about your Jitterbug? You got service?" He laughs to himself. "Wait... does a Jitterbug even get signal? Let alone calls?"

Bishop looks to the group. "What the devil's a Jitterbug?"

Kyle mutters, "A phone... for old folks."

Bishop breaks out into a hearty laugh—one that nearly turns into a cough.

"What's so funny?" Wayne asks.

"You, Wayne. You're a funny guy," Bishop says as he clears his throat and settles down. "Yes, I have a phone. However, if you want to see what I can do with two paper cups and a string, I'll be glad to show you."

Wayne rolls his eyes, though no one catches it.

The LED light above cuts off, earning frightened yelps out of some of the group.

"It's all good, people," Mike assures everyone. "Just turn on your flashlights."

Several bright white beams of light spill onto the tables, chairs, and conference room walls. They converge on the door. Mike grips the door handle, gives it several solid shakes. Still locked. He curses under his breath, then motions for everyone to back up. He raises his right leg and kicks the door as hard as he can.

Nothing.

Mike tries again, driving his heel into the door. The doorframe and the surrounding wall rattles, but the door doesn't give. He tries several more times, but to no avail. Taxed from the effort, he says breathlessly, "We gotta look for another way out."

"Or we could just wait?" Wayne suggests.

"You can." Mike wipes the fresh beads of sweat from his brow. "I think I'm with Kyle. I ain't sticking around here. This is crazy-ass nonsense. Locking us in a room like this. No thanks."

"Maybe it was an accident?" Wayne offers. "I mean, doors are unintentionally locked all the time."

"Unintentionally? And followed by power outages? No way," Mike argues.

"It's a new building from what I understand. Stuff like that is common in new construction," Wayne insists.

"Ok then, Mr. Architect," Kate jumps in, shining her light right in Wayne's face, "since you know so much, can you point us toward the nearest exit?"

"Wait a second. Why's everyone turning on me?" Wayne whines. "Wasn't it Crazy Kyle here who kicked things off with the mental break down?"

"Mental break down?" Kyle snaps. "Wake up, dumbass. They locked us in here to die–"

"HEY!" Mike shouts. "Calm down! I'm with you on the paranoia, but seriously relax." To the group, "Now, all of ya'll. Chill out. How about we focus on getting out of here?"

"I'm with you, Mike," Bishop says as he looks to the others. "Let's work together instead of fighting one another."

*Yeah... brilliant plan... Let's find a way out of a room with only one entrance,* Zander thinks. *Genius. I mean, never mind the fact that there might be a firewall separating us from the main room. But whatever.*

Cell phones cut swaths of white light through the room as the group inspects everywhere for some hope of escape. They scan the ceiling tiles. Move what little furniture there is aside.

Kate catches sight of the whiteboard. What was previously written on it has been hastily wiped away. Replaced simply with the following phrase, written in smeared red ink:

"The one you feed," Kate reads aloud. "Pretty sure that's not what it said when I came in here."

"Negative, Kate," Wayne confirms. "It was something about the world's your pearl–"

"*Oyster.*" Bishop's flashlight joins Kate's, highlighting the ghostly glossiness of the whiteboard and the contrast of the crimson marker. "*Why then the world's mine oyster, which I with sword will open.*"

"Shakespeare," Kate says with a smile, though Bishop doesn't see it in the darkness.

"Yeah. I was a big reader back in grade school," Bishop admits.

"I was too." Kate chuckles. "I mean... still am... a big reader, that is."

Mike aims his light on the ceiling tiles above. "Guys, maybe we should look up there?"

"I'll do it," Zander offers. *I bet you this wall is a firewall,* he thinks. *The way this day is going, I'm betting all four walls are firewalls.*

Zander hops onto the conference room table and pushes up on one of the tiles. With his cell phone, he scans the roughly eight-foot clearing between the suspended tile grid and the ceiling.

"See anything?" Bishop asks.

"Nothing but a mess of electrical conduit and fallen insulation."

"Anything like a hatch? An AC duct?" Wayne asks, his tone increasingly tenuous. "A ladder, for God's sake?"

"A... ladder?" Bishop chuckles.

Wayne shines his light on Bishop's face. "You never know, ok, old man?"

Bishop's laugh wanes. "Call me that again, and I'll show you what this *old man* is capable of. Now get that light out of my face."

Wayne does.

Zander gulps. "The hell is that?"

"What the hell is what?" Kate asks, the tension in her voice rising.

"I... I don't know." Zander stammers. "Not sure what I'm looking at."

"What do you mean?" Mike asks.

"I mean... it's... it's weird." Zander's throat grows dry as a desert. "The walls. They're... *wet.*"

"Wet?" Wayne shrugs. "Ok, big deal. So, what? So, they got a leak–"

"It's not a leak. It's..." Zander leans forward, and the upper half of his body disappears into the dark veil of the ceiling tile space. He crouches back down and extends a hand. "Someone get me a chair. I want to take a closer look."

Mike hoists up a chair onto the table. Zander uses it as a stepladder and peers higher, deeper into the ceiling space. The cell phone light whips around as he tries to make out what he's looking at. The others watch expectantly from below.

"Well?" Wayne demands. "You're keeping us in suspense here."

"Yeah, well... I don't know what I'm looking at." Zander tenses, as if zapped by a surge of static. "What the...?"

Before anyone can ask what he sees, several of the ceiling tiles vibrate in succession, shifting out of place, all heading straight towards Zander. He yells as he topples off the chair, bounces onto the table, rolls, and crashes onto the ground.

Mike quickly grabs him by his arm and pulls him to his feet.

Zander is dazed. Winking, as if awakening from a long nap.

"Hey!" Mike gives him a shake. "Hey... you alright?"

"Yeah... I'm fine."

"The heck happened?"

"Yeah, what was that?" Wayne prods.

Zander breaks away from Mike as if bothered by being touched. He leans against the wall, rubbing his arm where he landed. Before he can answer, the single LED light comes back to life above them. Everyone looks up, first at the light, then at the ceiling tile above the table. It is back in place. Undisturbed.

Along with the other tiles.

"How did you do that?" Mike asks Zander.

"Do what?"

"Put the ceiling tile back as you fell off the chair?" Mike prompts.

Zander shakes his head. "I didn't–"

All the LED lights in the conference room turn on now. Everyone nervously takes inventory of their surroundings. Aside from the ceiling tiles finding their way back into place, there are no immediate signs of danger. However, the words on the whiteboard have once again been erased, replaced with just one:

*Feed.*

Wayne examines the marker. The way it glistens against the glaring white of the dry-erase board. Thick. Uneven. Running...

Feed.

The letters seem to cry red ink.

Wayne fingers them. Still wet. He recoils. Rubs the sticky fluid between his fingers.

*Feels like blood,* he thinks. *Impossible. It's not blood!*

Wayne shakes the thought. "Ok. Which one of you assholes has the marker?" He turns on his heels. "Look, people. I declined a stellar gig at a call center in Miami for this job. Not to mention, the chance to meet Marcela in person."

"Who the heck's Marcela?" Mike asks, the question chased by a chuckle.

"My Colombian princess. She's from Bogota." Wayne lifts his chin, and there's an air of pride in his tone. "We met online. Been talking for months and now we're official."

"Congratulations," Mike says.

Ignoring him, Wayne continues, "And we were *going* to meet this month. But thanks to this baloney with SiDug, her and I must delay our rendezvous."

Bishop lowers his head, laughs to himself at the word *rendezvous.*

Kate rolls her eyes.

"Laugh all you assholes want," Wayne declares. "But this better not be some kind of stupid joke–"

"It's not a joke, dumbass." Zander shoves Wayne, then points at the ceiling. "I saw things moving up there. The walls were *wet*, dripping with black goo." He pauses. Trying to put into words what he saw. "There were also black wires... all over the place. Swinging around."

"Weird. Cables along the ceiling?" Wayne taps a finger to his chin, mockingly. "Who would have thought that there would be wires up there? I mean, the internet, electricity, that kind of stuff just automatically gets from one room to the next–"

"I know what a fucking network cable looks like!" Zander undoes his tie and tosses it aside. "And that wasn't what I saw up there."

24

"You said the walls looked black and wet," Bishop reiterates. "Could be mold."

"Ain't mold," Kyle says. "I've got a better explanation."

"Oh?" Wayne folds his arms. "Care to enlighten us?"

"Sure. I've finally done too much of my stuff. I'm beyond baked." Kyle motions to the group. "And you're all a part of my terrible trip. Probably the universe's way of punishing me for dealing."

"A little advice. Next time you get high," Kate says, "try not to manifest a sexist pig like Wayne."

"Hey, I'm not a sexist pig–"

"Everyone, shut up!" Zander shouts.

All eyes are on him now.

"Let's get back to leaving. Ok?" he asks the group.

And as if the conference room door heard him, it slowly creaks open on its own.

# Chapter 4–Enter The Office

The sharp creak the door makes as it opens could cut ice. It seems as though all the lights on the entire floor have just come back on. The air buzzes with the ambient whirr of computers coming to life, printers powering back on, and the indistinct chatter from the employees parked at their cubicles.

"Ok... so that was the world's creepiest power outage," Kate declares.

*That or something else,* Zander thinks as he eyes the ceiling.

*Oh, you know it's something else,* a second voice in Zander's head whispers, sending a chill through his body. *Something bad. Just like you. Just like how you deny the things you've done–*

"Send the scrawny kid out there first," Wayne says, nodding to Kyle. "He wants to leave anyway."

"Don't volunteer me," Kyle says with a snarl.

"Five minutes ago, you wanted to go."

"Why don't you go? Are you scared?" accuses Kyle.

"No." Wayne replies matter-of-factly, "*You* wanted to leave. So, go!"

Kyle glares. "Don't tell me what to do, you little bitch."

"I'm not little," Wayne taps his gut, "but that doesn't matter, since this pear-shaped body still gets me laid."

Kate makes a face in disgust. Utters, "Gross."

"Ok, let's just go!" Mike pushes between them and the rest of the group follows.

Within the main office, the everyday bustle has quickly resumed. Phones ring relentlessly in the background. Some employees busily work at their desks. Others slave away at copiers, filing paperwork, and running trivial errands.

The minor electrical disturbance was nothing more than a hiccup in the workday.

A pudgy man wearing a Marvin the Martian tie from Looney Tunes approaches. He's armed with a cream-colored coffee mug that shows a big fish chasing a little fish. Under the fish are the words *Never stop chasing what you want*, written in cursive. He nods at the new hires as he passes.

"Excuse me," Wayne says to the pudgy man.

The pudgy man stops short, a peculiar look in his eyes.

"What happened with the power?" Wayne demands.

The pudgy man recoils, bewildered by the question. He sizes up the group with his gaze. "Guess they'll hire anyone these days, huh?"

"What the hell's that supposed to mean, Marvin?" Wayne blurts out.

But the pudgy man blows them off with a huff and continues down the hall.

"I think he was only referring to you," Bishop tells Wayne with a bit of a cackle.

"Careful, Gramps," Wayne warns. "That laugh of yours sounds cancerous."

Before the group can get any more riled up, Mr. Gudu appears holding two coffee cups. On his face is a look of confusion mixed with worry. "Everyone all right?"

"We were until you locked us in the office," Kyle answers, a scowl cutting wrinkles across his brow.

Mr. Gudu appears taken aback. "Impossible. We have an open-door policy here at SiDug."

"Open door? Bullshit," Mike insists. "We were locked in there."

"An obvious accident." Mr. Gudu gestures for Wayne to take a coffee cup from his hand. "Your coffee, Mr. Sulkie."

"Ehh, I've had a change of heart." Wayne waves it off. "I'm stimulated enough."

Mr. Gudu frowns. Sets the coffee aside and sips on his own.

"An accident?" Mike gets in Mr. Gudu's face. "I've worked enough shady jobs to know something about you, and this place ain't right."

Wayne sneaks another look at his cell phone. Still no signal.

*Maybe it's just my service,* he thinks.

*Or perhaps,* a second voice rings in his head, *there's no one you need to call, Wayne, because no one misses you. Because you're a big, fat loser.*

Wayne goes stiff. *What the hell?,* he thinks. He looks at the others, wondering if they heard something as well, but the group is too preoccupied with Mike and Mr. Gudu's escalating conversation.

"No need to get upset," Mr. Gudu assures Mike as he brings his hands up in a sort of half surrender. "Please forgive us for the incident with the locked door and the lights. We know there are still some issues within the building that we are taking up with our contractor."

"What about that crap up in the ceiling?" Mike challenges.

"What are you referring to?" Mr. Gudu asks.

"Zander says he saw something *alive* up there," Mike replies.

Mr. Gudu glances up the tiles, "Oh, yes," then back at everyone. With a laugh and a calm smile, he explains, "We've got a bit of a rodent problem. This is par for the course for new construction. The local wildlife relocates when their habitat is upturned. Completely natural. No one likes to lose their home. Animals included." With a reticent sigh, he continues, "But we are dealing with it. So, I apologize for your encounter with them."

The words spill out of Zander's mouth, "You've got more than a rat problem."

Mr. Gudu snaps his head in Zander's direction. Smile fading, he says, "Well fortunately after this week, none of you will have to deal with our facility's issues, since you will all be working from home. And speaking of your training," Mr. Gudu makes a sweeping gesture with his coffee cup towards a group of cubicles at the far side of the room, "may I show you to your desks? I've got cubicles set up specifically for your team. I'd like you all to get acclimated quickly. We have a lot of ground to cover in a short amount of time. I'll need all of you to get your seats and monitors situated, and log into your training sessions."

Mr. Gudu takes off towards the training area. Everyone trades bewildered looks, then follow Mr. Gudu to their respective cubicles.

Mike and Bishop trail after the group.

"I think today's gonna be my first and last day," Mike whispers.

"I think I'm with you on that," Bishop whispers back.

Zander finds his desk, but glances back over his shoulder to find the pudgy clerk standing next to the copier. Mug still in one hand, his finger mindlessly presses the copy button over and over. A plastic smile is frozen on his face. Staring at Zander, he tilts his head to one side. Without breaking the stare, he snatches a page that just printed and snaps it up so that Zander can see what's on it.

Written in an almost childlike, crude font, an odd, foreign word:

*Muššagana.*

More copies print, and Zander is compelled to maintain the stare with the pudgy guy. He hears Mr. Gudu talking behind him to the others but is transfixed on this odd man glaring at him. Papers in hand, the pudgy worker holds them up and flips through them like rudimentary teleprompter cards.

It's the same word over and over.

*Muššagana.*

Pulling up the next page...

*Muššagana*

And the next...

*Muššagana*

Zander is about to call out to the pudgy guy to ask what *Muššagana* means, when he feels a firm tap on his shoulder. He spins around, face to face with Mr. Gudu.

"Did you get lost?" Mr. Gudu asks with a feigned chuckle. "You're at the wrong desk. Your desk is over there." He leans in so that the others, who are busily inspecting their cubicles, don't hear. "Even though it's only going to be a week, I gave you the best office chair in the building. One of those Serta memory foam models. It's my personal favorite. A dream for lower back pain," he says with a wink.

Zander fakes a smile and follows Mr. Gudu. He sneaks a look back over his shoulder. The pudgy man is no longer there.

Neither is the beast of a copier that was just there moments ago.

Zander is feeling like he's on stage in some chaotic play where the set crew keeps reassembling the stage, only he doesn't know what's real and what isn't.

*You'll know what's real when you stop denying it,* that cursed voice in Zander's head tells him. *And I'm going to show you!*

# Chapter 5–First Shift

It is one thing to think something. It is another to have a stray thought manifest on its own and plague your mind. Zander does his best to ignore this unfamiliar voice in his brain. He physically gives his head a quick shake, hoping that Mr. Gudu doesn't catch it–and fortunately, he doesn't.

While the others are already at their desks, logging into the computer and getting situated, Mr. Gudu shows Zander to his desk and has him take a seat. As promised, Zander finds his chair to be the most comfortable chair he has ever sat in–so comfortable, in fact, it seems to mold to his body.

Upon noting Zander's satisfaction, Mr. Gudu gives him a quick pat on the shoulder. He then circles the other cubicles, prompting everyone to grab their headsets and begin their training. "What you're about to see," he announces, "is a video series about SiDug, what we're all about, and what we expect from you."

Mike puts the headset on, then pauses, asking Mr. Gudu, "So, what do we do if the power goes out? Start the videos over?"

"I expect no more interruptions, as the facilities manager has been notified of the electrical issues. If the power drops again, do not worry. The videos will continue where they leave off once the power resumes." With a bit of impatience, he gestures for everyone to put their respective headsets on. "Now, if you all are ready, please double-click the SiDug Tech icon on your desktops. This will begin the training–"

"I'm sorry, dude," Kyle exclaims as he rips off his headphones and rises from his seat, "but I don't think this job is right for me."

Mr. Gudu expels a measured breath and lowers his head towards the floor, making an obvious show of his disappointment. "I understand. It is unfortunate that you do not share the same hunger as your team here." He motions towards the exit. "But I appreciate your honesty."

"Yeah." Kyle salutes the group. "If you guys are smart, you'll peace out too."

"Thanks for the advice. And if I might throw some knowledge your way," Wayne adds with a laugh, "lay off the caffeine."

Kyle walks backwards so that he can give Wayne the finger, then storms out.

Mr. Gudu watches Kyle go. Then says to the group, "If anyone else cares to leave, I would appreciate that you do it now." He moves between the cubicles like a prison guard keeping watch over the potential rebellion of his inmates. "I will gladly write you a check for a full day's pay today and see you off."

Silence follows as each of them contemplates staying or leaving, all mutually entertaining similar thoughts:

*SiDug pays great.*

*The benefits are amazing.*

*I finally get to work from home.*

*My own schedule. My way. My time.*

*Work-life balance!*

These thoughts briefly overshadow any of their individual desires to leave. At least for the moment.

No one says anything. No one abandons their desks. It's as if they are collectively wanting to know if this is going to unfold into something horrible, or if everything they have experienced so far was just a fluke. *Construction issues* as Wayne so vaguely reassured them.

"Great," Mr. Gudu proclaims while clapping his hands together. "I know we had some technical difficulties starting off, but from now on, I am confident that things will run smoothly."

Zander's mind wanders to the breathing walls at the mention of technical difficulties. The things he saw in the conference room but didn't get to fully express.

The swelling concrete.

The frothing liquid slipping down the façade.

The dark space just above where the average employee sits. The in-between. That interstitial area above the tiles but beneath the concrete and rebar of the next floor, where things slimy and slithering moved–

"Zander," Mr. Gudu says, "you still with us?"

Zander's eyes flutter absently. Entranced by the experience, he hadn't had time to process. It lingers in his mind like the bitter heartburn of a rotten meal. Off-putting and incongruent with the rest of the flavors he should relish:

The excitement of a new job.

The new crew.

The insanely good pay.

The movement towards a better life for him and Vicky.

Zander shows Mr. Gudu all is well with a thumbs up.

Satisfied, Mr. Gudu moves along and asks everyone to get on with the videos.

And that's when life for Zander and the others changes.

# Chapter 6–Training Day

A video window pops up on Zander's screen. He puts on his headphones, sinks into his insanely comfortable chair, and hits PLAY.

The video begins with a professionally dressed man sporting a power-red tie and an ivory button up. He has great posture, much like Mr. Gudu. Shoulders back and down, neck straight, head erect. The poise of a product spokesperson. He keeps his hands folded in front of him as he speaks. "Welcome to SiDug Tech! I'm Cory Lul, and I'm glad that you have joined us. We are one of the fastest growing IT companies in the Tampa Bay Area!"

*Cory. What an appropriate name,* Zander thinks. *Corporate Cory.*

As Cory goes on about the company, their history, and other innocuous details, Zander's mind drifts. He leans out from his cubicle and eyes the others. To his right, Kate absently picks her nose as she watches the video, apparently unaware anyone can see her. To his left, Mike is slouched in his seat, arms folded, glaring at the screen with a certain skepticism.

That same sense of doubt grows in Zander.

*Maybe that kid was smart to leave,* he muses. *Maybe I should do the same?*

*To do what? Rush home to be all alone?* that horrific second voice interjects. *To the mess you made!*

Zander freezes. *Where's that voice coming from?*

*From you,* the other voice informs him. *You're a fake. Stop lying to yourself about what you did–*

Zander rips off his headphones and starts to rise when a hand grips his shoulder.

"How's that chair treating you?" Mr. Gudu asks as he releases Zander.

"Good."

"Wonderful." As Mr. Gudu trots off to check on the others, Zander turns back to his monitor and slides his headphones on to find that Corporate Cory has just finished babbling on about SiDug's history. "That concludes our story! Now let's find more about you!"

Zander finds the way Cory speaks grating, almost condescending.

"SiDug Tech takes pride in caring about every one of our employees." Cory points at Zander. "We care about you. We care about your needs and treat them like they are our own. Because without you, there's no SiDug."

There's an awkward pause, as if Zander is supposed to respond but doesn't.

"Now let me ask you," Cory continues, as an image of a happy family of four appears next to him. The family is laughing, hugging. "What is your family life like?"

*I have no family*, Zander thinks.

The picture of a couple appears onscreen. They're in a kitchen, playfully feeding one another from a fruit tray. Cory asks, "What is your love life like?"

*Well, I have Vicky*, he thinks.

*Do you?* That secondary voice asks. The voice he is quickly growing to loathe.

"What does your future hold?" Cory asks with his perfect posture, hands neatly pressed together, fingertip to fingertip.

Zander senses his confidence in his decision to stay waning. The question posed by Cory seems odd for a "rah-rah welcome to the company" video.

"What is your purpose in this world?" Cory's eyes seem to darken with this question.

*What kind of training video is this?* Zander thinks. *Is this for real?*

Now the video jumps and crackles as though the streaming signal is getting corrupted. Cory's speech stutters. He jiggles in place, with that perfect poise, those transfixed dead-brown eyes of his, staring not just straight into the camera, but beyond. The features of his face become a blur. His body, a pixilated mess of multi-colored miniature squares.

The way Cory moves, twitching like a dying insect railing against its own demise, alarms Zander.

Just as Zander is about to kill the video—the feed improves.

Cory's image resumes in perfect 4K resolution. He reaches off camera, grabs a glass of water, sips, then pauses, savoring it as if it were melted from prehistoric glaciers. He closes his eyes, reveling in the water's purity, and Zander feels the tiny hairs on his entire body ripple on high alert.

*Forget the money,* Zander thinks. *Run!*

*Run now.*

*RUN RIGHT NOW!*

Zander reaches for his headset. He is about to yank it off when he hears Cory ask a question.

A question that no one...

A topic that not even his own mother knows about.

A subject he has kept from his best friends. His family. His therapist.

"Erik."

Zander's body locks up at the mention of that name.

"When was the last time you thought of killing him, Zander?"

Zander knows the answer to that question because he thinks about it daily. It is in his mind. In his dreams. He fantasizes about the blood pooling out from Erik's chest as he stares up at him with apologetic eyes—eyes that say, *I'm sorry for banging Vicky—*

*It's too late for you,* Zander thinks, *because you took advantage of a shitty situation when I needed you the most. You were nothing but a wolf in disguise. Loyal friends don't steal their friend's partner.*

The tirade, the mental avalanche collapses onto the forefront of Zander's mind. He can concentrate on nothing else other than this cerebral rant.

*We've been through it all, from elementary school to burying my father. But none of that mattered once Vicky showed up. All bets were off. The term 'best friends' didn't mean squat to you anymore because she was the prize.*

*You hung around. Not because you cared about me. But because you were keeping tabs. That way you could time when I was away and you could sleep with her, you scumbag!*

"When was the last time, Zander?" Cory asks once again. "When you dreamed of running a knife through Erik's heart, watching him squirm like a worm on a hook as he looked in your eyes–the last thing he saw before leaving this world?"

Zander rips the headphones off his head and jumps out of his chair to break away from this bizarre video training session–but doesn't get far at all.

Something clamps him to his desk.

# Chapter 7–Coffee Break

Zander leans forward to investigate what is grabbing his leg–when the lights cut off.

"Again?" Wayne groans aloud.

"Mr. Gudu needs to fire some people for this," Mike growls.

Zander reaches down to his feet, fumbling for whatever is tied around his leg. His fingers encounter something slippery, spongy, and soft.

The lights come back on.

To Zander's horror, there is a shiny, melanoid, serpentine rope wound around his ankle. He pulls his leg back but struggles against whatever this is. His first thought is that he somehow got tangled up with the network cables or electrical cords fed under his desk. *But why would network cables feel spongy?*

But then the black cord tightens its grip.

"Oh, God!" Zander bursts out.

"Whoa! Watch the language!" Mr. Gudu admonishes from behind him. Zander glances back and sees the boss man reaching towards him. "How in the world did you get yourself tied up like that?"

Zander looks back down at his leg. A blue network cable is hooked around his shoe in a single loop. "That's not what that was."

"What do you mean?" Mr. Gudu asks as he frees Zander's ankle from the cable.

"The cable. It was... it was black. Slimy," Zander stammers. "It... it moved."

Wayne and the others rise from their cubicles like moles curiously peeking up from their mounds. They look on as Mr. Gudu puts his hands on his hips and states, "I think you've got a case of new-job jitters. Is that common for you?"

"Not really," Zander scoffs. "But when weird things happen consecutively, it gets you worked up, you know?"

"I feel the same way," Kate adds. "I'm getting a little creeped out myself."

*Actually, more than a little,* she thinks. *More like a lot.*

"I am sorry to hear that," Mr. Gudu says with a hint of sympathy in his tone. "And I am quite embarrassed and frustrated with the issues the new construction has left us with. I feel like I've given you all a false impression of SiDug Tech."

*More like a weird impression,* Zander thinks. *Maybe I should have followed Kyle right out the front door too.*

*And give up the new place?* that second voice in his head asks. *Give up on your new life, to go back to working crappy jobs, living in overpriced, termite-infested South Tampa dumps? Is that what Vicky would want you to do?*

This time, instead of feeling anxious about that secondary voice, he feels a sense of concurrence.

*That is true. I just need to get through training,* Zander assures himself. *Then I'll be working from home.*

Mr. Gudu puts a hand on Zander's shoulder and gives it a firm squeeze, shaking Zander from his thoughts. "Maybe you should go get yourself some water. A snack or something? Blood sugar affects anxiety from what I understand."

*My blood sugar is fine,* Zander thinks. *Something about this place isn't. Something about you isn't right either. But I can stick it out a week if I have to.*

Zander fakes a smile. "Ok."

Mr. Gudu points with his great hand towards a door on the left. "Snack bar is that way. Down the hall, and to the left. Can't miss it. Take as much time as you need." He turns to the others. "Everyone else, please resume your training. As I mentioned, it will pick up right where you left off."

The group settles back into their cubicles, except for Mike, who watches

39

Zander leave. The two exchange an uneasy glance.

Zander enters a long corridor that is well lit. The snack bar is off to the left, just as Mr. Gudu mentioned. At the end of the hallway is a glowing red exit sign. Before entering the snack back, he stares at the sign.

EXIT.

*Exit. Not a bad idea. Maybe I should leave–*

His cell phone vibrates in his pocket, and he checks it. Vicky texted him: *How's it going?*

A welcome elation courses through him as he thinks, *Thank god. I have signal.* It's only two bars but beats no service at all. Not wanting to waste a ton of time texting back and forth, he responds: *Can I call you?*

Wanting more privacy, Zander ducks into the snack bar, which is also amply lit. It is lined with contemporary couches, sporting an IKEA-inspired coffee table, decorated with a vase full of black roses. Along the wall is a foosball table and an old-school upright PAC-MAN arcade game. In the corner sit two vending machines and a self-serve coffee maker.

He heads for the coffee machine. More caffeine is probably the last thing he needs, but he's too anxious to eat, and his throat is growing drier by the minute. It is a high-end coffee dispenser with a touchscreen. There are several images of varying beverage types, a menu of icons representing a slew of choices from shots of espresso to lattes. He follows the instructions printed alongside the touchscreen, pops a Styrofoam cup under the spout, and presses the icon for regular coffee.

The machine buzzes, almost as if he chose the wrong answer on a trivia game. Zander nearly jumps back. He tries the button again, but the machine buzzes so loud, he questions if the rest of his team hears it in the other room–though he doubts it given the noise-canceling nature of their headphones.

On that note, a brief thought slips into his mind: *I wonder what Corporate Cory is telling them?*

The screen on the coffee maker goes black and then comes back to life. This time, two rectangular buttons appear side-by-side:

Coffee or Truth.

Zander mutters, "The hell?"

He tries one last time. Selects coffee and winces, waiting for the machine to buzz loudly again.

But it doesn't.

Instead, coffee pours from the spout and fills his cup. The phone vibrates. He glances at his cell phone, annoyed by its unpredictably intermittent signal, and finds that Vicky replied:

*Sure, give me a minute. Just getting out of the shower. I'll call you.*

The coffee finishes pouring and the next options on the menu screen appear:

Cream or Truth.

Zander shakes his head. He presses the Cream button, but the machine squeals with that horrid buzzing sound. The Cream button fades and the Truth button fills the small screen, blinking sporadically.

Zander takes a step back. Then hesitates. Part of him wants to know if someone is screwing with him. The other part wonders if he is going insane.

He extends a shaky finger towards the screen and presses the Truth button.

The screen goes black. Then comes back to life. It's a camera view of a bedroom. A familiar bedroom.

His bedroom!

Zander steps closer. Eyes glued to the screen. *Did someone install a camera in my house?*

There are voices, diminished but audible, coming from the coffee machine's brittle speaker. One voice he immediately recognizes.

*Vicky.*

*She's... giggling?*

Vicky comes into view. Nude. Breasts staring back at the camera, swinging freely as a man comes up from behind her. Fingers wrapping around her from behind. Cupping her breasts. She's swung around in a half-circle and is tossed onto the bed, giggling some more. The man's head is cut off by the camera as he walks towards an eager Vicky.

Zander grips the sides of the coffee machine, and his teeth grind as he utters, "What is this?"

The man forces Vicky into a doggy-style position and she obliges with a throaty laugh. He then mounts Vicky from behind and a furious session of sex, noises, and groans proceeds.

Zander's fingernails dig into the metal skin of the machine.

A breathless Vicky rolls onto her back. Chuckles as she pulls the man down on top of her. He turns to the camera, as if aware of its presence, and grins at Zander.

*Erik!*

Zander pounds at the side of the machine with his fist.

Erik smiles wide, then peppers Vicky with an assault of kisses accompanied by playful laughter. The screen goes black.

"Screw this place, and screw you, Erik!" Zander swats away the coffee cup from under the spout, splashing the brown liquid everywhere. He spins around back into the hallway, and his cell phone rings. Without looking, he answers.

"Yes?"

Vicky asks, "Hey love, how's training going?"

# Chapter 8–Call With Vicky

"Babe?" Vicky sounds distant. As if calling from Antarctica. "You there?"

Zander's indignation over what he just witnessed makes everything a blur. Vicky's voice seems so far away. With a great concentration he answers, "Yeah. What? I'm here."

A cautious pause. Then, "Everything okay?"

Zander glances at the coffee machine. There's no pornographic feed. No scenes of Erik aggressively pumping Vicky as if she were the last woman on earth.

No. Only the innocent menu of caffeinated beverages on the small screen.

Zander clutches the back of his head, hoping that his skull does not split apart given the madness of it all.

The madness brought on by Erik.

An image of Erik pressed up against Vicky springs in his mind.

Erik used to be his best friend until the breakup–or simply *the break* as Zander labeled it more comfortably. Zander had floundered within his career choices and hated most of the places he worked, complaining constantly. He'd overshadow Vicky's needs, her concerns, with his own. He'd suck the air out of the room and steal the conversation. When he tired of hearing himself whining to Vicky, he'd quit. Then the cycle would start again, where he'd spend months unemployed, depressed, mopey and on the verge of going broke. Pounding fast-food, playing video games, growing flabby and grumbling how life wasn't fair.

One day, the cycle broke. Vicky had had enough, ending things unexpectedly.

This caught Zander by surprise. He took the following six months to get his act together. Worked on his resume. Reached out to other contacts. Networked like a beast.

But while he was busy getting his life in order, Erik the vulture swooped right in. Entertained Vicky. Took her out. Wined and dined her. Made her feel special. Actually listened to her instead of talking over her. By taking Vicky for granted, playing the victim of his circumstances for too long, Zander had given Erik the opening to weasel right in.

"Vicky, can I ask you something?" The question spills out from his mouth before Zander can hit the verbal brakes. "Did you ever have feelings for Erik? I mean, even before we took the *big break*?"

A long pause follows.

Zander senses her retreating through the phone. Before she can respond, he blurts out, "Never mind! I-I'm sorry I asked that."

"Uh-huh."

"Look," Zander presses a hand against his forehead as if suppressing his brain from exploding. "I don't think this job is for me."

"Wow." Zander practically hears her shaking her head in disbelief. "You're kidding, right? What about the new place, Zander? A place that we can't afford if you quit!"

"I'll find something else—"

"You'll find something else? Something that pays double what you were making before, to do the same amount of work, and *not* require more time away from one another? Seriously?" There's a virulence in Vicky's tone that Zander hasn't heard since that day she left him. "Make up your mind, okay? You want us to get to that next level? Then you need to stick with this for now. It's only temporary. Get through the training. Then come on home. It's a small sacrifice."

"I understand that," Zander explains, "but it's not just about the training. I don't feel right here. Something is off with this company."

Vicky sighs.

"One of the new hires already quit."

"So? So what? People quit all the time, Zander. Just like you have, many times."

The words cut deep, piercing Zander's heart in a way he's never felt before.

"This is a new chapter in our life," Vicky continues, "and it's time you embrace it and not just quit and hope for the best like you have in the past!"

Zander hears what she's saying, but the gnawing distress in his stomach is just too undeniable.

"We're making a fresh start, right?" Vicky asks Zander this, but all he can picture is the video he saw. Erik mounting her. Thrusting his body into hers as if he was trying to break her–

Zander presses his thumbs against his temples at the imagery.

*Is that what happened?* he wonders. *Is that how it went down?*

"Baby?" Vicky presses.

*Baby...?* The word sounds so hollow to him.

"Did you call him baby?" Zander demands, and once again, shocks himself with his frankness.

"Who?"

"Erik."

"Erik?"

"Yeah, Erik. Did you call him *baby*?" Zander finds it almost impossible to stop himself from continuing, "When he was inside you?"

There's a beat. Then Vicky becomes unhinged. "You asshole. How dare you!?"

Zander eyes the coffee machine. The small screen flips on, displaying a shot of his bedroom.

*Their* bedroom.

Erik moves onto the bed. His nudity partially shielded by a comforter. He gazes back at Zander–

"You want to quit?" Vicky's voice trembles. "Fine. Quit. I don't care. Do whatever you want to do!"

The image on the coffeemaker fades out. Then fades back in, and now Erik is riding Vicky from behind, a snarky grin plastered on his face. With a wink, he smacks Vicky's ass and then flicks off Zander.

45

The feed stops.

"Just like you did, right?" Zander snaps. "Like when we broke up, and you hooked up with Erik, right?"

He pauses. Catching himself.

*What the hell has gotten into me?* he thinks. *I would never say this kind of crap. Why now?*

*Because it's how you truly feel,* that troubling voice answers.

*Shut up,* he mentally screams at the voice as he smacks at his forehead. *Shut up! Shut up! SHUT! UP!*

A faint click registers from the cell phone.

"Vicky?" he says tepidly.

Silence.

"Vicky? Are you there?" He glances at the phone. She hung up. "Damn!" He tries calling her back, but his phone cuts out immediately. "What the–"

He checks the phone. No signal.

*That's it. I'm leaving,* he tells himself. *I need to get home and straighten things out with her, since I went and screwed it all up again!*

Zander makes for the hallway, heads towards the exit. He glances over his shoulder, half expecting to find Mr. Gudu staring him down, a disappointed look on his face.

But no one is there.

Zander decides to leave and not say a word. He pushes on the exit door's panic bar. It clicks but doesn't open.

Frantically, he tries several more times.

*Click–click–click–click–click.*

Nothing.

"Are you serious!?"

The exit sign flashes above him, dying out moments later. The ceiling lights in the hallway pulse violently, then go out as well.

Zander's chest tightens in the darkness. Anxiety squeezes on his lungs, on his heart, on his mind. It feels as if the unending dark of the hallway is going to swallow him up.

This dread is heightened with the steady footfalls of something coming straight at him.

And that *something* is in a hurry to get to him.

# Chapter 9 – The Hallway

Zander braces against the exit door, readying himself for what is headed his way.

A sharp, concentrated light flicks on and penetrates the shadows, bumbling toward Zander like a drunken bird.

"Who's there?" Zander calls out.

The undulating beam of light slows, then levels with his eyes, blinding him temporarily.

"Zander?" a familiar, deep voice asks.

"Yeah," Zander says, shielding his eyes.

"It's me." The voice turns the light toward themselves, casting a ghastly shadow under their eyes. "It's Mike."

"Oh. Hey," Zander says as he catches his breath, still a bit shaken.

"You taking an extended break?" Mike asks as he approaches.

"The kid was right. We should leave. So, I'm out."

"I'm a hundred percent with you." Mike reaches past Zander, tries the door which clicks, but still does not open.

"Did that already."

"Well, I didn't want to challenge Mr. Gudu in front of everyone, but I've done enough construction jobs to know this is more than 'new build' issues."

*Tell me about it,* Zander thinks as he recalls what he saw both in the ceiling and on the coffee machine display.

"And I hate to use up my battery like this, but after what I saw on those training videos," Mike pauses, recalling what he saw, "that crap has got me shook."

"What crap?" Zander asks, feeling some base level of comfort that he might not be going crazy.

"I'm talking about that dude on the video. Casey. Carrey–"

"Cory."

"Yeah. Him." Mike exhales deeply. "This is going to sound crazy, but Cory was talking to me about stuff that no one knows about. No one except for a few people I haven't talked to in years. I'm talking about folks that are dead, jailed or M.I.A."

"What did he talk to you about?"

Mike hangs on that question for a moment. Then replies, "You know. Stupid teenager stuff from back in the day. Nothing that I'd put on blast." He changes the subject back to the situation at hand. "Anyway. How we gonna get out of here?"

"You got signal?"

Mike checks his cell phone. "Nah. You?"

Zander checks. "Same. I mean, I talked to my fiancé just before you came stumbling in here. So maybe there's a chance that I'll get signal again."

*Fiancé, huh? Zander thinks. That's assuming she'll still want to talk to you after your Spanish Inquisition over the goddamn phone, you stupid idiot! Who the hell are you to give her the third degree? You are the lazy-ass who could never get your crap straight. You are the one who could never hold down a steady job while she supported you. Put up with your manic-depressive ways. Who are you to think that she's going to stick around–*

"Shut up!" Zander exclaims aloud as he clutches his head. "JUST SHUT UP!"

Mike turns to him. "What?"

"N-nothing."

"The fuck's gotten into you–"

The lights in the hallway come to life. Mike and Zander eye them, then each other, then the sprawling hallway behind them that leads back to the main office. Several doors line the hallway on either side.

"We got to find another way," Zander announces. "Maybe one of those other doors–"

Behind them, a woman's scream pierces the door from the office they came from. Her shriek is followed by the sound of heavy footsteps, havoc, and people crying out in agony. Then Mr. Gudu's muffled voice playfully asks with a laugh, "Where is everyone going? Training is just getting started."

As the cries grow wilder, Zander and Mike trade glances, then try every door. One after another. But each one of them is locked.

"Run all you want," Mr. Gudu shouts, his voice curiously clear through the door, "but you're already in my stomach. Because the one you feed..."

Zander goes for the last door on the right.

Mr. Gudu sounds eerily close. "Is me."

The door handle gives. Zander motions Mike to follow him into wherever it leads, just as the lights in the hallway go dark once again.

# Chapter 10–Wayne

Wayne awakens at his cubicle, slumped over his desk. Face down, his cheek presses against his keyboard. He whimpers as if stirring from a bad dream as he shoots up, erect in his seat. He rubs his eyes to find that the room is obscured in a flaxen haze, a veritable fog. As hints of carbon and smoke waft into his nose, he thinks:

*Fire!*

*This place is on fire!*

He practically jumps out of his chair—but his head is yanked forward, accompanied by a brutally sharp pain within his sinus. He gasps as he processes what he sees:

A black, barbed cable runs out from his nose and dives under his desk.

"What... what the hell?"

He touches the cable warily, as if unsure it is even real. It is. He tries to pull it out but is rewarded with a scathing lightning bolt to his head. Another wheezed gasp escapes him. He kicks his chair away and drops to his knees. He reaches under the desk, feeling around for where the cable ends, but is pierced by the cable's barbs. He curses, flinches, and pulls his hand back, whipping it in the air hoping to shake off the discomfort.

Panic settles in as Wayne wonders if this is just a dream. Wonders if perhaps he fell asleep at his desk during one of Cory's monologues. But Cory's ramblings had derailed into something more sinister, something more intimate. They devolved into a tangent about Wayne's past.

Into his childhood.

Into his father's disappointment.

Into his ritualistic taunting by school bullies.

The fact that Cory knew such specific details told Wayne everything he needed to know.

*This is just a nightmare!* Wayne closes his eyes, willing himself to awaken. *Come on, Wayne! Wake up!*

Wayne opens his eyes to find that he is still in the darkened room, kneeling at his desk, with something attached to his nose. His heart quickens. Sweat dampens his shirt, soaking the center of his chest and his armpits. He takes a deep breath and clutches the cable. Thorny barbs dig into the flesh of his hands. It hurts like a bastard, but he knows he has got to get this thing out of his nose—whatever it is!

Then these odd, random thoughts call out to him from the corners of his mind:

*Stay with me, Wayne.*

*Feel what I have to give.*

These thoughts are followed by a brief sense of euphoria, akin to the warmth of a narcotic or the high from a joint. Both of which he's very familiar with.

But the peaceful sensation is swiftly dwarfed with distress.

*Stay with me, Wayne.*

*We'll dine together.*

The weird thoughts send a shiver coursing through Wayne's body like an unwanted side-effect. He pulls at the cord once again, and the pain is immediate, excruciating, and emanating from within the wall of his nostril.

*Come on, Wayne,* he thinks. *Get this thing out of your nose!*

Wayne squeezes his eyes tight, pulls, and yells.

It doesn't budge.

He pauses, recuperating. Giving himself a moment to recover from the white-hot sensation. He opens his eyes and shouts, "Hello!"

Only the empty hush of the room responds.

"Can anyone here me? Is anyone there?"

Nothing.

Wayne huffs and goes at it again, gradually pulling at the cable. The pain is instant and intense. He can't help but cry out as he pulls. But he can only try for so long, as the discomfort makes him dizzy. He pauses. How much or how little is hooked inside his nose is hard to tell. The fiery sensation makes comprehension and measurement difficult.

"Mr. Gudu?" Wayne calls out. "Kate? Mike?" He blanks on Bishop's name. "Bob?"

*Bob? You really are a selfish idiot, you know that?* that crooked voice inside him asks. *Can't even remember the old man's name. Worthless. See, that's why no one likes you.*

"Shut up," Wayne whispers to himself.

*It's the just pain,* he thinks. *The pain from this thing in my nose! I got to get it out.*

Something rustles on the other side of the cubicles.

Wayne's body locks up. "Is anybody there?"

"Yep," a man's voice responds, "I'm here."

Wayne looks in the voice's direction, careful to not test the slack of the cable. Still gingerly holding the thick wire, he peeks above his cubicle and watches as the flimsy walls of other cubicles wobble in place like bowling pins on the verge of tipping over. "Who's... there?"

All movement stops. "You know who it is, *Eggie.*"

*Eggie?*

Wayne hasn't heard that name since high school.

"Come on. Who do you think it is, Eggie?"

Wayne swallows what feels like a chunk of wood in his throat as he realizes who it is. The name Chet McKalister illuminates within his mind like a theater marquee lit up by two-thousand bulbs, bordered by a flickering cherry-red neon strip.

Chet.

The one person Wayne reviled the most on this planet.

Chet was a mouth-breathing bully who hunted Wayne the way a cheetah spoors a gazelle. Chet would embarrass Wayne publicly by tripping him in front of his classmates or flipping his lunch tray on his lap. Privately, Chet would stalk Wayne in the gym locker room after class, sneaking up on him with a wet towel, wound tight, delivering an unwelcome surprise whipping that left Wayne's back full of welts.

"Are you still there, Eggie?"

Eggie was short for egghead–Chet's endearing sobriquet for Wayne, since he often made fun of Wayne's oval-shaped head.

"Oh, Eggieeeeee..."

*That can't be Chet,* Wayne thinks as his lower lip trembles. *There's no way! Unless... he works for SiDug too. But what are the odds?*

The voice grows loud and lethal. "EGGIE, I'M TALKING TO YOU!"

Wayne holds his breath.

An unsettling quiet hangs in the air as the nubilous misty fog slides through the room, occasionally obscuring what dim lighting there is above.

"SAY MY NAME, YOU LITTLE PUSSY!"

Wayne says meekly, "Chet?"

"BINGO, GENIUS!"

Wayne's breathing quickens. His heart pounds in his chest with the troubling tempo of a Taiko drummer signaling an impending attack–

There's a thundering of objects being thrown around the room. Wayne peeks out from behind his desk to find cubicle walls flying upwards, much like cards jumping out of a magic deck from Hell. They shoot up in succession, one after another flung into the air, heading in a straight line towards him.

*Think, dumbass! Think!*

Wayne turns his attention back to the thorny cord keeping him prisoner to this cursed desk and pulls hard on it. Blood drips from his hands and from his nose as he howls, pulling with all his might, besting the pain, and he finally yanks the end of the cable free from out his nose. A bridge of blood trails from his nostril to the rope's hooked end, cascades, and spills on the floor.

*Did I just yank out a vein?* he wonders. *A blood vessel? Half my goddamn sinuses?*

But the madness closing in on him instantly breaks his thoughts. He guns it towards what appears to be an exit door.

"Where are you going?" Chet calls out from behind him.

Wayne bursts through the door, slamming it behind him. He presses his back against it, gasping wildly, as he stares down a long hallway with a break room area off to the left.

Chet slams into the door with a resounding boom. Wayne's body shakes as he steadies himself against the Chet's pummeling. Feels as if the man is literally throwing himself at the door.

The thuds continue for what seems like an eternity. Wayne closes his eyes and grits his teeth, praying inside that Chet's muscle doesn't overpower his own frumpy physique—

The onslaught abruptly stops.

Silence falls.

Wayne remains glued to the door, panting uncontrollably. He listens intently without moving a muscle. Blood seeps from his nostril, and tickles his upper lip, then his chin. He wants to wipe it away, but he's not letting a hand or any part of his body off this door until he knows that Chet, or whoever is there, cannot push their way through.

Some time passes.

Wayne is not sure how long, but long enough for his muscles to quake with fatigue. He licks his lips, tasting the metallic tang of his own blood. The inside of his nose stings with unremitting agony, overshadowed by the adrenaline coursing through him.

He peels himself off the door, as if carefully slipping away from the grasp of a sleeping bear. He and takes a step forward—

BOOM!

Chet slams into the door.

Wayne yelps. Without looking back, he bolts down the hallway, testing every locked door along the way until he finds one that opens. He yanks it open, dives in, and slams it shut behind him.

# Chapter 11–Cubicle Hell

Z ander and Mike sit in total blackness. The huffs of their panicked breaths claim the air. Mike fumbles for his cell phone. As the screen comes to life, the curved edges of his face glow.

"My battery's low," Mike pronounces. "Didn't bring my charger because I didn't plan on being on my phone all day."

Zander checks his phone. "I'm at fifty percent."

"Beats nineteen. Won't be long before mine dies."

"Cut off your Wi-Fi. Lower the brightness. Kill any apps that are running."

Mike follows Zander's advice. "Mind taking over flashlight duty?"

*Want me to hold your hand too?* Zander thinks. *I didn't ask you to team up with me.*

"I... guess."

"That ok?" Mike asks, the question hanging on his tongue.

"Yeah, yeah. That's fine."

*Sure, let's use up my battery. Why not?*

Zander grudgingly flicks on his flashlight and scans the other room. From the scarce funnel of light the cell phone provides, they are greeted with the slate gray walls of cubicles directly in front of them. Beyond that, their surroundings are engulfed in unyielding blackness.

"Maybe I can find a USB cable somewhere," Mike says. "Charge my phone."

"With what power?" Zander asks in an acidulous tone. "The lights are off."

"Yeah, no crap. I meant once the power comes back on."

The two men progress deeper into the room, occasionally bumping into the low profile, carpeted cubicle walls and random chairs strewn about carelessly. The stillness is deafening. The ceaseless caliginosity of the room is unrelenting. The air reeks of new carpet accented with a fetid undertone.

Mike catches a whiff. "You smell that?"

"How could I not?" Zander asks as he leads the way. "It smells like death."

*And you know this smell all too well,* that secondary voice shouts in Zander's mind. *You can pretend you don't, but you do–*

"Maybe something died in the walls," Zander suggests, hoping to interrupt the unwanted thoughts plaguing his mind. "Mr. Gudu mentioned a rodent problem."

"Right." Mike laughs to himself. "Rodents. Sure, man."

They continue for another ten minutes, pushing further into the belly of the room. Zander keeps the cell phone light aimed ahead, swinging it intermittently from left to right, hoping for any sign of a way out, but only the dull scenery of cubicles flanks them on either side. These cubicles appear unused and bare. Completely absent of personal items, portraits of loved ones, or even post-it notes.

*This is probably just a new wing,* Zander tells himself. *Set up for other new employees. Not everyone gets to work from home, right?*

"This place goes on forever," Mike says. "Feels like we've walked a mile."

Zander stops short. His light catches something to the right.

Mike sees it too.

They move in for a closer look to find what appears to be a child's drawing pinned to one of the cubicle's walls. Dead center on the picture is an enormous, charcoal-black oak tree, surrounded by several stick figures. A wild mane of branches shoots up from the tree's trunk, while a chaotic mess of roots takes up the bottom-half of the picture. Those roots weave around the page in a frenetic manner, ending at the stick figures' heads. Written in crayon, crude letters spell out: FEED. Scrawled below that in smaller letters, the word *Muššagana*.

"Mussa-what?" Mike asks.

"It's kid jargon, dude," Zander explains. "They make up words. You were six once, right?"

Mike rolls his eyes.

They explore the rest of the cubicle and find a telephone, a computer, and two side-by-side monitors. Lined up along a shelf just above the monitors is a collection of snow globes. He shines his light on them, one at a time.

The first snow globe is of downtown Chicago, featuring the Willis Tower, John Hancock, and its other quintessential skyscrapers in miniature form.

Followed by downtown Detroit.

Then Cleveland.

Then New York, Boston, Nashville, Columbia, Atlanta, Miami, Orlando, and Tampa.

Mike takes the Orlando snow globe—its downtown skyline is shared with the iconic buildings of the area's prominent theme parks.

"This is my hometown." Mike gives the glass orb a hearty shake. Flecks of chalky plastic stir within the liquid, shedding snow on a city that possibly hasn't seen snow since the 1970s. He turns to Zander. "Place has changed a lot since I grew up there."

Zander eyes the globe, then swipes the Tampa one. Something compels him to shake it. He does, and instead of white, plastic snow, tiny red flecks, glimmering with an almost golden hue, flare upwards above the city skyline. For a moment, he thinks he might have something wrong with his eyes. Perhaps the lighting is not helping. He brings the light closer to the globe as he gives it another shake again.

This time the liquid in the globe darkens, obscuring the miniature buildings completely.

Zander drops the globe where it lands on the carpeted floor with a vacant thud. "You saw that, right?" He looks to Mike, who's facial features are barely lit by his cell phone, yet clearly communicating with wide eyes and a worried sneer that, indeed, Mike saw what he saw.

Mike snatches up the desk phone and puts the handset to his ear. No dial tone. He swears under his breath. Grumbles, "Figures."

Zander would have been surprised at this point had it worked. "Let's keep moving," he tells Mike. "There's got to be a fire exit somewhere."

*Some way out of this cursed place,* Zander thinks. *The sooner I can get out of here, the quicker I can fix the mess I made with Vicky!*

*It's a little late for that,* the secondary voice taunts.

"Shut up!" Zander lets slip.

"What'd you say?"

"N–Nothing."

Mike pauses. "You wanna rest for a second?"

Zander puts a hand to his head. "No. Come on."

"Ok." Mike watches him go on first. Lets him get a few steps ahead.

*Gonna keep an eye on you, bro,* Mike thinks.

They move on, finding nothing but more cubicles and unremitting quiet, layered with the subtle, malodorous scent of decay. They might as well be on a highway, in the sticks, in the dead of night, staring down an endless road ahead of them.

"You're totally right," Zander whispers, "this place really does go on forever." He feels something snap inside him.

*Hold it together,* he thinks. *There's got to be an explanation for all of this.*

*Really?* that interloping voice from the back of his mind asks. *An explanation for the pornographic live stream of Erik and Vicky grinding into each other?*

Zander clinches his jaw. Fights away the image, the burn in his chest and the flush of anger. Wanting to distract himself, he assures Mike that there has got to be an exit coming up.

They press on.

Walking ceaselessly, as if on a treadmill to nowhere.

"Honestly," Mike breaks the silence, "I don't remember the building being this big outside. Tall, yeah. As wide a shopping mall? No."

They keep walking. Occasionally Mike glances behind him at the enveloping pitch black that swallows up their trail like an encroaching black hole.

"Did we get turned around?" Mike asks.

"How so?"

"Well we can't tell where we're headed," Mike replies. "Could be walking in circles for all we know."

While Zander might be unsure of what he saw in the crawlspace, and of the validity of what transpired on the coffee machine, he is certain that they have been going in one direction this whole time. They never turned once.

"We're not," Zander states as though reassuring himself. Then stops short.

Mike practically bumps into him. "What's up?"

Zander's cell phone battery is down to twenty percent. He shows Mike, who responds with, "We've been walking that long?"

"Long enough," Zander says grimly.

"Maybe you've got a crappy battery?"

"It never drains this fast."

"When's the last time you went for a hike using your cell phone as your guide?"

Zander steadies himself. Avoids retorting. "I've got an idea," he says instead. He aims the light ahead at the immeasurable path that creeps deeper into the room. Then back at Mike. "Let's run."

"Run?"

"Yep. We're going to bump into a wall, a cubicle, or an exit."

"Alright." Mike pauses for a beat. "After you."

They take off running with Zander in the lead. The cell phone light cuts white swaths through the pitch-black room. Their shoes thumping as they sprint breathlessly–

Something crosses their path in a blur, quick as a deer cutting across a deserted dirt road in the black of night.

The two men stumble to a halt.

"The... heck..." Mike asks, panting between words, "was... that?"

*You're asking me?* Zander thinks. *Maybe it was the one of the others? Maybe everyone followed Kyle and left?*

"No... idea." Zander does his best to catch his breath. "Let's just... keep going,"

Mike checks his phone. Five percent battery. No service.

They continue, but not before something trips Zander. He tumbles forward and the cell phone goes spinning out of his hand, swirling off into the shadows. "My phone!"

Zander spies a sliver of bleached light flowering out in a subtle circle on the callous Berber carpet. The phone has landed face down just a foot away, under a desk. He lunges for it, hand open, outstretched–

*Another* hand steals it and kills the light.

# Chapter 12–Kate

Kate's eyes flutter open and she is greeted by the murky haze of the room's brumous lighting. Tufts of fog pass above her in waves, masking the taupe ceiling tiles above her. Her head is all the way back in her chair. She rolls her head forward to find that she is at her desk. The computer monitor is off. Her cell phone lays face up next to the keyboard.

*Oh crap,* she thinks. *Did I fall asleep during the training?*

She adjusts her glasses. The lenses are fraught with smudges. She moves to wipe them off, but a brutal stabbing pain stops her short.

"Ouch!" Warily, she touches her nose.

*What the heck is this?*

The black cable identical to the one that was lodged inside Wayne's nostril is hooked in her nose as well.

Kate notices the icy tingle of anxiety spreading over her body as a panic attack takes root. She grabs the cable with both hands–the vicious barbs prick her soft skin and she winces, hands retreating. She shakes her hands in an inefficacious attempt to quiet the discomfort.

"Oh, God, please," she mutters to herself. "Please, God. What is this?"

Leaning forward, she sees that the cable disappears under her desk. Taking a deep breath, as if preparing to take a high dive off a precipitous sea cliff, she grasps the cable once more. Braving the sting of a dozen black teeth biting into her palms, she yanks the cable desperately. Deliberate, knuckle-whitening tugs. But the harder she tries to remove the hooked end, the more it hurts.

The computer screen in front of her comes to life, flashing erratically as the desktop tower tucked by her feet forces it out of hibernation. She pauses. Gives her haggard breathing a chance to catch up. The punishing pangs in her nose beat like a bass drum. She grinds her teeth, fighting back the sensation, and stares intently at the screen.

A picture fades into view, as if being downloaded via an old dial-up connection. At first the image is blurry, but gradually sharpens. Kate watches and another inexplicable cold flush of apprehension spreads throughout her. As she makes out four figures, her palms instantly go clammy, her glasses fog, and her breathing hastens.

Kate feels a worm of worry slither inside her like a redacted phobia reluctantly resurrected, re-surging from the depths of a black and reviled corner of her mind that her younger self had amputated—but now was back.

The image's resolution enhances, bringing into focus the horrid faces of the monsters that scarred her as a child.

Faces that she would later laugh at as she grew up. She admonishes herself, wondering, *How could I have feared a bunch of dudes in make-up, clad in black leather, and wearing four-inch heeled boots? Even if they were adorned with horns and the angered faces of dragons, it was all just a show! A rock and roll show!*

But the terror Kate is feeling now is anything but laughable.

She is seven again.

When Kate was a kid, her loathsome aunt, Mina, used to be her sitter. Kate's mother was a nurse and often got stuck working nights, leaving her in Mina's care, which she abhorred. When Mina babysat, it meant at some point she would pull out that fearful picture of the four men—members of a glam-rock band, dressed in costume armor, faces obscured by black-and-white face paint, representing their individual characters within the band.

The first member in the picture was a human feline known as *Fang-Man*, who had bloody incisors, crooked whiskers scribbled across his cheeks and shamrock green makeup highlighting his eyes. Leaning against Fang-Man stood the lead singer—a hellishly tall monster, known simply as *The Beast*, with clawed black marks that stretched across his eyes like the jetty wings of a bat and an unusually rangy tongue that drooped down to his chin.

The other two men had stars decorating their eyes. *Blackstar*, who had a black star on his right eye and *Mr. Shimmer*, who had stars covering both eyes—one coal-black, one glittering silver. Between the four men, Mr. Shimmer unnerved Kate the most, as he liked to bare his jagged, serrated teeth between tar-colored lips that arched upwards into the strained smile of a jester.

At first, the band's photo was used as a behavioral device. If Kate misbehaved, Mina would punish her by showing her the photo of the four men and warn that if she didn't shape up—going to bed when she was told to, finishing all of her vegetables, or following any sort of rule that Mina felt was broken—that *they* would show up late at night and get her.

Mina told Kate that if she were lucky, she would hear them coming first. Their big boots. Clamoring on the floor like the footfalls of giants. Menacingly slow, steady, and drawing disturbingly close. If she wasn't lucky, then she'd simply awaken to the four men. Their horrid monochrome figures floating above her bed like a pack of ravenous hyenas, preparing to pounce on her.

This imagery was enough to ensure Kate followed Mina's strict babysitting rules to the letter.

Unfortunately, Mina quickly grew bored with Kate's compliance. Missed taunting her. Missed her tinny, shrill shrieks. So, with a snarky grin, Mina would randomly catch Kate watching cartoons or coloring with her crayons and whisper, "Hey, Kate. Guess what I got here?" Then she would slide the photo out of a manilla envelope like some top-secret document borrowed from the devil himself, earning horrified high-pitched screams from Kate. "They're coming for you."

Some nights, Mina would mix it up. Hiding pictures of the four men throughout the house. The backs of cereal boxes. Inside toilet lids. Under pillows. Folded neatly between the pages of whatever books Kate was reading.

Finding these pictures became the Easter eggs of Kate's nightmares.

Kate pleaded for Mina to stop with the photos, but her aunt couldn't. She got a rise out of hearing her scream. Enjoyed the game. But that game devolved into something more disturbing as Mina's tortuous creativity evolved. Mina purchased used two masks off eBay. One of The Beast and one of Mr. Shimmer—the two characters that Kate grew to revile the most. Whenever the mood struck her, she'd don one of these masks and randomly pop out of a closet or the bathroom and scare the life out of Kate. Occasionally, Mina would wake her up in the middle of the night and toss her into the closet, imprisoning her for hours on end via locks and threats, warning her that if she tried to get out or tell her mother about this, The Beast or Mr. Shimmer would show up and hurt her.

One night, when Kate was pulled out of bed and forced to hide in the closet, she dared to ask Mina, "Why do you do this to me? Why do you hate me so much?"

"Why?"

Kate nodded, tears spilling from her eyes.

"Because I hate your mother."

"But... why?" she asks through her sobs.

"Because she's a whore."

Kate had no clue what that word—

"Do you know what a *whore* is?" Mina asked. "Of course not. You're seven." She paused, searching for a way to relay it to Kate. "A whore is a thief. You know what a thief is?"

"Yes."

"It's someone who steals things, right?"

"Yeah."

"Well, your mom stole your dad from me. He was mine first." The words shot from Mina's mouth like little bullets. "How do you think they met? Through me. Did mommy ever tell you that?"

Kate shook her head no.

"Course not. Because mommy withholds the truth. She lies." Mina touched a lock of Kate's hair. "Just like she probably tells you you're pretty, right?" She then moved her hand to Kate's chin, giving it an unwelcome pinch. "But not with that big ol' moon chin of yours."

Kate pulled away. "Stop it."

"I'm not your mommy, which means I'll always tell you the truth," Mina said. "You're nothing but a crybaby who's going to get uglier as you get older. Boys won't like you. Girls will make fun of you. And you'll be lonely for a very... long time."

"Stop it!" Tears welled in Kate's eyes.

"The only things that'll love you will walk on four legs and require you to sift through their poop every few days."

"STOP IT!"

"Yell all you want. Your mom won't tell you the truth, Kate, but I will."

Kate snarled, "I hate you!"

Mina snatched Kate by the cheeks, squeezed hard as she hissed, "And I *hate* your mom." She tightened her grip and continued, "And if you ever say anything about this little talk, I'll make sure the monsters will come for you. I'll make sure all four of them chew you up, starting with your toes."

The four men glare at Kate from the monitor.

*This is fake,* she tells herself. *They're just a rock band from New York, and Mina was the actual monster!*

The men stare Kate down with their vile grins and fiendish armor.

*You met the lead singer, remember?*

The men's eyes twinkle like distant stars from a dark dimension.

*The guy was super down-to-earth. Even signed your T-shirt! He's not a monster. None of them are!*

The stark achromatic makeup on their faces makes them appear evermore evil.

*You even told him what Mina did to you as a kid, and you both laughed about it! Heck... he even wrote 'Mina is a bitch!' on your shirt!*

But as much as her mind tries to reason, tries to take the sting out of that childhood trauma, the four figures on the monitor glower at her as if she is a meal they didn't get to devour when she was a child.

Kate sucks in the stuffy air as The Beast moves. Lowers his head ever so slowly until Kate can barely see his eyes beyond his furrowed brow. Eyes that remain locked on her.

The screen flickers several times.

Then the picture fades back in once again.

Now the outfits on the men have changed from that of glam-rock gods to reptilian freaks. Their faces droop and glower. Their hair sags, like the saturated threads of a dirty mop head. They have morphed into something significantly more malefic, worse than any picture that Mina showed her. She's staring at men no longer, but four creatures that have seemed to have melded with their makeup.

The Beast, head still lowered, eyes glaring straight at Kate, sticks out his tongue and wags it like the brassy bob of a grandfather clock.

Kate's breathing stops for a moment.

The monitor cuts off, followed up by the sounds of footfalls in the far corner of the room.

Several hulking footsteps.

Prickles of anxiety explode across Kate's body. She cries out as she resumes pulling at the cable nested inside her nostril. Searing pain gets her eyes watering. As the heavy boots close in, she feels the floor vibrate.

Kate pulls with all her might. Barbs cut into her hands, ripping through the delicate inner walls of her nasal cavity. She feels that she almost has it free, as a shadow catches her eyes. The heads of tall silhouettes waver in the distance, highlighted by a few dim LED lights here and there.

*They're coming for you, Kate.*

Kate yanks as hard as she can. The footfalls grow and the ground beneath her shakes as the cable finally snaps free from her nose. A stripe of her blood hits the monitor. The blaring pain is insane, but the thought of meeting the four men in the flesh eclipses all physical sensations right now. She launches from her chair, forgetting her cell phone in her haste, and takes off running.

Without looking back, Kate bumbles through the dark room, banging into any obstacles in her wake—until she finds a door. She rams her body against it, forcing it open—

But not before the lights cut out.

And something catches her shirt from behind.

She whips around to a pair of bedeviled eyes ogling her, accompanied by a long, wet tongue.

Kate breaks free and slams the door in the creature's face. The lights come back on and she's in a long hallway full of doors along either side. Sprinting as fast as she can, she grasps the handle of the door closest to her and hurries inside.

There's a commotion in the hallway. One—or all of them—are right behind her.

# Chapter 13–Wading Through The Darkness

Disbelieving, Zander reaches out into the blackness. He pats the surrounding ground, trying frantically to locate his cell phone, hoping to brush upon it. Finds nothing.

*Was that really a hand I saw?* Zander asks himself. *No. No, it wasn't. The screen just cut off. That's all.*

"Mike?"

"Yeah, man," Mike answers. "I'm here."

"Here? Why don't you turn on your flashlight so I can find you?"

"Because five percent battery just went to almost zero, ok?"

"Fine. Just stay put and keep talking," Zander says with a huff. "I'll find you by the sound of your voice."

"What do you want me to talk about?"

"I don't care. Whatever." Zander stands, palms out, and progresses through the room. "Just keep talking."

"Well... to be honest, I'm sorry I took this job. I mean, there like ten other gigs I applied to that were closer to my house–"

"That paid less?" Zander asks as he tracks Mike's voice.

"Well, yeah." Mike seems *further* away now. "Now I know why."

"Why's that?"

Mike's voice is even further as he replies, "Because we got lured into some messed-up shit."

*He can't be that far from me,* Zander thinks. *We were right next to each other. It's not like we ran off in opposite directions.*

"Are you walking around or something?" Zander asks.

"No."

"Because you sound further away."

"Maybe you're walking in the wrong direction?"

*But I'm not,* Zander thinks. *I was walking straight towards you!*

"Ok, keep talking then," Zander tells him.

"Bro, I can't think right now—"

"You got a girlfriend? Wife? Boyfriend?"

Mike manages a laugh. "None of the above. Just a dog."

Zander bumps into a cubicle. Feels the synthetic fibers carpeting the wall crunch under his fingertips.

"Just a super loyal dog who smiles every time he sees me."

Zander steers around the obstacle, hearing Mike more clearly now.

"Don't matter what time of day or night," Mike continues. "He's always right by the door, wagging that little nub of a tail. Smiling, the way dogs do when they love their owners."

*Did this room grow?* Zander wonders. *Did the walls up and move?*

"What kind of dog is he?" Zander asks.

"Pit bull. Best dogs in the world. At least, in my opinion."

"That's not a popular opinion." Zander bumps up against something cold and metallic. He feels around. It has handles on one side.

*File cabinet?*

"Pits don't stink. Don't bark a lot. And they don't bite—unless you train 'em that way. That's why they get a bad rap."

"Contrary to what the news says about them, right?" Zander moves past the file cabinet. Mike sounds incredibly close.

"Screw the news! They never report about those other ankle-biting breeds that go mad and attack their owners. You ever seen a chihuahua when it's pissed?"

*Found him,* Zander thinks. *He's right in front of me.*

"Your dog got a name?" Zander puts out a hand, grasping at the empty air until he feels Mike's fingertips. Their hands slide together and with a solid hoist, Zander leans back and helps Mike to his feet.

"Thanks, man," Mike says. "So, do we keep holding hands in the dark? Or what?"

"Hilarious," Zander says sarcastically. "But first I kind of need to find my cell phone, or some sort of flashlight."

"I still got mine, brother."

"But you said your battery is at zero."

"I said almost," Mike says as he powers on his cell phone. "Was trying to conserve every bit of light I could."

"Fair enough," Zander watches as Mike brushes his thumb across the phone's screen and flips on the flashlight. "So, you didn't tell me what your dog's name is."

Mike shines the cell phone light on himself.

Zander senses the color emptying from his face.

"My dog's name," Erik says with a nefarious grin, "Is Erik."

# Chapter 14–Bishop

Bishop awakens to a sharp pain in his nose. Eyes flicking open, he stiffens. Scans his surroundings. The room is scarcely illuminated. A nicotine-tinted cloud drifts above the cubicles like a sea of ghosts, shrouding the few lights that remain on overhead. His gaze levels with his computer screen. Catches a reflection of himself. Along with something black and spindly coming out of his nose.

*What on God's green earth?* he thinks.

Bishop brings a wary hand up to touch it. "Jesus..."

The other end of the cable disappears under Bishop's desk. He leans forward, examines closer.

*The hell's it attached to?*

Bishop's arthritic joints complain as he slides off the chair, lowers himself, and seizes the cable. The prickly cord bites into his skin the moment he clutches it. Ignoring the pain, he coils the thorny rope around his hands, presses his feet flat up against the wall of the cubicle, and gives it a solid tug. Pulls back on the vile rope as if trying to uproot a stubborn weed from its concrete home.

It does not budge.

Corralling much needed stamina, he goes for round two. As the virgula dig unbearably into his weathered skin, he grinds his teeth, and throws his back into dislodging the cursed cable.

With a resounding *thwap*, it snaps free.

Bishop takes another moment. Breathing heavily. Dizzy and borderline nauseous from the effort, he leans back against the cubicle. The hard floor presses unapologetically into his tailbone as he contemplates pulling the cable free from his nose now.

*This is going to hurt.*

Bishop fingers his left nostril. The cord goes deep. But how deep?

*Doesn't matter. Gotta get it out.*

He grips the cable. The barbs prick his skin. Wraps the bristled wire around both fists.

Counts down in his head:

*Three.*

Deep breath.

*Two.*

Exhale.

*Dammit, this is really going to hurt!*

Deep breath.

Exhale.

*One!*

Teeth clamped. Eyes tight. Muscles locked. Fists quivering. A grievous groan escapes him as he pulls downward. Feels like he is fishing a razor blade through his nostril. The crescendo of pain builds, until at last, there is the unsettling *snap* of cartilage or flesh tearing as Bishop rips the cable's barbed end free from his nose. A mixture of blood and mucus follows, and he unleashes a harrowed groan that resounds within the vacuumed hush of the office.

Woozy from the extrication, Bishop takes the bottom of his shirt and dabs his nose. Summoning whatever energy he has left, he pushes himself off the ground with an anguished grunt. He rests a hand on the cubicle wall, steadying himself.

The stillness of the room is unsettling. There is not an inkling of sound. Not the electronic chatter from computers or their peripheral devices. Nor is there the hushed whoosh of the AC cycling on, recirculating the stale air tainted with hints of decay.

The quiet makes Bishop's tinnitus more noticeable. His ears have always rung, the result of spending a lifetime working with power tools and lawn equipment. Not to mention the security detail. Bouncing for local rock venues during the Eighties. Ear plugs were a passing thought in those days. At least for him.

The lights click off.

A low, grinding sound breaks the room's silence.

Bishop's nerves light up. Heart fluttering. Pulse quickening.

The grinding noise draws towards him.

*What... is... that?*

The noise is now accompanied by a persistent squeal. Distinct protests from wheels in need of a healthy dose of WD-40. The closer the screeching wheels get, the more Bishop fills with dread.

*I know that sound.*

Bishop reaches in the darkness. Clutching the cubicle walls of his desk, he uses them as a sort of railing, guiding him out from his workspace—at least, as far as he can tell. One hand on the walls. The other extended in front of him. A blind mouse in a big maze.

The wailing wheels abruptly cease.

Bishop freezes. Waits. Listens. Nothing stirs, save for his uneven breaths—then he hears something that makes the gray hairs on his skin stand.

He hears a woman whistling a song that he has not heard in decades.

The whistling grows close.

Then the whistling turns to singing.

And then she croons the chorus about 'making up one's mind.'

About 'being her angel.'

Asking, does he 'want to die?'

The lyrics pound at Bishop's brain like a migraine. He recognizes the song as *Possum Kingdom* by *The Toadies*. Larissa had been in her forties when that song came out.

They met at a biker bar. A ramshackle dump called The Stuck Pig. Touted the best BBQ on the Florida West Coast. Bishop hadn't gone there for the pulled pork. He had just finished a job helping the owner build a storage shed out back. The work was rewarded with a series of cold Budweisers, whatever he wanted to eat, and an earful of bad karaoke.

Larissa had been on the mic. Belting her lungs out to that song. When she was done, she found a stool next to Bishop. He offered her a beer if she promised never to sing again. She laughed, took him up on the brew, and soon after, they started dating.

Larissa was brassbound, cursed like a stand-up comic, and rode Bishop like he was the last man on Earth. Initially, she made him feel like he was worth something. That he was not a miserable, lonely wreck of a person. Not meant to be cast aside—the way his mother did when he was a boy. Threw him to the wolves of the state. Left him moving from foster home to foster home.

After a lifetime of instability, Larissa had proven to be the only thing that kept Bishop grounded. She was his glue. He was with her for a year, which was a lifetime in his dating years. Never once thinking of moving again or switching jobs. He didn't want to leave her side. She was his sunshine. His everything...

But her love came with a price.

Larissa liked to get drunk. Blackout drunk.

'Tell me my name,' drunk.

'Let's do dirty things to each other and not tell the world,' kind of drunk.

But kinkiness aside, there was a darker side of her. And that fluctuated with her mood.

There was rage.

And, boy, she could rage. Seething with this fermented furor that effervesced from some childhood trauma. Within her was unresolved angst that clung to her soul, stained it the way wine does an ivory dress. Unapologetic. Undeniable. It was there, and it was not going away.

There was no removing it.

There was no disregarding it.

It was there.

Always.

Perhaps sometimes a mere ghostly shade of pink. A trace of red. Halfway gone, but not forgotten. A stain is a stain. Ignore it. Treat it. Paint it. It never leaves. It just takes a new form. A revised narrative shapes to frame how the stain came to be. Larissa's stains from her past could not be forgotten or masked, and alcohol uncovered them.

And when she drank, those demons that talked of her past came out.

The fights between Bishop and Larissa were monumental. She loved to argue about money. He was a dyed-in-the-wool factotum, and she looked down upon that. She ranted about how he didn't make enough as a handyman or doing whatever odd job he had at the time. How he didn't take her out enough. How he didn't dress nicer. She especially enjoyed picking on his weathered work boots. Often, she would comment about how other men had better shoes.

*But did they bring you flowers like I did?* Bishop pondered, but never asked. *Did they give you flowers for no occasion at all, and not to make up for some stupid mistake, but because they loved you? Did they surprise you with the fresh loaves of Cuban bread you coveted from that quaint bakery in Ybor City? Or the raspberry sangria you enjoyed? The bottles delivered straight from Spain to our grocer's shelves? Did they take you to the doctor when you got sick? Did they fix your toilet or hang shelves so that you can buy more clothing for yourself, while you give me a thank-you card and a five-dollar lottery ticket on my birthday?*

*No. They just had better shoes than me.*

Larissa came from a family that liked to show off their Mercedes lifestyle while secretly living paycheck to paycheck. Bishop, having come from humble, if not impoverished beginnings, knew only that he needed enough to live, eat, and sleep. If his belly was full and there was a pillow under his head and he was above ground, things were alright.

*Alright* wasn't good enough for Larissa. And at their one-year mark, this internal unrest manifested into her seeking outside entertainment. There was this new bar she frequented, Lucky Toads. The only luck she found there was at the bottom of a bottle and whatever beer-brained toads hit on her. They would ramble about trucks and fishing. Larissa would listen so long as they paid her toll, buying her drinks.

Drinks always lead to more drinks.

Following an argument with Bishop one night, she found respite at Lucky Toads. After a session of Long Island ice teas courtesy of a sharp-dressed stockbroker with pristine Cole Haan loafers—who was clearly out of his element but had a generous way with gifting drinks—she drove back home hammered. Ran a red light and nearly clipped a parked car.

Larissa stumbled to the door of her house, so drunk that she could barely put her key in the lock. Breath reeking of booze, mind still seething from the earlier quarrel, she shook Bishop awake. He nearly fell out of bed, scared out of his mind. Disregarding his reaction, she ranted. Told him he needed to earn more money. Needed a bigger place. Needed a better job. If not, she'd find a man who could give her those things.

*A man like the one with the pretty shoes*, she had thought. *Bet he drives a Beemer.*

Bishop didn't respond the way she had hoped, neither protesting nor rebutting. He seemed dumbfounded, droopy-eyed, sitting there half-awake and trying to process everything—

She slapped him and continued her verbal assault. She told him about her wonderful evening with the smooth-talking stockbroker. Told Bishop how much he didn't compare to the stylish stranger.

Bishop simply glared, speechless.

As the drunken, slurred words spilled out from her mouth, specks of spittle sprayed him. "Say somethinnnn, god-dammmmit!"

It was the first and last time Larissa had ever gotten physical with him.

Bishop brought a hand up and rubbed his cheek. Took in the moment. Her assaults, both oral and physical. Then said, "Since you're so unhappy with me, then maybe you should find someone else." He moved her aside, leaped out of bed, and dressed. "I think it is obvious by now that I'm not good enough for you."

"What?" Larissa stood here and stared with incredulous, wide eyes. "What... what did you say?"

But Bishop did not repeat himself. Years of gypsy life taught him when it was time to move. He calmly packed what scant items he had as Larissa broke out into a full-blown tantrum. Stomping her feet. Throwing up her arms in protest. A waterfall of tears streaming down her face, turning the fine-lined black mascara around her eyes into muddled streaks.

She asked him what the hell he was doing. But it *was* apparent.

He was done.

Against her pleas, her violent sobs, and screams, his countenance never faltered. He wished her well and drove off, glimpsing her defeated expression as she stood there on the porch. It was as if life itself had leaked out from her soul.

Larissa was shocked by his abrupt exit. Stunned. No one had ever done that to her. She called him repeatedly. Begged and pleaded via countless voicemails. But he never talked to her again. She tracked him down at his job, but he had promptly quit... just like she wanted. She tried to track down where he had moved to, but Bishop's itinerant nature kept him on the go. Bouncing from spare rooms, to trailer parks, to wherever he could find a comfy pillow and a warm bed. Content with just being. Nothing fancy.

Larissa did not share that same sense of self.

Following Bishop's exodus, she could not bear to be alone. She filed through a series of other men. Men who hurt her instead. Assholes who took Larissa's berating as a challenge—a chance to retaliate their inebriated authority, using fists and curse words to express their lowly regard for her.

But she put up with it. Gave up. Settled for the new deck of cards she felt life—not her own actions—had handed her. Internalizing the anger. Instead of blaming herself for her mistakes, she blamed Bishop. While he was not perfect—and he would concur himself—he took no umbrage in their arguments, nor her alcohol-infused words during their heated conflicts.

Still...

Larissa blamed him. Her last voicemail to him was her, several glasses into whatever she was imbibing, telling him, "You left me. You gave up on me. You abandoned me!"

The message, like most of Larissa's messages, hurt his heart.

"Run away, you lousy quitter!" Larissa had been a poet of vulgarity. "It's what you're good at anyway."

Bishop wanted to respond, to tell her he still loved her, but stood firm. He knew it would reopen a regretful door to a continued life of drama. To the maudlin miasma that clung to her like a foul stench. As adept as he was at fixing things, Larissa was not for him to fix. So, with tears in his eyes, he deleted her voicemails.

All of them.

Then changed his number. The last nail in the coffin of ending their communication permanently, hoping Larissa would move on.

Regrettably, she never did. One night after attempting to drown her sorrows with Jack and Coke, she made the lamentable mistake of not taking a cab home.

Bishop later discovered her fate on the news. There was a head-on collision on I-75 involving a drunk driver. Larissa had gone the wrong way up an off-ramp. Drove right into a semi-truck that was barreling down the ramp. She was not wearing her seatbelt. While the truck driver was unscathed, she sustained severe head injuries, rendering her a vegetable.

When Bishop heard the news, he had to see her. There at the hospital, a nurse wheeled Larissa out to greet him. She was unrecognizable. Her pallid, jaundiced skin was the color of a tangerine. Her misshapen head was wrapped in bandages. With only the left half of her face exposed, she stared vacantly through Bishop as if he were just a piece of furniture and not her former lover.

Knowing there was not much left that could be said or done, Bishop simply placed his hand on hers—which was cold and clammy—and told her he was sorry. It broke his heart to see her in such a depressing state. He forgave her for her wrongs and did not wish this upon her.

As the nurse rolled Larissa away, the caster wheel of her wheelchair squealed. A shrill, cringe-worthy creak. The nurse cursed inaudibly, grumbling to Larissa that no matter which wheelchair Larissa was in, she somehow always made them squeak. Bishop was about to offer to fix it, but just like Larissa, he realized some things were not his to repair.

When Bishop returned to his car, he cried his eyes out. Banged his fists against the steering wheel and slumped over sobbing until he had no more tears to shed. Distraught that he couldn't make their relationship work.

Before he could fall asleep that night, he stewed over his choice to leave.

Could he have given her more time?

Had he given up too quickly?

After hours ruminating over the varying regret-based scenarios, he finally drifted off to sleep. The next day, he awoke to something interesting. Something odd.

There was a voicemail on his answering machine. When he listened to the message, his stomach dropped:

It was from Larissa.

Bishop was dumbstruck. He had changed his number, yet somehow a message got through. Baffled, he replayed the recording again.

"This is all your fault, Bishop."

*But how could she have called me?* he wondered. *She's paralyzed.*

Bishop's question was never answered, because when he went back to visit her a week later, they said that she passed because of complications from the injury suffered.

Bishop was in shock.

But he was more disturbed when he received *another* voicemail from her the next day.

"I died because you left me."

Bishop told himself these were simply old messages, helplessly lost in the telephone network. Floundering aimlessly within the system like a stray canine seeking a home.

This was over a decade ago. Since then, he hasn't received any more communications from her.

The lights in the room come to life. Then turn off. Then on. Off. On. Off. On. Bishop curses in frustration. Feels his cell phone vibrate. He checks it.

There's a new text from Unknown:

*I'm coming for you.*

The message is followed by the familiar cries of squeaking wheels, drawing closer by the second.

# Chapter 15–Erik Sends A Text

The cell phone highlights the undersides of Erik's face, making him appear as if he is about to tell a scary story. Before Zander can process that his former best friend and now nemesis is standing before him, he's given a hard shove backwards. He hits the floor and the base of his skull rattles against the unforgiving Berber carpet.

"You can't leave," Erik informs him from somewhere above Zander.

Zander's eyes nictate vigorously, vision spinning, the vague accents of light along Erik's body loop in a sideways blur.

"Training's not done yet, stud," Erik says.

Zander presses a hand against his forehead, hoping to calm the dizzy spell. Erik's voice is painfully loud–at a volume capable of triggering the worst of headaches.

"You've got so much to learn!"

Zander tries to get up, but Erik's foot lands on his chest. Pins him against the ground with uncanny force.

"And while you're busy learning new things about SiDug... and yourself," Erik pauses, chuckles lightly, "I'll be busy teaching Vicky what it feels like to have her nipples tingle as the inner walls of her pus–"

"SHUT! UP!" Zander grasps Erik's leg with both hands. Groans as he fights to get Erik off him, but he might as well be trying to heave a car off his chest.

"Don't tell me what to do!" Erik leans in, placing more pressure on Zander's chest. "You didn't know what you had with Vicky, you ungrateful slob."

Trapped between the floor and Erik's leaden foot, Zander strains to breathe.

"But that's ok, because I'm going to have fun with you." Erik drives a bony heel into Zander's sternum, earning a strained groan from him. "Then I'll end your relationship for good."

Erik seems to weigh a thousand pounds. Zander worries his chest is going to cave in at any moment. Then Erik dangles the cell phone above Zander's head so that he can see that it's *his* cell phone and not Mike's.

"Going to send Vicky a quick text," Erik tells him as he licks his lips. "And your days with her are done." Zander's cell phone casts an unnerving glow on Erik's face, highlighting the vicious twinkle of delight in his eyes as he thumbs a message.

*How can he send a text,* Zander asks himself, *if I don't have signal? And how did Erik get in here? Does he work for SiDug too?*

"There." Erik chuckles, amused with himself. "It's sent." He releases Zander, taking a step back into the coverture of the shadows.

Zander sits up and winces, rubbing his sternum. It throbs as if he took a hammer to the chest. "What's... sent?"

"Oh, this," Erik tosses the cell phone next to Zander where it lands with a thwack. Zander picks it up. On it is a picture of him with a brunette woman he has never seen before. It's a selfie of the couple smiling back at the camera.

Zander looks up at Erik.

"Keep swiping," Erik tells him.

As Zander swipes left, the pictures become more sexual. The next few photos feature the brunette in various stages of undress until she is fully nude and sprawled out on the bed, legs open, exposing her most intimate details to a dumbstruck Zander.

*Who is this woman?* he asks himself.

He continues swiping to uncover a montage of the two of them in the throes of ecstasy, sweat-soaked, twisted up in a mess of bedsheets. All taken from crude angles, leaving no curve of flesh concealed from the camera.

Zander feels his heart drop like an elevator.

"Now read the message I sent her," Erik taunts with a wink.

Zander swipes up on the screen, reads:

*I have to come clean, Vicky. I've found someone else, and I'd rather be honest than hold back any longer. You deserve better. I won't be home for a bit—training is going crazy good. So, take from the apartment whatever you feel is yours. I'll be staying in a hotel. I'm sorry for ever hurting you. Wish you all the best.*

Underneath the message is a validation showing that the message was sent.

Several animated dots appear as Vicky responds:

*Go to hell!*

*And your new bitch!*

The messages might as well have been bullets, the way they pierce Zander's heart. His mind races. Speechless. He tries to think, but a panic worse than any other has overtaken his brain.

*Who the hell's that woman? Was I drunk or something?*

The doubt creeps in like an unwanted guest.

*No! I would never do something like that! These pictures must be Photoshopped or something. Erik is just screwing with me!*

Zander tries to text her back but can't.

NO SERVICE.

Zander senses his world collapsing. "No-no-no-no-no!" As he gets to his feet, he stares into the darkness. Asks Erik, "What did you do, you asshole?"

"I did what you could never do." Erik steps forward and Zander aims the light at him. "Finish something!"

Zander is horrified to find that Erik is naked from head to toe. A bloody gash runs along the left side of his chest—

A hand comes sailing from the shadows as Erik swats the phone out of Zander's hand. It goes skidding off. Erik follows with a swift kick to Zander's stomach, stealing his breath. He drops to the ground and curls into a ball, eyes tight and teeth grinding.

"Sorry," Erik says, "but we're going to have to cut your training short." Zander hears Erik fumble with something, followed by a grunt.

The lights in the room come on.

Zander opens his eyes. Finds a stark-naked Erik hoisting a monster of a printer above his head.

83

The lights go out.

"No!" Zander shouts, anticipating the commercial printer slamming down on him with all the weight of a fridge. He shields his head with his arms just as−

A cell phone light comes to life, and a hand is extended to Zander. "Found you!" And before Zander can respond, Mike pulls him up. "Come on. Let's go."

Mike runs, but stops short, glances back at Zander, who is just standing there with this listless look.

"Hey!" Mike barks. "Come on, man!"

Zander locks up as his mind goes into overdrive, processing the fact that things with Vicky could be completely over. That he almost died moments ago. Trying to decipher which is worse.

*Losing Vicky*, his mind responds. *That's worse−*

"COME ON!" Mike gives Zander a shove, snapping him out his spell and the two take off running.

# Chapter 16–New Year's Resolutions

The light of Wayne's cell phone is met with endless cubicles and empty chairs. Beyond that, the shadowed depths of the room await. He makes his way, diligently moving in one general direction—straight.

*There's got to be an exit around here, somewhere—*

A door opens and shuts behind him.

Wayne turns to stone.

*Oh... no.*

Footsteps shuffle within the umbra.

*Please don't tell me Chet followed me in here.*

Neck muscles moving like molasses, he slowly turns his head and glances over his shoulder.

Something gallops his way. Footsteps trampling the floor at a frenzied pace. Thump-thump, thump-thump, thump-thump.

Wayne shrieks as he breaks into a full-blown sprint. Cell phone light careening from one side to the other as he charges ahead. Bounding down the aisle like a frightened pony, his feet pound clumsily as his paunch jiggles. A stitch forms along his side.

*Should've kept to my New Year's resolution for once!*

Every January, Wayne professes on social media that this will be the year of change. *New year, new me. Self-care is self-love. Mindfulness is happiness.*

Insert the mantra-of-the-year here, and Wayne is posting about it on January first.

Weight loss has always snuck its way into his annual promises to himself. He starts the year strong, like many do. Hitting the gym three to four times a week. Sprinting on the treadmill with the exhausting intensity of an antelope outrunning a lion. Two weeks into his gym membership and diet plans, life gets in the way, self-loathing rears its head and that internal, unrealistic critic blasts him for not having a six-pack by the end of the month.

*I wish I stuck with the stupid gym now,* Wayne laments as his legs burn with lactic acid. Joints grinding. Lungs aflame. He totters to a halt and keels over, propping his palms against his knees. He gasps for air, sucking in big, stuffy gulps. He glances back, shining his flashlight and praying Chet hasn't followed him. Nothing there but empty cubicles and vacant office chairs.

He takes a moment and, still huffing, he places a palm along the side of his belly. That nasty cramp runs up his torso, sparking an excruciating jolt with each breath.

He arches his back, grunts as he tries to stretch out the cramp at his side. The constricting muscles of his abdomen go as taut as steel cables.

*I'm so out of shape.*

Head throbbing, veins pulsing throughout his flabby physique, he feels like he's been running a marathon, though here in the dark it's hard to tell how far he's actually gone. Or how big this place is. The room seems to expand with each step.

"What the hell did you get yourself into?" Wayne asks himself aloud. His voice is trailed by dead air, a noiselessness that sends a shiver through him. "You got yourself into a fine mess. Why? Because you're an idiot."

"You got that right," a raspy voice whispers from behind.

Wayne's heart flutters. He spins around, cell phone cutting blessed swaths of light wherever he looks.

"Who—who's there?" He asks aloud.

No one responds.

Wayne gathers every diminishing ounce of courage to mask the fright in his voice and shouts, "I know someone's there!" He surveys the room, finding only an empty aisle that extends infinitely in either direction, framed in by what appears to be an expansive honeycomb of cubicles. Anything beyond what his cell phone's light can illuminate is choked with shadows. "Quit wasting my time and come out already!"

The room remains library quiet.

*Ok, so should I run or stay put?*

Before his mind can answer the question, a horrible thing happens.

The light from his cell phone dies.

Wayne curses. Anxiously taps the screen, but it's dead.

*Oh, no-no-no-no-no-no-no-no.* His mind races. *This can't be happening right now–*

"Oh, but it is, Wayne," that same raspy voice whispers. "And I assure you, I'm not wasting your time. In fact, nothing about you is going to waste."

Wayne's pulse quickens, an uncoiling unease unravels inside him. "Who-who said that?"

"Me, you big dummy."

"Who are you?"

Silence.

Then the voice replies from another direction, "You know who I am, *Eggie*."

Wayne turns towards the voice. "Chet?" Anger floods him. He bites his lip then belts out, "Did you invite me here to torture me?"

The voice laughs.

Chet's hearty, hateful laugh.

"What? Did you miss me?" Wayne seethes, the anger superseding his nerves. "Still can't get enough bullying me, huh?"

*This is just a prank, and this jerk is behind it!*

Chet laughs again, but this time, his chuckling comes from another direction.

"Yeah, laugh it up," Wayne says. "You want to play games with me? Well, I've got a lot of friends. Lawyer friends. And they'll sue the piss out of you and this bogus company!"

The laughter bounds about the room.

Limbs trembling, Wayne rallies against his nerves and shouts, "I'm not playing, Chet! I'm going to take you to court for false imprisonment, kidnapping, and harassment! You hear me! We're not teenagers anymore, jerk-off!"

Chet's laughter grows so loud, it grinds on Wayne. He squeezes his fists, ready to knock Chet out.

Then the laughter stops.

Wayne, shaking all over, spins around in the shadows, adrenaline and festering adolescent angst briefly igniting a renewed fire in him.

*He thinks he's going to bully me as an adult,* Wayne thinks. *Well, he's got another thing coming to him. With money and experience on my side, I'll take him down the smart way. The legal way!*

Quiet blankets the room once again. Beyond his own shallow breathing, Wayne listens intently, no longer hearing whispers or laughter, but something else.

Footsteps.

Coming closer.

Anxiety overrides angst as apprehension squeezes Wayne's chest.

The footsteps hasten, transitioning from walking to running.

Wayne's hairs stand on end. Goosebumps form along his body. The footfalls thud against the ground with the uneven cadence of a galloping beast. He screams as Chet comes straight for him—

The ceiling lights in the room come back on, and Wayne catches Zander and Mike running straight for him, just milliseconds before they collide into each other.

# Chapter 17–Kate's Motivational Experience

T he lights above Kate unveil a small lounge filled with contemporary Scandinavian furniture. The air is musty, rank with the odor of unattended mold left to spread unopposed like some nanoscopic army. Off to one side is a refrigerator with a built-in LED flatscreen in the door that promises to entertain or reveal what is cooling inside. Huddled against it, a microwave and stainless-steel Keurig. Both look unused. Decorations within the kitchenette are sparse, save for a set of art deco letters in the vintage marquee style of a retro theater. Fixed above a minimalist leather couch that hugs the wall, the letters spell: FEED.

For a moment, she stares at the appliances. The microwave beeps suddenly. Across the digital display, a message scrolls from right to left. In dull, amber characters, it reads:

U READY?

Kate's skin frosts over with fear.

The microwave kicks on, humming with electricity as if something is being cooked inside as it counts down. While the interior light never comes on, the accompanying noise of the carousel wheel grinding as it twirls the thick glass disk inside is there.

The display blinks.

5.

4.

3.

2.

1.

*BEEP!*

The beep is jarring, earning a startled gasp out of Kate. She doesn't know why, but she jumps. It's not like she's never seen or used a microwave before. It was her entire kitchen when she worked retail. Mall food and fast food got expensive on a retail wage, so she lived off of the cheap and the microwavable. This diet included frozen burritos that could have doubled as doorstops or sodium-laden stir-fry bowls that pretended to be healthy.

"Pop 'em in the microwave, heat 'em and eat 'em." These foods were *shovel ready*, as she'd tell her coworkers. Especially those who complained about the cost of eating out or the lack of adequate shift breaks.

"Forget the food court, for starters. It's a rip-off," she'd explain. "And second, you don't have time to play with forks and knives when you're trying to push Indonesian wicker furniture or overpriced Italian Damask pillows. I've learned you've got to have shovel-ready food. Crap you can either eat with a spoon or shove into your face. Customers don't care if you haven't had a lunch break on a long shift. They just want to know if their twenty percent coupon from two years ago will still be honored. Or if you can fully refund their purchase of a Moroccan ivory and gray trellis rug that has Cabernet stains on it that somehow *we* put there, and not them."

When Kate was hungry or had been deprived of her hours in favor of other employees, these types of angst-infused lectures reared their head and resulted in a barrage of complaints to her colleagues. Even to her own surprise. Not one to be confrontational ever, she had always made it a point to keep the peace, be agreeable. But sometimes things leaked out of her. The buried negativity inside her, tucked away like a diary full of terrible memories—sometimes it seeped into her daily life. And she owed that all to Mina.

Eventually these soapbox rants made it to the ears of her manager and lead to her firing.

And her ultimately finding work...

With SiDug.

The display on the microwave now reads: OPEN PLEASE.

Kate feels her heart dance within her chest like a small bird fluttering wildly within someone's cupped hands. Part of her is compelled to do as the appliance is telling her to. The other part is wondering what the hell she is thinking.

*Leave the creepy thing and just go,* her mind shouts. *Go, already!*

She turns and runs–

*BEEP! BEEP! BEEP!*

Kate takes a clumsy step forward, leg midair, pausing, then clapping her foot against the ground. She halts. Gazes squarely at the peculiar box as it chirps once more.

The text scrolls quicker now: OPEN... PLEASE!

OPEN PLEASE.

OPEN PLEASE.

OPEN PLEASE.

Her body seems to move on its own–against the grumbling of the rational-minded complaints of her brain. Arm extending, she wraps her hand around the handle. Gives the muddy amber display another glance.

OPEN.

A pause. Next message:

PLEASE.

The microwave door emits a muted click as she opens it. The interior light finally turns on. Parked on the circular glass tray is a glossy piece of paper. Scribbled across it in black Sharpie:

*Who's the bitch now?*

*Love, Mina.*

Kate's body shivers, icing over with apprehension. She cautiously flips the photograph over.

It's the four men.

A sputtered insufflation escapes her. Covering her mouth with her hand, she flings the photo aside as if it had caught fire.

The LED screen on the refrigerator powers on. Corporate Cory appears, rigid in his perfect posture and professionally folded hands. Suddenly the picture jitters and sputters like damaged frames from an old film reel, twisting Cory's body into impossible angles.

The image rights itself. With a broad wave and plastic smile, Cory says, "Hi, Kate! Hope training is going well. Should you need a break, please make yourself comfortable in our lounge, as you will be with us for a long time." His specious smile widens to the point of appearing painful. "An insanely... long... time."

Cory's image fades and is replaced by a close-up of The Beast, whose ghastly mouth opens, unfurling an elongated tongue that stretches downward. Through the greasy white face paint, he stares icily at her with oily black eyes that shimmer like pools of freshly poured tar.

Kate freaks, guns it towards the nearest door and finds herself in an unfamiliar room. She slams the door behind her and throws her back against it, panting. Heaving with panic, she surveys her new surroundings.

This room is well lit, as wide as it is long. In the center is a mishmash of trashed desks, broken cubicle walls, and upturned chairs, piled up like some bizarre office bonfire waiting to be set aflame by a disgruntled employee. The walls are a somber shade of gray. If depression had a color palette, it would be this paint scheme. Ironically, decorating these walls is a contrasting collection of framed motivational posters. Some hang crooked, some are impeccably level. At the far end of the room is a garish peach colored sofa that somehow survived the 1970s and end up here. Beyond that is the exit door.

The space is alarmingly quiet, with only the sound of her throttled breaths filling her ears. The stench of decay flirts within the air of the closeted atmosphere. With each shallow breath, she inhales the rancid air. She coughs, expelling the foulness from her lungs. She wipes away the drops of sweat that have congregated along her brow and on her glasses. Then she peels herself away from the entrance and takes a wary step forward.

She eyes the posters along the wall. The first one is that of a group of divers, jumping off a steep cliff. Captioned in big letters: DESCEND. Underneath the photo, in a smaller font: *Down we go. Together we flow.*

Kate makes a face as though she just tasted something sour.

The next poster is of a rat struggling to free itself from a mousetrap. Mouth agape, frozen in misery. Eyes forever soulless and wet with finality.

Caption: TETHER.

Underneath: *That which binds us, frees us.*

*What is going on?* she thinks.

The next one features a jovial group of people gathered at a campfire. They're mid-conversation, as if this moment was stolen from a commercial peddling outdoor camping equipment. The camp-goers are armed with cans of beers and roasting sticks, surrounding an amorphous hunk of meat ablaze above a fiery pit.

Caption: FEAST.

Kate leans in for a closer look at what's being roasted. "Oh God." Reeling back from the image, she fights the urge to vomit as she realizes the slab of flesh is not a foul nor a swine, but a human. The armless, legless stump of a torso.

Caption: *Food brings folks together.*

Kate's knees suddenly wobble, as though composed of gelatin and not bone. Her stomach does cartwheels. She skitters sideways, nearly tripping, and props a hand up against the wall, stopping herself from falling. Gasping, she gathers herself. Shakes her head.

*You're not going crazy, Kate.*

*You're not... going... crazy*!

As Kate moves along, she passes one more poster. There's no subject in the photo, only a black square where the picture should be. This poster has a caption though:

FOOD.

The smaller caption here reads: *Come... closer...*

Terror floods Kate as she shakes her head no. Whatever kind of joke this is, she's not falling for it–

The words on the poster fade away.

Kate pauses. The anxiety wanes momentarily as several rational thoughts pop into her mind:

*Maybe these aren't posters.*

*They're just flatscreen TVs.*

*And this is some jerk's elaborate prank.*

The words *come... closer...* reappear. A picture comes into focus and Kate sees herself on the screen. Shocked at her reflection, she recoils. The unyielding lights above rain down their unapologetic light, rendering her features sunken and haggard. The color of her skin appears wan, washed out. She brings a hand to her face, adjusting her drooping glasses, shocked at how horribly frightened she looks. What is this place doing to her–

*Stop it*, she thinks. *Just a stupid TV in a screwed-up place. I need to find the camera. There's got to be a camera somewhere!*

Kate examines the monitor and the immediate area around it. No cameras. Words pulse on the screen again:

*Come...*

*closer...*

"Who are you?" she asks aloud. "Why are you watching me?"

No response.

"Answer me!" she shouts as she takes a step closer, feeling momentarily brave. "Who are you? Why are you doing this?" Sweat beads moisten her nose, forcing her to reseat her glasses once more–

Her body locks up.

The Kate in the live feed hasn't touched her glasses. In fact, she's *folding* her arms.

Kate glances down at her own arms.

They're not folded.

Kate shudders. She looks up, and the screen is black. "Why are you doing this?" she asks, her voice the shakiest she has ever heard it. "Who are you?"

*C'mon, Kate. Why are you trying to figure this out?* she thinks. *You're not a detective. Get the hell out of here!*

But curiosity overrides her apprehension. Kate needs to know who is behind this.

Words materialize on the screen:

*Want to know who I am?*

There's a flash of white on the TV and Kate is staring at herself again—only her skin is cracking, blistering, and flaking off her face. Blood seeps between the fissures. Kate brings a trembling hand to her face, touches her skin.

But the reflection doesn't mirror Kate's response. "Who am I? I'm you, Kate." It leans forward, bowing its head, eyes locked on her. "I'M YOU!"

Kate kicks backwards on her heels, loses her footing and lands on her tailbone. Her jaw clacks as she connects with the ground. She's stunned for a beat, then checks her hands. Fingers quivering, she finds no traces of blood. Confused, she looks to the screen to find the dancing, gory version of her writhing unnaturally. Sweating blood from its skin. It moves closer to the screen, head lengthening, as it cranes its neck left, then right, studying Kate through the monitor as if she were a specimen on a microscope slide.

With its chaffed skin, chapped lips, and blood-stained teeth, the face murmurs, "Why am I doing this?"

Kate hops to her feet and starts running, heading towards the far end of the room where the exit door is. Beyond that, another door? Another hallway? Possibly a way out of here? She doesn't care. It's just not here.

Behind her, she hears the creature from the TV yell, "I'm doing this because I'm hungry!"

Kate glances back at the monitor for a second, ensuring nothing is following her.

"I'M HUNGRY FOR YOU, KATE!" the TV bellows.

She dashes around the pile of trash at the center of the room but hits the brakes just shy of the peach-colored sofa.

Someone is sitting there.

Someone that wasn't there before.

Kate can only see the back of their head, as they stare straight ahead at the very door she was going for. She eyes the greasy, onyx, wiry mane of the person sitting in the chair, and it's enough to send her heart into a fluttering panic.

That someone...

Is one of the four.

# Chapter 18–Bishop & White Diamonds

The way the room's lights are blinking, Bishop might as well be at a nightclub. LED lights rarely flicker unless there's an abrupt surge in wattage, blown capacitor, or a loose wire in the circuit breaker. He knows this, having installed enough of them in offices, garages, trailers, and living spaces.

Yet the lights above him nictitate ceaselessly, winking on and off with the irritating bursts of spasmodic strobe lights. The ones directly above him struggle to stay lit.

Then cut off completely.

Bishop grows more angered by the fluctuations than scared.

The set of lights ahead of him ignites in succession. One, then another. And another. Again, in a steady sequence, forming a straight line then veering a hard right directly above the aisle between the cubicles. They delineate a clear path like a series of runway lights, leading straight toward the screeching sound of–

Wheels.

Those horrid wheels.

Squeaking like the hateful trilling of a cricket chittering near his bedroom window at the darkest hours of the early morning.

*That could be anything,* he tells himself. *I've inhaled enough WD-40 lubricating things to know corrosion happens, bearings wear down.*

The squealing wheels close in. Bishop's gaze follows the path of LED lights illuminated above from where he stands to whatever is at the end of the aisle beyond the cubicles.

Bishop could imagine a million possibilities for what that sound could be. But he catches a whiff of something undeniably Larissa.

The fragrance of White Diamonds.

It's the only thing Larissa wore–and she hated other perfumes and body sprays. But White Diamonds. Boy, did she have a thing for the late Elizabeth Taylor's opulent scent. Clean, floral, with notes of oranges and lilies. If white had an odor, indeed it would be this. Bishop recalled a woman at one of the department stores referring to it as an "old lady scent." Given his age–and what would have been her age now–perhaps that would be right. But he never cared.

It was *her* smell.

He could bathe in it, just as he bathed in her until it all ended.

But now, now that smell was as undeniable as the Florida heat. Wafting into his nose then fading. Under normal circumstances, this aroma would incite a bittersweet sense of reverence for Larissa. A mixture of sadness and the recollection of the love they once shared.

However, standing here in the dimly lit office, having just yanked a cable from out of his nose, hearing that distinct and eerily familiar creaking of wheels dragging along the carpet–there was not a drop of reminiscing–only confusion and an unrelenting sense of dread.

"Hello?" Bishop calls out. "Who's–who's there?"

Silence.

Then the wheels respond with a brief chirp.

More silence.

Then a waft of White Diamonds.

"Larissa?" Part of Bishop ponders why he just called out her name. Another part of him, a foreboding and intuitively aware part of him, knows why.

Nothing.

Bishop's throat goes dry. He swallows hard, choking back a knot of nerves. His nostril weeps blood and he wipes at it.

The wheels roll closer, then stop.

"Is that you?"

White Diamonds drift into his nostril. He's about to call out her name once more, when his cell phone vibrates, startling him. From Unknown:

*Come say hi.*

"No." Bishop shakes his head. "No-no-no-no-no-no." He clenches his fists, digging fingernails into his skin, trying to bring some other sensation to the forefront of his brain other than unease or madness. "This isn't happening." He smacks himself with his hand. "This... isn't... real!"

The sound of his slap is crisp yet quickly swallowed up by the undiscernible emptiness of the room.

His cell phone buzzes. Another text:

*This.*

*Is.*

*Real.*

*Yes, it is,* Bishop thinks. *You have finally lost it, old man. You're probably passed out on someone's tile floor, half-finished, exhausted from overwork. Tirelessly slaving away for some hipster flipping houses using daddy's money and yet not paying him a decent wage for his level of experience. His craftsmanship.*

His age.

*Yep, that's it.* He muses, ignoring the pulsing ache in his nostril. The burning scrape of his fingernails once again biting skin. The unforgettable aroma of White Diamonds. *I've finally lost my marbles.*

He receives another text. Eyes glossy with worry and impending insanity, Bishop reads the message:

*Come see me, old friend.*

Bishop grits his teeth. Shakes his head once more.

*Fine,* he thinks. *I need to know if I am losing my mind. Let's do this.*

Bishop marches towards the source of the squeaking wheels. He follows the lights above, rounding the corner where he is led into a large aisle flanked by cubicles on either side. Some fifteen feet ahead of him is a frail woman, head drooping, face obscured by a canescent mop of thin, thready hair that clings to her skull. She is seated in a wheelchair too big for her skeletal frame.

"Dear God," he utters in a low voice.

*Is that really her?* he *wonders.*

*No way.*

*It's impossible.*

*She died.*

However, there under the foggy, unreliable LED lights, this gaunt woman sits, slumped forward in her wheelchair. Her identity masked by her hair.

"Larissa?"

The woman does not move. Sits still as a statue.

Bishop's old heart rams against his chest so hard he questions if he's about to have a heart attack. Panic sets in as he debates whether to approach her or take off.

"Larissa, is that you?" he asks, unnerved by the tremble he detects within his own voice.

The woman remains motionless. She might as well be dead. Bishop questions if she is.

He receives another text:

*Yes, it's me.*

Bishop glances back at the woman, studying her. She doesn't have a cell phone in her hand.

*Someone else in the room is doing this,* he thinks. *Someone is screwing with me. They have my phone on file. Wouldn't be that hard to—*

Another text comes in.

*I'm so excited that we're going to be together again, Bishop.*

The lights above die. The light of his cell phone dims. Panic intensifies within him. Breath quickening, his heart crashes wildly within his rib cage as if it were trying to break free from his chest.

Another text:

*Together forever.*

The cell phone fades to black, powering off on its own once more. Bishop fumbles as he tries to turn it back on, smashing every button. He finally turns the flashlight on. Aiming it ahead, he finds the woman in the wheelchair is gone. He whips around—

Coming face to face with a pasty, sallow-skinned Larissa. Emaciated and semi-decayed. Jaw slung crooked. Her features are sunken, desiccated, as if all manner of hydration and fluids had been siphoned out of her. The bandages loosely wrapped around the right side of her face unravel on their own, revealing a cavernous dent in her skull. There's no eye socket, only a puckered scar outlining the cavity, a remnant set of holes for nostrils, and a jagged cheekbone that juts downward like a stray tooth.

Bishop gasps. Stammers. Speechless at this horror that was once his beloved partner.

Larissa leans her head back, opens her hooked jaw impossibly wide as if it were a trap accepting bait. She emits a shriek that could make glass explode.

Bishop panics. Clutches Larissa by her shoulders, feeling her spongy flesh give, bones crunching as if composed of eggshells, and shoves her back. He breaks in the opposite direction, keeping his cell phone aimed ahead. The light coming from the ever-weakening battery barely illuminates the hungry dark ahead.

"Why did you leave me?" Larissa begs. Her croaky, gravelly voice booms through the office.

Bishop's knees click as he hurries away, shooting splinters of pain up and down his legs.

"Why, Bishop?"

As he hears the grating wheels grind behind him, he dares not look back.

"I thought you loved me!"

Bishop's legs and lungs are on fire. Heart beating so fast, he feels his pulse in his eardrums. Right when he thinks he's about to collapse, he spies a door ahead. Like a welcome mirage in the tenebrous desert of cubicles and darkness, he races towards the door, throws it open, and slams it shut behind him.

From the other side, Larissa bangs incessantly. "You left me, you worthless bum!" she screeches. "You always were useless!"

Wheezing, dizzy, Bishop slumps to the ground, gasping for air. Woozy and fatigued, he gathers his strength, keeping his hand locked on the door handle, not wanting Larissa to follow him.

*I'm not sure if I can keep this up,* he thinks. *And I wish this friggin' door had a lock!*

"Just another non-committal man with nothing to offer!" she shouts as she jiggles the handle.

With a shaky hand, Bishop brings the cell phone up. Casts the light ahead, finding himself in a hallway lined with doors.

Larissa shakes the handle once more, but Bishop's iron grip holds steady despite how exhausted the rest of his body is. "Open up, you flake!" She bangs on the door. She is hammering it with unbelievable vigor, considering her feeble state.

He rises, knees firing uncomfortable twinges up his legs. He staggers toward the closest door. Thankfully, it's unlocked because as he enters, he hears Larissa burst into the hallway screaming with that ghoulish wail of hers. A disturbing cry that will no doubt haunt his dreams forever, should he survive this ordeal.

He shuts the door behind him, grateful that it has a deadbolt, which he promptly engages.

# Chapter 19–Heart Box

With all the force of a head-on collision, Zander and Mike plow into Wayne. The three of them take a tumble. Wayne and Zander land the hardest. There's a mess of grumblings, groans, and curse words exchanged. Mike quickly recovers, helping the other two back up with a solid yank.

Zander dusts himself off. Annoyance is plastered on his face.

"The hell?" Mike blurts out.

Wayne nervously scans the room. No sign of Chet.

"Wayne?" Mike asks, confusion in his tone.

"In the flabby flesh." Wayne is drenched in sweat. Eyes wide and worried. Nose bleeding. He wipes his face with his hand, then asks, "Can I say the same for you guys?"

"Did we not just knock you on your ass?" Mike answers.

"Yes," Wayne replies. "And now I what a bowling pin feels like."

"Sorry about that." Mike taps his nose. "And the nose. Hope I didn't break it."

Wayne shivers at the thought of what he had to go through to yank that cord out. Choosing not to relive the experience, he simply says, "No permanent harm done. I'm fine." He casts a backwards glance. Still no sign of Chet.

"So, what the heck were you running from?" Eyes narrowing, Mike asks, "And why do you keep looking over your shoulder?"

"Just making sure I'm still not being followed."

"Followed?" Zander finally joins in on the conversation. "By whom?"

"This bully from high school named Chet. I think he works here at SiDug." Wayne lifts his shirt up, dries the fresh sheen of sweat off his face. "Were you guys in this room the whole time I was?"

Mike's hulking shoulders heave as he shrugs. "No clue."

"Did you see the lights flickering?" Wayne asks.

"Of course we did," Mike answers. "But then, that's been like everywhere we've been in this place."

"What about the laughter? Did you hear Chet laughing?" Wayne demands. "Did you see him?"

Zander groans. "Seriously, we've got no clue who or what you're talking about."

*Now, if it were Erik, that'd be a different story.* Zander thinks. *Did Wayne see Erik? Naked, angry, bloody, and poised above me? Ready to crush me like a cockroach?*

"What about us?" Zander asks. "Did you hear us?"

"I-I don't know," Wayne admits, mind reeling. "Hard to tell, since this place makes no sense. It's a funhouse from Hell."

*A Hell where Erik lives*, Zander thinks.

"Where were you guys running to anyway?" Wayne asks.

"Anywhere but here," Zander answers, avoiding the details of Erik's sudden appearance.

"Yeah," Mike agrees, "we were leaving when we literally ran into you–"

"Hey, people," Zander interrupts as he gestures in a general direction, "mind if we get back to finding a way out of here?"

*Because I don't want to bump into Erik again*, he thinks. *Or see either the smirk on his face or that gash on his chest.*

"Alright," Wayne says, shooting Zander a cross look. "Let's go."

The men explore the room. There's nothing distinctive about it. Nothing differentiating it from any other office within the building so far. Just a warren of cubicles, Berber carpet, autumn orange walls, and fake plants. There are three doors at the far end of the room.

"Come on." Mike leads them toward the doors.

"How do you know where we are going?" Wayne asks. "How are you sure that we're not walking in circles? I mean, the room was pitch black."

"I don't," Mike admits. "But what's the alternative? Stand around? Wait for Mr. Gudu to show?"

*Or Erik*, Zander thinks. *No thanks.*

The men reach the doors. One of them has the word *Manager* on it. One is blank. The other says FIRE EXIT.

Mike goes for the fire exit. He pushes on the panic bar, but the door doesn't budge. He hammers the bar several more times. The acrylic exit sign comes loose, leaning at an angle now.

Mike faces the others. "I thought you can't lock these doors. It's against fire code."

*Not sure if you've been keeping up with things, dumbass*, Zander thinks, *But I don't think this place cares about building codes.*

Wayne compulsively reaches for the exit sign to straighten it. When he touches it, it drops, stopping just short of the floor. Suspended by a black cord above the floor where it dangles like a yo-yo.

"Is that glue?" Zander asks.

"Looks more like black caulk," Mike answers. "They must've been in a pinch. Can't always make it to Home Depot, you know? Sometimes you gotta improvise when you're in the middle of a job."

"Feels like this whole place in an improvisation," Zander complains. "Whoever built this nuthouse should be strung up by their balls. *Then* taken to court."

"Bit extreme, don't you think?"

Zander's eyes bore into Mike's as he says, "No. I don't."

Mike brushes him off. *Creep*, he thinks.

Wayne investigates the piceous cord: spinous, scraggy, and the same material that was lodged in his nose. His stomach quivers as he replays the agony of ripping it out.

Mike catches Wayne's reaction. "What's up?"

It takes Wayne a moment. Gaze sliding from the cord to Mike. "One minute I was watching those freaky videos starring Cory. The next, I'm waking up at my desk with this," Wayne points at the rope, "*thing* hooked inside my nostril. Practically ripped my face off trying to get it out."

"Jesus," Mike mutters, trying to picture the ordeal.

"Yeah, and it still hurts like a mother," Wayne says as he dabs at his face again with his shirt, exposing part of his potbelly. "I'd kill for some ibuprofen right about now." An opaque blood stain flowers across his shirt and he does his best to wipe it away, rubbing profusely with his hand. "Did the same thing happen to you guys?"

"Same thing as in what?" Mike asks.

"Did you wake up with *that* attached to your schnoz?"

"Nope," Mike answers.

Zander responds with a curt, "No." He cuts between Mike and Wayne, goes for the middle door. It swings open with ease.

Wayne and Mike draw back, spooked by what they see. Disgusted by what they smell. Mike shields his nose with his forearm. Wayne his shirt. Zander stares on, unmoved, undisturbed by the sight or the odor of what is before them.

It is a basic janitorial closet, replete with common supplies stocked on shelves that run along the opposing walls: commercial soap dispenser refills, paper towels, bottles of bleach, scrub brushes, and an assortment of brooms and dustpans.

Centered among these items is something unrelated to maintenance or cleaning.

"Somebody want to tell me what the hell that is?" Mike asks, his voice partially blocked by his arm. The stench is so rank, so fetid, it seems to burn his eyes and he winces.

"No. Freaking. Clue." Wayne stammers. Does his best not to hurl.

Directly in front of them is a standard, four-tier utility shelf. Instead of being stocked with custodial supplies, it is smothered by a pink and black striated web of flesh that reeks of rotten meat. Its thin, diaphanous muscles cling to the shelf the way a giant squid would its meal. Roughly the size of a duffle bag, it pulsates like a giant heart. Its fleshy skin glints under the vibrant LED lights above it.

Wayne turns his head and heaves.

"You gotta be kidding me," Mike says as he and Zander study the animated heart. Dozens of black cords, similar to the one attached to the exit sign, dangle down from openings in the ceiling tiles above, almost like network cables fed into the room from another world. "Am I the only one seeing this?" Mike asks, wanting to confirm that he isn't going crazy and that the other men are really there with him.

"Unfortunately, no." Wayne wipes the vomit from his lips, and points at the beating heart. "Because *that*... that right there is the grossest thing I've ever seen in my life."

Mike shakes his head, wishing he had an answer. There's no logical explanation for what he's witnessing. Perhaps he's dreaming this? Perhaps he drank himself to sleep, just like he does when he can't sleep—when thoughts from the attic of his subconscious leak into his conscious to remind him of poor Nigel. Nigel... his former best friend from middle school. The one he inadvertently helped to–

Zander pushes past Mike, knocking him aside. Mike snarls. "Excuse you."

"What are you doing?" Wayne demands.

*I'm doing what I've done before,* Zander thinks.

Something inside Zander compels him to pick up a broom. He jams the tip into the door jamb and pulls back on it until it snaps with a resounding *crack!*

Wayne protests. "Zander, what–"

"Shut up!" Zander has converted the broomstick into a makeshift spear. He wraps his fingers around it, and with one steady thrust, drives it straight into the humongous black heart. It thrashes violently, oozing blood the color of burned motor oil, as it emits a shrill cry that carries throughout the office, permeating doors and walls.

It's as if the entire building screamed.

This prompts the men to take a cautious step back, eyes trained on the ceiling tiles.

Wayne looks to Zander. "What'd you do that for?"

Zander retrieves the broomstick from the wriggling organ. It shudders momentarily, then sags, lifeless and bereft of animation. He turns to Wayne, closes the gap between them. "When's the last time you saw a beating heart, the size of a Great Dane, tucked away in a storage closet?"

Wayne stutters, words and thoughts escaping him. "N-never?"

Zander nods and then says, "Exactly."

Mike takes two broomsticks. Follows Zander's lead, breaking off the end to make a weapon for himself. He hands Wayne the other one. "Zander's onto something."

Wayne asks with a nervous laugh, "What's that?"

"Being armed."

Wayne takes the broomstick, sticks it into the doorjamb. Tries to break it as easily as Mike and Zander did, but fails.

Zander huffs, takes hold of it, snaps the end off in one go and shoves it into Wayne's chest. "You want us to hold your hand too?"

Wayne snarls as he snatches the stick. "You know, you don't have to be such a dick."

"And you don't have to be such a pussy," Zander retorts.

There's a creaking sound that draws the men's attention.

"Check it out." Mike nods toward the noise.

The manager's office door has just opened on its own.

# Chapter 20–Couched Demons

U pon seeing the back of that creature's head, every inkling of hatred that Kate held for Mina, the loathing that she had long stuffed away inside of a box, inside of another box, hidden in her mind like some Russian nesting doll–that hatred resurfaced. A seething escaping the mental packaging she had so meticulously interred it in.

Curse Mina for torturing her with those pictures. Those scary men dressed in all black, wearing monstrous boots, faces painted like felines, spacemen, and monsters. Curse her for instilling this fear in Kate of a rock band that wasn't remotely as frightening as the photographs Mina tormented her with.

That mixture of abhorrence and alarm churns within Kate's stomach. Roiling, bubbling, and finally flooding her with nauseating dread as she stares upon the unctuous inky weave of hair and that signature black ponytail sprouting from the top of The Beast's head like an overgrown weed.

Kate wants desperately to scream but suppresses the urge by biting her lip and stifling her breath. The door is just beyond the sofa where The Beast sits. That bastard faces it, with its wide shoulders and disgusting mess of hair.

*I'm going to have to run,* she thinks. *To book it past this thing and pray that door is not locked. It better not be locked!*

But there are no guarantees. Especially the way things have been unfolding within this sinister building. The only promise this sprawling facility keeps is that nothing is reliable. Nothing makes sense. In keeping with that promise, somehow one of the men from her childhood nightmares is now lounging directly in front of her.

*Maybe it's not him,* she reasons. *Maybe that's just an employee.*

A shiver ripples through her, eroding these fragile thoughts.

*No, you idiot, because he wasn't sitting there before. Maybe this... person... came from the very door I'm trying to get to?*

Her rationale is quickly struck down by the other voice in her mind by a single question:

*But you didn't hear a door close, did you?*

Kate stops short of the sofa and gets a whiff of the funk emanating off him. It's a fecal odor. An amalgamation of rot and sulfur that seems to have come out of nowhere, as she hadn't picked up on it before. She makes a slight choking sound as she represses a gag-reflex brought on by the stench.

As Kate covers her nose, her mind goes into overdrive. A succession of rapid-fire thoughts:

*Maybe this is a corpse?*

*Maybe someone died here? How did I miss this?*

*Is this place haunted?*

*Am I stuck in a dream? Am I asleep?*

She stares at the back of the unmoving head. Its coal-black hair glistening. The stench of his body wafting into her nose. She catches herself holding her breath and exhales a steady, yet trembling gasp as she braves to utter, "Hello?"

The head doesn't move.

*Oh, God. Should I see if he's alive?* she asks herself. *Or just go for the door?*

"S-Sir?"

*Come on, Kate. Decide.*

*Check the body or make a break for it!*

But she's unexplainably drawn by an insatiable curiosity to know if this is one of the four.

Or just someone. It is as though her mind hungers for reassurance that the miscreated quartet from her childhood couldn't possibly be a reality.

Her hand hovers in the air, quaking, as she moves it towards the man's shoulder. Her trembling intensifies as she reaches...

Reaches...

She lets out a stuttered gasp. Her hand is inches from his imposingly large shoulders—which have swelled during her approach, as if inflating with each step.

She's just about to touch his shoulder when she stops short.

*What if this really is The Beast?*

*Then what?*

She argues within her head.

*Then you'll rush the door and get out of here.*

*But what if the door's locked?*

*Maybe it is and maybe it isn't. But I need to find out if I'm alone.*

*And if this... if this is him.*

She extends her fingers and holds her breath, leaning the rest of her body back as if she's reaching toward the trigger of an explosive device.

Tap.

Nothing.

The body doesn't move.

"H-hello?" she says once more.

Only the stretching stillness of the room and the billowing stink of his body respond.

She timidly touches him again.

Tap.

*Ok, maybe he's dead*, she thinks as she tries her hardest not to freak out and start crying hysterically. *And maybe it's not even him! Just some stinky corpse with equally awful hair.*

She takes a cautious step back. Surmises how quickly she could make it to the door if she ran.

*You don't know if he is dead!*

Kate wonders if maybe she should find out.

She takes a deep breath and starts around the side of the couch, eyes locked on his head. To her dismay, she finds the man's face is hidden behind the black veil of hair that spills over his brow. He's wearing dark, theatrical faux armor, furnished with shoulder pads she swears weren't there moments ago, a black and gray leather chest plate with a dragon's head relief, black leather pants, and a pair of massive boots that she could fit both of her arms into. The man's hands are cradled in his lap.

She looks upon this giant with welling trepidation. It is definitely The Beast. She is so sure of it, her knees sway as she finds herself racked with disbelief that this corrupt thing from her past now sits in front of her, lounging on a couch as if enjoying a siesta between inbound customer calls.

She steps backwards, towards the hopeful exit door. Eyes fixed on The Beast. Praying that he doesn't move. Once her back meets the wall, she reaches behind her and feels for the door handle.

*Where is the handle?*

She slides her body to the right, thinking that perhaps she misjudged where the door was. Gaze still locked on that formidable creature napping or rotting and hopefully not watching her, just sitting there like some noble warrior, decked in battle attire, waiting patiently for his favorite TV show to come on.

*But maybe the show's already on,* she thinks. *Maybe I'm the show.*

For a split second, she glances over her shoulder using the peripheral vision of her eye, verifying the door is right behind her. Hand fumbling, she smacks it against the door, searching frantically.

*Oh, my god, where is the door handle already?*

She finally finds it.

Without taking her eyes off The Beast, she tries the handle. A sliver of relief fills her as the door registers a gentle click as she backs against it, opening it.

Thankfully, The Beast doesn't move.

*You just stay right there,* she thinks. *Whoever you are!*

The Beast does just that.

Still as a corpse.

*I'm going to spin around and shut this door behind me. And I pray there's a lock, so I can seal you in here.*

With one monumental step backwards, she clears the threshold, eyes glued on The Beast. She's about to slam the door—when it stops short.

*What the heck?*

Still grasping the handle, Kate gives the door a shove, but there's something stopping it from shutting on the other side—

A figure slides out from behind the door, dressed in black and gray armor. An array of spikes adorns his shoulders. His hair is flared out, styled, exposing his gleaming ghost-white face, and the sparkly stars outlining his eyes—one black, one silver.

The milky skin around his cheekbones bunches up into two knots as Mr. Shimmer smiles devilishly.

Kate releases a scream that could be heard across the ocean.

# Chapter 21–Speak To The Manager

W ayne, Mike, and Zander stare at the manager's door as it sits ajar.

"Who wants to go first?" Mike asks.

"Move," Zander says as he slowly pushes it open. The office is well lit, thanks to the eminent white light of the fluorescent tubes above.

*Fluorescent and not LED*, Zander notes. *Interesting. Maybe they ran out of money and had to switch to these instead of the LEDs.*

The room is roughly twelve-by-twelve. A slew of pictures covers the walls: a balding white man and his wife, the same man with his children, the four of them standing next to a cruise ship, bordered in a beach-themed graphic and captioned with *Nassau, 1996.*

Slumped over, resting his head upon his keyboard as if it were a pillow, is that same bald man. Behind him is an old CRT monitor, something Wayne and Zander haven't seen since the nineties. On the man's desk is a nameplate with a dash of blood spatter on it: *Henry Thorzac.*

Next to it, a smaller nameplate reads: *Head Asshole in Charge of the Assholes.*

Henry has his back to them, so it's hard to tell if the guy is passed out, awake or dead.

"Hello?" Zander says as the other two file in cautiously behind him.

Henry doesn't respond.

Zander moves closer and finds that Henry's eyes are shut. A black cord hangs from one of his nostrils, disappearing under the man's desk.

Wayne immediately feels his own nose throb. Recalling his experience with the cord, he touches his nose absently. Finds a pearl of blood on his fingertip–

Henry suddenly sits straight up in his chair, and the three of them hop back.

"Jumping Jesus on a pogo stick!" Wayne exclaims as he hides behind Mike.

Henry's eyes flutter open. He leans back, woozy, as if awakening from surgery. Upon seeing them, he groggily asks, "You... you guys new here?"

It takes a moment for one of them to respond. Mike finally answers, "Maybe."

"Who are you?" Henry asks.

"I'm Mike. This here is Wayne." Mike looks to Zander who has a scowl planted on his face. "And that's Zander."

Henry sighs. "And I'm..." Dark blood seeps from his nostril where the cable resides. "I'm so sorry."

"Sorry?" Mike asks. "For what?"

Henry sighs deeply. "I'm just sorry for you. I'm sorry *it* got you." A tear slides down from his eye and he wipes it away quickly. "It tricked you here."

"Yeah, we thought we were getting hired to work from home. We came here for training," Wayne tells him, peeking from behind Mike's frame. "Not to wake up chained to our desks by our noses, stuck in this madhouse with psychos."

Mike turns and shoves Wayne aside, commands, "Get off me, man," under his breath.

Henry retrieves a tissue. "That sounds about right." Dabs at his nose as he goes on, "It tricked you all into coming here. Just like it did to me."

"It?" Mike asks and steps forward.

"Yes. It." Henry waves his finger in the air like a wand. "As in SiDug."

"SiDug put that thing in your nose?" Zander asks, tapping his nostril.

Henry brings a hand up the cord, and touches it gingerly, as if discovering it for the first time. "Oh... this.... this is its umbilical cord." He stares blankly ahead for a beat. Then looks back to the men. His demeanor, posture, and timbre in his voice changes as he explains, "It keeps me connected. It wants to nourish us. To fulfill us. To get to know us more than any other human cares to. Humans are selfish by nature. SiDug is not."

"Can't you pull it out?" Wayne asks. "I mean, it was painful as all get out, but I did it."

Henry glowers at Wayne. "Why would I want to do that? It nourishes me. Feeds me wisdom. Pleasure. It is far superior to any booze or barbiturate."

"Have fun with that," Mike says. "Just tell us how we get out of this building?"

Henry pauses. Offers grimly, "You don't."

"What? You can't keep us here!" Wayne shouts, spittle flying from his mouth.

Henry leans forward. Rests his elbows on his desk in an *I'm-the-manager-here* fashion and shares, "When I was a kid, my dad got me a Chinese finger trap. Ever played with one of those?"

The group says nothing.

"It's a simple device. A small cylindrical tube woven from bamboo." Henry points his index fingers at each other, end to end. "You put one finger in each hole in either side, and your fingers get stuck. The more you struggle to pull them out, the harder it is to free them." He smiles, and it looks completely bizarre given that there's a shiny black wire dangling from his nose. "Just like here."

Zander practically dives onto Henry. Snatches him by his collar. "If you don't tell us how to get out of here—"

"You'll what, Zander?" Henry's crooked smile spreads across his face. "Tell me, please." There's a glimmer in his eyes, like the glint from a dark star winking as it's snuffed out, that unnerves Zander. "I already know what you'll do, Zander, because I've seen it."

Mike raises an eyebrow. "What's he talking about?"

Zander releases Henry, steps back. "He's talking nonsense." He looks to the others. "He's trying to screw with us, with our heads, just like this place."

Wayne taps Zander and Mike on their shoulders and whispers, "Can we talk for a second?"

"You guys want to speak privately?" Henry calmly motions for the door.

"Be my guest. Take all the time you need. You're not going anywhere, anyway."

The men step outside and make a tight circle. Wayne keeps his voice low, as he looks back to see Henry has already spun around in his chair. He's typing away at his keyboard. The same word appearing over and over on his screen: *Feed*.

"What's up?" Mike asks.

"Look, I've got a crazy idea," Wayne says, "but I think we should do it."

"Which is?"

"Clearly this guy knows something, right? I mean, the way he's talking."

"What do you mean, *clearly*?" Zander asks with a scowl. "Obviously he's a nut job."

"Right. First, he tears up. Then acts nutty," Wayne says. "So, I say let's yank that cable out of his nose."

Mike recoils. "What? Why?"

"Because when I had that thing in my nose, I felt weird too. Like I was on my old Vicodin prescription. Euphoria. Withdrawal. Crazy thoughts."

Zander looks back at Henry. The man is still busily clacking away at the keyboard, typing the same word repeatedly: *Feed*.

Wayne goes on, "I think if we remove that cable–the umbilical cord or whatever–he might talk more sense. Maybe tell us how to escape."

"I hate to agree with the moron," Zander admits, "but it's worth a shot. Maybe he has something to do with it, or maybe he doesn't, I don't know."

"I'm not a retard," Wayne huffs. "I've got an IQ of one hundred and fifty. I could run circles around you."

"I don't think you could run circles around anything."

"Both of you. Shut up." Mike mulls over Wayne's idea. He glances at Henry, who's still furiously beating on the keyboard as if toiling away at the longest memo the world has even seen.

However, instead of the word *Feed* on-screen, there's a picture of an African-American boy who makes Mike's blood go cold. Followed by a name that springs in his mind:

*Reggie–*

"So?" Wayne prods. "Are we doing this? I mean, maybe we'll be saving him too."

Zander nods.

"Yes, we are," Mike agrees as he eyes Henry's screen again. The picture is gone. The steady stream of the word *Feed* continues scrolling upwards.

The three men walk back into Henry's office. The balding man swivels around in his chair. "Your meeting go well?"

"Yep," Zander responds.

"Great." Henry folds his hands together, and a plastic smile stretches across his face. "Can I interest you men in some beverages? Coffee? Tea? Water?" He looks at Zander. "I hope some of you visited our break room during your tour of our facility."

*I did,* Zander thinks, *and it wasn't quite the break I wanted to experience.*

"Sometimes, the best things get revealed when you step away from your desk and take a breather," Henry says. "You know, like a revelation in the shower or when you're at the gym."

Mike looks to Wayne and Zander and the three of them move in and surround Henry.

Mike tells him, "Yeah, we could definitely use a revelation."

Henry trades glances between them, curious what they are up to.

Wayne and Zander lurch forward, grabbing hold of each of Henry's arms, pinning him. He squirms, resisting. "You insubordinate ingrates!" he protests. "What are you doing? I'll call security!"

Mike grasps the cable, which instantly digs into his skin with a thorny vengeance. At first, the thorns catch him by surprise, and he flinches, shaking his hand in pain. Then he takes a breath and grips the cable again, braving the blistering bites. He uses all his strength, Henry crying out in agony all the while. It's like tugging on barbed wire, but given Mike's muscle and leverage, it doesn't take long for the hooked end of the cord to make an excruciating exit from the manager's nostril.

Mike staggers backwards as the cord gives. Henry cries out in agony. Wayne and Zander release him. Everyone in the room is heaving, gasping for air. Mike checks his hands. They are cut up and bleeding as though he's fought a rose bush and lost.

Henry has sunk forward, head down on his arms, sobbing.

"You ok?" Mike asks, still catching his breath.

Henry sits up, throwing his head back in his chair. Tears stain his face. He brings a hand to his nose, which bleeds copiously. He wipes his nose on his sleeve, marring his shirt with a pinkish streak. It takes a moment for him to respond, but when he does, his tone is frail, dejected. Not like the oddly stoic speech pattern before. "No. I'm not ok."

"As far as your nose goes," Wayne assures him, "you'll live. The pain's annoying, to put it lightly. Though, we should get you to a hospital soon. Last thing we need is a nasty infection–"

"An infection won't kill us," Henry interrupts as he dabs at his nose with his shirt. "This place will. And I'll tell you why."

# Chapter 22–PUCKR Up

Now inside the room and hovering in front of Kate, lips black, slick, and grinning, Mr. Shimmer's face is as vivid as a full moon at night.

Beyond him, the couch lays vacant. The Beast has vanished. Before Kate can react, she feels hands grab her and she's spun around, greeted by the monster himself. The Beast's tongue rolls out from its mouth, unraveling like a pink and purple spongy coil, forked at the end.

Kate breaks away, running away from both men. She finds the nearest door and throws it open, rushing down a narrow, sparsely lit hallway. Behind her, she hears the door slam. A quick look over her shoulder reveals that they're following her–

Kate trips. Goes skidding forward. Lands painfully on her side. She quickly peels herself off the rough skin of the carpet. Glances near her foot. A footstool was carelessly placed in the middle of the hallway.

Though *careless* is an assumption in this place.

The men march toward her, towering within the mouth of the hallway like pillars. They are taller than normal men.

*Are they even men?* Kate wonders.

Her question is answered when the men's faces distort. Bodies elongate as if made of rubber, teased upwards by invisible hands. Their ghost white face paint is starkly contrasted against the hard, black lines and smothering silver makeup surrounding their eyes. She looks on in terror as the faces of the two creatures stretch, mouths yawning, bearing shark teeth as they let out an unsettling, creaking *ahhhhhhhh*, sound. A tonal, vocal fry of the most unnerving kind.

Kate backs up until she's against the wall.

The room darkens. LED strips above fade as if a movie is about to start–a horror flick starring her and two of the four. The lighting is just abysmally ample enough to make it appear as if their heads are volitant, gliding in her direction like stray soap bubbles. The ceiling lights appear to track the men's faces, casting an uneven glow onto their waxen, milky appearance, their soulless eyeballs, accentuating the forked black streaks of makeup that curl up from The Beast's brow and the argent tinsel stars encircling Mr. Shimmer's eyes that spangle supernaturally.

Kate's glasses fog from the moisture of her rapid breaths. She slinks along the wall, sliding deep into the ever-widening gloom as the hungry creatures close in–

There's a noise behind her. A loud click. Then a sliver of light from another room spills onto the floor, tracing a line then expanding out in a triangle of yellow.

Someone else is coming. Joining her nightmare.

Kate looks to the open door, expecting to see the other two monsters, Fang-Man and Blackstar, but to her relief, neither are there.

It's just an old man with cartoonishly large forearms decorated with weathered tattoos, and a bewildered expression on his wrinkled face.

Bishop.

The Beast and Mr. Shimmer break into a run. With one swift motion, Bishop seizes Kate and yanks her out of the hallway just as the monsters slam into the door, pummeling it with all their unnerving might.

# Chapter 23–1997 Called

H enry frantically searches his desk until he finds a box of tissues. He pats his nose and asks Mike, Wayne, and Zander to take a seat. The men check in with one another, trading uneasy looks.

Noting their hesitance, Henry pleads, "Please." Henry's tone rises as he wipes away his tears. He gestures with his free hand. "We have little time."

The men comply, sitting in Henry's leather-wrapped seats. Weapons still in hand. Ready.

Henry rises, moves to shut the door. The three of them turn in their seats, watching his every move. The second the door's latch finds the strike plate, he sighs in relief. "Can't let SiDug hear us."

"What are you talking about?" Wayne surveys the ceiling. "There hidden cameras somewhere?"

"Not exactly," Henry replies.

"What's that supposed to mean?" Wayne's pitchy voice is unnervingly loud and annoyance is reflected in Henry's disapproving gaze. "And what kind of company are you all running, anyway?"

Henry smacks the desk. "Look! SiDug isn't a company!"

"Then what is it?" Wayne shouts back, the veins in his neck bulging. "A front? You guys working for the Mafia? Ex KGB? Are you all drugging new employees then harvesting their organs?"

"Whoa. That got dark," Zander taunts with a smirk.

*You're one to talk, Zander,* that unwanted voice says in his head. *Think about the things you've done.*

Wayne shoots Zander a look that could rip his head off. "Dark?" He points at his own face as he fumes, "That was my first thought when I woke up with that *thing* in my nose! Someone drugged me!"

"He's not too far off," Henry mutters as he shakes his head, surrender in his expression.

Everyone looks to Henry now.

"Come again?" Wayne asks.

"What you said about harvesting," Henry explains. "That's not too far off the mark."

Mike rolls his head from one side to the other as if gearing up to fight. "Cut the drama. What's up with this place?"

Henry pauses. Folds his hands in a prayer-like fashion. Leans forward, burying his face between his thumbs. Produces a murmured, "How do I explain this?" He exhales as he leans back. In a matter-of-fact tone, he tells them, "SiDug is a trap."

"A... what?" Wayne asks with a bit of a scoff, not sure he quite caught what Henry said.

"We're trapped here. This place..." Henry raises a finger, gestures to the room itself and beyond. "I mean most of this... is... *fake.*"

*Fake? No way,* Zander thinks. *What I saw wasn't fake!*

Images cycle within Zander's head:

The things above the conference room ceiling.

The video on the coffee machine.

The full-frontal nude presence of Erik.

The creepy heart blob in the closet.

His mind tries to rationalize these encounters. Massaging them like mental clay into a something realistic, plausible.

*Erik was definitely in front of me. That video? Easily streamed or programmed with the right technical tools and know-how. But what about what I saw in the ceiling? What was that?*

*A leak? Fungus? A growth?*

*A hidden mold growing unchecked within the architecture like a cancer?*

*It reached for me! Swatted at me!*

Zander's gaze shifts to the pictures on the wall. Namely the Nassau photo, where Henry and his family stand proudly. Beaming as brilliant as the Caribbean sun. Decked in floral pattern shirts, shorts, and flip flops. Behind them is their cruise ship—a ship that looks rather dated and small compared to the luxury ships he's seen.

His eyes trail to the CRT monitor. An old ViewSonic. Thing looks to weigh about forty pounds. Zander wonders why they'd use such ancient technology, but then again, maybe SiDug spent all their money on the building? They had to cut corners somewhere.

*But an old ass CRT*, Zander thinks. *Why use one of those when flat-screens are dirt cheap?*

To the right of the monitor is something he hasn't seen in decades—a black Motorola pager.

*People still use those?*

Zander spies an old GI-Joe action figure named Snake Eyes who stands ready. Propped up against a framed, yet faded ticket stub. He strains to read it:

*Goo Goo Dolls. May 1997. Florida SunDome.*

The tiny details of the room, Henry's scattered belongings, are almost like a time capsule. A nostalgic Easter-egg hunt.

*This guy is clearly a collector of retro stuff*, Zander thinks.

Henry continues, "Yes. This whole place... it's all a mirage."

"So, where are we then?" Wayne throws a hand in the air. "In the desert?"

"The desert of the mind." Henry studies everyone's expressions. They're not following. "Look, SiDug is... how do I explain it—"

Henry winces as a barrage of dark thoughts explode in his mind.

A montage of madness. A flutter of images of people in various forms of torture. Skin being peeled back, separated from flesh like husk from ears of corn. Bodies mangled and writhing in a bath of blood, flesh pulpy and ruby red, shimmering at the base of a great, charred tangle of knotted wires and coarse cables. The bodies reach out to Henry. Jaws slung open, groans escaping. Eyes empty of color, now black pearls reflecting the soulless fluorescent lights of the office.

A word escapes the gaping mouths of these blood-soaked bodies:

"FEED."

Henry bolts up from his chair. He squeezes his eyes shut at the thoughts and presses his palms against his eyes. "No more!"

Mike, Wayne, and Zander jump to their feet, weapons aimed at Henry as he melts down.

"Yo! What the hell?" Mike grasps the staff so tightly, his knuckles swell.

"I'm... I'm sorry." Through his hands Henry mutters, "I'm having a hard time keeping my head straight."

"We can tell," Wayne says.

"The images in my mind... just now..." Henry drops his hands, exposing his nose, which weeps snot and blood. "They're not mine–"

A buzzing noise interrupts. Mike's pocket glows. "Hold that thought." He keeps his spear on Henry as he fishes out his cell phone.

*How's this thing still working?* Mike wonders.

"What kind of beeper is that?" Henry asks.

Without looking up from his phone, Mike answers, "W-What?" He has just received a text from *Unknown*.

"That a new Motorola?" Henry asks. "Never thought they'd make pagers that thin."

"A pager?" Wayne laughs. "It's a cell phone. Hello? Who uses pagers anymore?"

Zander snarls. "Some hospitals do, dumbass."

Wayne makes a sour face.

"There are some hospitals out there that are dead zones for mobile phones," Zander explains. "When you have walls that can stop X-rays, or metal roofing, cell service gets screwed up. Pagers use radio signals, so they don't have the same issue."

"Great. Thanks for educating me, Dr. Prick."

Zander salutes him. "Thank my time at the hospital's help desk."

Wayne makes a petulant face, twisting his lips into a half-snarl.

Mike stares at his phone and a shiver courses through him. On the screen is a picture, a yearbook photo of that same African American boy that was on

Henry's screen earlier.

Reggie.

Reggie, his childhood friend from middle school.

Another message pops up right after that one. It's the same photo, only someone has drawn a red skull head over Reggie's face. It is followed by a text that makes Mike's insides constrict.

*Captain Cody got me. He should've got you too.*

Mike's hand shakes.

"I know what cell phones are, guys." Henry pulls his cell from out of his desk. It's an old Nokia. "But yours is so thin. I mean, compared to mine."

"What third world country did you pilfer that from?" Wayne approaches Henry, ogling the relic. "I haven't seen one of those since, like 1997."

Henry narrows his eyes. Cocks his head, perplexed. "But it *is* 1997."

Unknown sends Mike more texts:

*I'm gonna get you though.*

*You ain't leaving here, Mikey.*

*You, me, and Captain Cody gonna see the stars and then the black void.*

Mike drops his phone, and it clatters on the floor. He's suddenly sweating profusely, as if trapped in his own personal sauna. He puts a hand to his heart, feeling it thump against the walls of his ribcage.

"The heck is wrong with you?" Wayne asks.

Mike searches the expressions of the others, wondering, *Did you all see what I just saw?* Of course, they hadn't. His gaze falls to the phone, and the image of Reggie smiling sends him backing into the corner. Head shaking from side to side as if trying to shed the ensuing panic. The tingling shivers cascade along every inch of his body, driving him to run.

But there is nowhere to run to in this hellish place.

Nowhere to go in this *trap*, as Henry called it.

The other men eye the phone, curious about what Mike saw. Wayne scoops it up. The screen is off. He tries to hand it to Mike, but Mike refuses. "I don't want *that*."

"Why not?" Wayne gives the phone a second glance. Still off. "What'd you see?"

"A ghost," Zander interjects with a wry smirk. "He looks like he saw a ghost."

"Yeah," Mike says. "That's exactly what I saw."

# Chapter 24–Mean, Mean Mina

Bishop and Kate cut through a narrow conference room and open the nearest door to find that somehow they are back in the hallway again, which sends Bishop's mind reeling. This building makes no sense. He asks himself, *Is Larissa here?*

Thankfully, she's not.

It's just he and Kate–who backs against the wall, shielding her body from Bishop with her arms.

"Kate! It's me, Bishop," he tells her, hands raised in surrender.

Kate warily lowers her guard.

"You're safe now." He assures her. "Alright?"

Kate nods. Glasses foggy and smudged. Her hair spills over her brow, matted to it by sweat.

"I'm not going to let those things touch you either," he says.

*You sure about that?* Bishop's mind asks. *You don't even know what they are. You couldn't even handle seeing Larissa.*

*Putrid, ravaged, Larissa.*

Bishop brushes off the unwelcome thoughts. Asks, "Are you ok?"

Kate cleans her glasses. "I'm... I'm fine." Whatever *fine* is right now. If fine means not having two of the four, or *any* of the four stalking her, she's *more* than fine. Fortunately, the monsters don't try the door. They don't knock. Nothing. Not a peep. It's just the two of them in this long, empty hallway. Could be the same hallway from before. Could be a different one. Everything is blurring together in this maze of barren offices and vacant rooms. However, at the far end of this hallway appears to be a stairwell door.

"What's going on?" she asks.

Bishop shakes his head. "I don't know."

Kate collects herself, steadying her breath. "Those things back there," she says, "you saw them, right?"

Bishop nods.

"Well... they're... they're from my nightmares. From when I was a kid."

Bishop more than just *saw* those faces.

He recognized them from PUCKR.

It was the Hot Lixx Tour back in '77. PUCKR, suited up in their trademark flamboyant armor and touting their respective musical weapons, played to a sold-out crowd in California. For him, it was the best show ever, and whenever they come on the radio, Bishop is instantly brought back to that concert.

Twenty years later, he took Larissa to a see them in San Antonio during their Pucker Up Tour, and those over-the-top, costumed rockers from New York City brought the same energy as they did two decades prior. Gave the crowd their all and then some. Bishop revered them as genuine artists that loved their fans and performing for them.

But there was no love in the ghastly, putrid paled faces he saw back in that room. Those things were not the energetic quartet he admired.

No.

Those *things* were nightmarish caricatures of the actual band members, recreated with the chaotic accuracy of a distraught child's drawing.

"When I was seven," Kate begins, "I had the unfortunate experience of having my hateful Aunt Mina babysit me. She made a hobby of taunting me. Got off on showing me pictures of those dudes from PUCKR in full makeup, outfits and all. And for some stupid reason, seeing those pictures always freaked me out."

"It's not stupid. You were seven."

"Well, I felt stupid. And scared. It was the way Mina would go about it."

"How so?"

"She'd put effort into it. She'd go to Toys R' Us, steal one of their bags, then she'd act like she was surprising me with a new Barbie or something." Kate frowns. "Nope. It'd be a picture of the PUCKR. The band members all hunched together with their creepy faces. Some of them smirking. Some with their tongues out. All of them staring at me with their crazy eyes. She'd say they were coming for me, so I'd better be good. Which I was. I followed her rules while mom was out working, but it didn't matter."

Bishop seethes at the thought of a grown adult scarring a child like this. "Why not?"

Kate exhales an extended, exhausted sigh as she says, "Because she got bored with me behaving. So, she took it up a notch."

Bishop listens intently, eyes narrowed and brimming with intensity as she continues.

"Sometimes, if she was drinking, she'd wake me out of bed, shove me in a closet and lock me up for hours. I'd bang away at the door, and when she'd finally let me out, she'd be standing there wearing a PUCKR mask, usually it was The Beast or Mr. Shimmer, because she knew those two scared me the most, and then she'd chase me around the house, screaming and laughing all the while."

As he takes this in, the somber look on his face hardens into anger. "Why did she do that to you?"

"Because she was a sicko. Because she hated me. And she hated my mom." Her eyes gloss over. "She loved making me cry. Loved calling me a crybaby. Said I'd grow old alone. I mean, look at me." As she wipes the tears away, her gaze meets his. "Was she wrong?"

"Yes. She was. And it's totally ok to be emotional. Especially given the situation," he tells her with a gentle nod, knowing how much he cried over Larissa. "Did you ever tell your mother what Mina did to you?"

"I did." Kate shrugs. "I mustered up the courage a few months ago actually..." Her words trail off, reliving the moment with her mother–

"And?"

"She didn't believe me."

"Unbelievable." Bishop chokes back the anger. "What about your father?"

"What about him?"

"Did you tell him?" Bishop presses.

"No."

"Why not?"

"Because he died not long after he and mom married. Just before I was born. Pancreatic cancer. It took him quick." Kate stares blankly at the ground. "And that's what made Mina so mad. He was gone and she would never have him. Ever."

"God, I'm sorry. No child deserves that."

"Doesn't matter, right?" She looks to Bishop. "Heck. I mean, she ended up being right. I'm alone now—"

"You're not alone. You're not old, kiddo. You're all of eighteen and you've got your entire life ahead of you—a life that you can make your own. And we're getting out of here so you can go live that life, ok?"

"Ok..." Kate's gaze drifts off.

Bishop grinds his teeth, the muscles in his jaw pulsing with rage as he entertains the thought of confronting Mina himself.

"Want to hear something ironic?" she asks.

"Sure."

Kate chuckles lightly as she says, "I got to meet the lead singer not too long ago at a comic book convention. No makeup, thankfully. Guy was super chill. Nothing like the monster Mina him out to be. He even autographed my shirt, which I showed her. She went all nuclear. It was great."

"Good!"

A smile breaks across her face as she says, "Yeah, he wrote 'Mina is a bitch!' on the back. Just above their tour dates. She was livid, but I didn't care. It kind of felt like I got even with her on some level. Here was a band she loved, and loved to torment me with, and with the stroke of a Sharpie, I got back at her."

"She deserves that and more. Much, much more." Bishop clenches his fists, though Kate doesn't notice. He clears his throat, shaking off the thoughts of vengeance against this nasty aunt of hers and revisits the situation at hand. "Now, as far as what *we* saw back there... those things weren't human. I've seen PUCKR live. They're just musicians in gaudy costumes. Those *things* in there..." Bishop points to the door. "They're something else." And as he says this, he feels everything come together.

Someone or something is unearthing their fears and the unspeakable memories buried in their minds. Kate saw monsters inspired from Mina's photos of the band.

And he saw... Larissa.

Or what has been hideously translated as Larissa. She'd been inhumed in Bishop's brain under layers of guilt and compunction, which took years to process. But like that wine stain on a white dress, a mark remained no matter how many times he tried to cleanse the traces of her from his head.

"Look, I saw something too. Back there. Someone I loved dearly named Larissa. Sitting in front of me," Bishop reveals. "But I know it wasn't her. Couldn't have been her."

"How are you so sure?"

"Because I read her obituary, Kate. She's been dead for nearly twenty years." Bishop gapes at the floor, searching for answers. "There's no way that was her."

"Then who was she?" she asks.

Bishop meets her gaze, trying to restrain the concern in his eyes. His gut tells him if he reveals how rattled he really is, she'll cave too. At a loss for explanations, he offers a simple, "I don't know."

Kate scans the hallway for cameras. "You think we're being watched?"

"Maybe."

The door behind them rattles. They glance at it, then at one another.

"Come on, kiddo." Bishop makes for the stairwell door. "Let's go."

Kate follows him without objection. On their way to the exit, they pass another hallway, one they somehow missed. Given the nondescript decor of the office's interiors and its random, sprawling nature, navigating SiDug was proving to be an impossible task, especially when coupled with their anxieties.

This particularly hallway boasts cracked blue paint along its walls and various flowering moldy stains suggesting water damage. At the end of this hallway is an elevator. Doors open. Lights on. Almost... beckoning them.

Behind them, the jangling door explodes, falling onto the floor like a life-sized domino.

Kate slinks back into the shadows as the lights in the hallway go out. Two beaming, white demons appear: Mr. Shimmer and The Beast. Their heads gravitate towards them like luminescent balloons.

Bishop eyes the darkened hallway ahead and then the well-lit elevator down the blue hallway. *Pick one, old man.* And pick quick, he thinks. *Stairwell door? Or the elevator?*

Kate freezes. Shouts Bishop's name. Eyes glued to the greedy grins of the creatures traveling toward them. Faces elongated and freakishly oval. No longer human, but ghoulish. Mr. Shimmer chatters his teeth with an unsettling, rapid-fire *clack-clack-clack-clack-clack-clack.* The Beast flicks his serpentine, forked tongue at Kate.

Bishop takes Kate by the wrist and guns it for the exit door since it is closer. "Come on!" He pulls her into the ominous hallway, heading in the general direction of where he recalled the door was. His hand connects with the panic bar. Jiggle-jiggle.

Locked.

"Dammit!" Bishop spins around, taking Kate with him with such force, she uses her free hand to prevent her glasses from sailing off and being swallowed into obscurity.

The creatures draw close.

"Bishop!" Kate screams.

Bishop leads her into the blue corridor and yanks her into the elevator. The interior is decked in dated brass and gold accouterments. Marbled white and pale gray tiles cover the floor. Bishop stares down at the elevator panel.

*What floor, old man?*

"They're coming!" Kate shouts as she backs into the corner of the elevator, gaze glued on the monsters as they approach with their tongues wagging and teeth chattering. "Bishop!"

Bishop smashes buttons. Second floor. Third floor. Sixth floor. Whatever floor. Whatever button will make this elevator shut its doors and put a barrier between them and those freakish things.

"Bishop! Do something!" The way she screams at him makes his skin crawl. Her panic is infectious.

"I'm trying!" Bishop presses every button on the panel.

The creatures' heads bob up and down as their boots thump along the carpet. The closer they get, the louder Kate gets.

Bishop hammers the DOOR CLOSE button with the bottom of his fist. The elevator chimes.

Finally, the doors slide shut.

Several feet away, mouths yawning open, the creatures extend their hands like zombies reaching towards their human meal.

Bishop pounds the button repeatedly. "Come on! Come on! Come on!" The doors are inches away from sealing shut—

The creatures reach into the gap between the brass doors, and they struggle to close, jiggling against the clad-black leather gloved hands, as their filthy digits snake inside.

Bishop hammers at their fingers with his fist, but to no avail. He takes a step back, ready to make a last stand. Puts himself between Kate and the beasts. Arms raised and ready to punch the hell out of them.

But the doors continue to close. The face-painted freaks on the other side screech with the harrowing cries of trapped wildlife. The doors shut and their fingertips are sliced off, dropping onto the elevator floor like a handful of grapes.

The elevator hums as it moves.

Bishop slumps back against the elevator wall, spent and breathless. Adrenaline courses through him like a drug. Steadying himself, he braces his body by putting one hand flat against the mirrorlike brass above the button panel. He glances back at Kate, who is balled up in the corner, arms wrapped around her knees. She stares at the floor, glasses fogging with each heated breath.

"You ok?" Bishop asks.

She doesn't respond immediately, continuing her staring match with the marble floor.

"Kate?" Bishop asks her as the elevator purrs, ascending to God knows which floor because all the buttons on the panel are unlit.

A moment passes but it feels like an eternity, occupied by only the drone of the elevator and their panicked breaths. When Kate finally locks eyes with him, she asks, "Are we in hell?"

"Maybe."

# Chapter 25–Santoku

I *ain't going out like this*, Mike thinks as he snaps out of the spiraling panic Reggie's photo has gotten him into. He tosses his spear aside, shoots around Henry's desk, and hoists him up by his tie. "What the hell is going on here? Huh? Tell us!"

"Whoa!" Wayne yells. "What are you—"

"Shut up!" Mike casts a sideways glance in Wayne's direction. "This asshole knows what's going on." Lips curled into the unapologetic snarl of a growling wolf, he tightens the newfangled noose. Henry's pallid skin flushes red, veins along his neck and temples fattening with blood. "And he's going to start talking right now!"

Henry's nose weeps, face swelling as if his head is about to pop.

"Jesus, let him go!" Wayne protests. "You're killing him!"

"Fine!" Mike releases Henry and backs away.

Henry slumps against his desk, gasping for air. Between breaths, he utters, "Fine. I'll cut right to it. But first, answer me this." He clumsily undoes his tie and rips it off his neck as if it were a leash. "What year is it?"

Mike cocks his head to the side, not sure if he heard Henry right. "Come again?"

"The year... what year is it?"

Mike picks up his spear. "Ok, now you're just messing with us."

"No, I'm not." Henry throws his hands up. "Just... answer my question. What year is it?"

"It's 2018," Wayne says.

Zander shoots him a look. "What?"

"*It's* 2018."

"No, it's not."

"I don't know what planet you're from, crazy boy," Wayne retorts, "but it's definitely 2018!"

*Crazy.*

The word triggers Zander. His mind opens like a black hole that he sinks into. Mike and Wayne argue about what year it is. Henry chips in as well, but it all becomes the indistinct background chatter of a restaurant, as Zander locks onto the word: *crazy.*

One night, he and Vicky got drunk off wine, and he said something offensive. Something he claims he didn't say, but she swears he did. Swears he told her that if she ever cheated on him, he would "*lose his shit.*" That he would kill the asshole that dared break them up. And that's when she asked him if he was crazy.

*No,* he recalls telling her, *I was just drunk. Drunk and saying stupid things. Not crazy.*

*I wouldn't kill anyone. Though, yes... Erik would be at the top of my list.*

This thought is immediately followed by a sequence of images in Zander's mind:

Erik is in front of him.

There's a bright flash of light.

Zander stares down at his hands, holding a seven-inch Santoku knife. It was one of his first culinary purchases at Williams Sonoma. He had promised Vicky he'd start cooking for them more at home to save money, and this knife had been his first investment. His foray into attempting to whip up other dishes outside of hot dogs, ramen, and soggy chicken tenders. His plan was to grab a bunch of used cookbooks and shake things up in the kitchen.

The saleswoman at Williams Sonoma told him she preferred it to a traditional chef's knife because it was thinner, lighter, more balanced, and allowed for more precise, refined slicing. She then explained that the word Santoku—which translated to *three virtues*—described what the blade was best used for: chopping, dicing, and mincing.

However, she never mentioned how it would work on human flesh.

On the flesh of Erik's chest.

The vision now plagues the forefront of Zander's mind:

Erik. Naked, palms up. Pleading for his life.

The Santoku knife sits in Zander's hand. Its wafer-thin, precise blade, brimming with kinetic potential. Its expert craftsmanship, handmade with the same love and care–the same raging passion–that burns in Zander's now broken heart.

Erik pleads, but Zander answers his cries with the crisscross slashes of his Santoku. Like a movie swiftly devolving from R-rated to snuff film, the vision devolves into something far more malefic than he expected.

Erik backs away, face contorted, eyes glistening with disbelief.

Zander advances and watches on in third person as his hand does all the dirty work, slicing horizontally at Erik's palms, where a red line forms as the skin splits open. Erik howls, stumbles, and collapses onto the very bed that Zander and Vicky share. A woman screams in the background. Shouts for Zander to stop.

But he doesn't, wielding the Santoku with such vengeful accuracy that Erik, even with his CrossFit physique, is no match for the relentless slashing of this exquisitely crafted blade that is wreaking havoc on his mind and body. Death by a thousand cuts. Zander goes at Erik like he's cutting at a wild bush with a machete.

*Swipe-swipe-swipe–*

Mike gives Zander a hard shove. "Hey, he asked you a question!"

Zander shakes his head. Looks to Henry.

"What year is it on *your* planet?" Wayne asks.

"2021," Zander responds. A trickle of goosebumps cascade across his body. "It's... 2021."

"Ohhh-kay." Wayne groans, "It's official. Everyone's crazy in this place but me."

Zander explodes, "I'm not crazy!"

The other three men flinch.

"It's 2021! Not 1997. Not 2018," Zander insists. "It's 2021!"

"No, it's not!" Wayne shouts, waving a dismissive hand in Zander's direction.

"Everyone, please!" Henry says as he falls back into his chair, eyes drifting absently to the floor. "This is not the first time this has happened. And it certainly won't be the last. I've managed many people here at SiDug. Employees who have been with us for weeks. Some for decades."

Wayne extends his arms with a sarcastic gesture. "So, like every company in the world?"

Without acknowledging Wayne's comment, Henry continues, "I've met people who claim it's 1910, 1966, 2001. I don't know what year it is anymore, and neither did they."

"And what happened to these other employees?" Wayne folds his flabby arms, making them appear slightly more muscular under the overhead lighting. "They still work for you?"

Henry scrounges up more tissues. "The better question is..." Wipes at sweat on his forehead and the drying blood under his nostrils. "Are they still alive?"

"Boy, you better stop talking riddles," Mike threatens, popping his knuckles.

"Look, SiDug is not a company. It's not anything you think. And all of this," Henry gestures around the room, "some of it's real. Some of it's something else." His leg shakes in place, as if he's got to piss. "This place. This building... it's..."

Wayne interjects, "Haunted?"

Henry shakes his head no. "That would imply that what you, I, and every other lost soul in here are going through is powered by some force beyond the grave—"

Images flash in Henry's mind once again. A macabre montage of images:

Cadaverous bodies writhing, bathed in blood, tethered to one another by blackened, thin appendages.

The outlines of screaming faces pressed against slimy walls composed of a substance more malleable than gypsum.

A room cluttered with cubicles. People suddenly rising from their desks. A black cable fed into their noses. They scream out in unison, "FEED–"

Henry shudders.

"YO!" Mike shouts.

Henry's eyes are unnervingly glossy. Distant. Unblinking. As if he's stared into the void and what he's seen has left him scarred forever. Bearing witness to unspeakable things no drug or therapist could ever sever from his mind.

Henry stares down Mike. "This place... it isn't haunted. It's *alive*." All color and life has left his face. "SiDug is alive and we're very much inside it."

# Chapter 26–Elevator To Where?

The elevator stops suddenly, sending Bishop and Kate stumbling against the wall.

Bishop grimaces as he rubs his arm. The hum of the elevator goes quiet. "We've stopped."

Kate rises. Glances at the ceiling. The lights above coruscate sporadically. The elevator does a little hop. Kate yelps. Bishop puts his hands out, as if on a surfboard, steadying himself.

Kate's breathing staggers. She closes her eyes tight and prays aloud, "Please God, don't let this elevator fall. I don't want to die like this."

"We're not going to die, okay?" Bishop kneels despite his body's complaints and places a hand on her shoulder. She flinches at first, then looks up at him through those steamed glasses of hers. "We're getting out of here."

"Ok..." Kate nods, wipes the moisture from off her lenses. "I'm thinking God sent you. I mean, you saved me from those things."

"Not sure if God sent me or not." Bishop hides his worry under a wrinkled old smile. "But I know there's got to be a way to escape and I'm going to do my darndest to make that happen, alright?"

Kate nods again, feeling a mustard seed of confidence take root within herself.

Bishop gives her shoulder a squeeze and slowly rises with a grunt. "I tell ya what... getting old sucks."

Kate watches him stagger towards the button panel. Not wanting to fixate on the possibility that this elevator could drop at any second, she distracts her mind by telling Bishop, "Just so you know, I'm not a bible thumper. But I have my faith... something I normally keep to myself."

Bishop presses at the elevator buttons. No matter which floor he chooses, the buttons refuse to respond.

"I've learned to keep a lot to myself," Kate shares as she unconsciously taps her foot against the elevator floor. "People are judgmental. Christian or non-Christian. Liberal or conservative. Doesn't matter. People are people. They love to judge."

*Just don't think about the elevator dropping,* Kate thinks. *Keep talking.*

She goes on, "I learned to lean on God on my own. Kind of discovered my faith at a young age. Mina helped with that. Had to believe in something to protect me from her and her monsters."

*Don't think about the elevator.*

*The fall.*

Kate taps her foot faster, unaware she's even doing it.

Without looking back at her, Bishop examines the elevator doors, the panel, everything. He finally mutters, "Uh, huh."

*Keep talking to the old man. He's going to find a way. I know it. God knows it. He sent Bishop to protect me.*

"You believe in God?" she asks.

*Yes, keep talking,* Kate tells herself. *Don't think. Keep talking.*

Bishop lets out a *Huh?* as he sticks his thick fingers into the slit of the door. He tries to pry them open with all of his might, but can't.

"Do you believe in God?" she asks again.

"I–I don't know."

"Are you an atheist? Agnostic?"

"I'm a realist." He scans the ceiling for a hatch. While climbing might normally be impossible for Bishop given his age, after the things he's seen in this place, the fuel in his tank might be just enough to push him through this supernatural gauntlet.

*I'd rather die trying,* he thinks, *than sit and wait for this thing to fall.*

"So, what do you think is going on?" Kate asks. "This place is cursed? Haunted? Maybe some kind of hell mouth? A portal to the underworld?"

"I don't think this place has anything to do with voodoo, ghosts, or demons."

"What makes you so sure?"

Bishop takes a moment. Asks himself that same question. "I don't know." He stares at the ceiling. Got to be a hatch around here somewhere. "But something inside just tells me so."

A thought pops inside Bishop's head like a mental firecracker: *Not something, Bishop. Me.*

*Me!*

*I'm the one telling you so.*

Bishop presses a palm to his head. Grimacing. The thought felt like the spark of a nasty migraine.

"Bishop?" Kate pushes her body as flat against the elevator as possible. "What's wrong?"

Bishop takes a second. "N-nothing. It's just my head. It's... it's killing me."

Kate frowns, not buying what he's saying.

*Don't worry, Kate. God's got you in the palm of His hand.*

*He sent you Bishop.*

Kate suddenly feels a similar sensation in her head, and she gasps. A foreign voice inside her head exclaims:

*No, I've got you!* the voice says. A voice that is not her own. *You belong to me now.*

*You're in the palm of my hand. And I'll prove it to you!*

*I'll prove it to you both!*

Before Kate can open her mouth to tell Bishop about the unwanted voice in her head, she feels the floor beneath her lighten as the elevator drops.

# Chapter 27–SiDug's Wi-Fi

The lights in Henry's office glint. He glances up at the fluorescent tubes as they sputter. Flinching as if he knows something the other men don't regarding the power outages and lapses in lumination.

"It's hungry," he murmurs.

"Huh?" Wayne says. "Who's hungry?"

"SiDug. The building. The beast." Henry stares above. "We're in the beast's belly."

"Hey! Focus!" Mike smacks the desk, vying for Henry's attention. "What'd you mean SiDug is alive?"

Henry glares at Mike. Doesn't immediately respond.

"Aw, forget him." Wayne waves Henry off. "Dude's a loon—"

"I know it sounds crazy!" Henry suddenly bolts up from his chair. "Hell, I think I've gone crazy! But this building. This place. This tomb... it's *alive*." He points at each one of them as he goes on, "And for the moment, you're safe because it's low on energy. Everything in the universe runs on energy, right? Well, this creature is no different."

The men gawk, trying to understand.

Henry sighs. Frustrated at how insane he sounds. "Look, to put it simply, we're a bunch of little fish in the belly of a bigger fish—one with an insatiable appetite. And we're slowly being digested."

Mike makes a face. "That's the most wack thing I've ever heard."

"I agree one-hundred percent," Wayne says.

*And I don't know what to think about any of this*, Zander thinks, *because my mind's as clear as fog.*

What isn't muddled in Zander's brain is a vision of Erik standing before him. The slash across his chest, pink and puckered like a pair of bloody lips, grins at Zander. He rubs his eyes, fighting away the image.

"I don't care if you guys believe this or not." Henry holds up the frayed end of the toothy black wire. "But if you found yourself anchored to your desks with this crammed up your nose, then SiDug has gotten a taste of you and it's going to want more."

Wayne subconsciously touches his nostril. The pain, having previously subsided, starts again. Psychosomatic or genuine, it's hard for Wayne to say. But the pang of panic pulsing inside him feels very real. "I had that same wire hooked in my nose."

Henry's eyes lock with Wayne's. "You did?"

Wayne nods. "Yes, but I was able to get it out, thankfully."

"What about you guys?" Henry asks. "You find yourself with this tethered to your nostril?"

Mike shakes his head, no.

"Nope," Zander replies.

*No, you didn't wake up to a hook in your nose, Zander thinks, but you sure as hell had a run in with Erik. And he's stalking you now. Going to put him down before he tries to put you down.*

"You sure?" Henry prods.

"I'm sure. Think I'd remember if I had barbed wire shoved up my nose," Mike snaps.

"Yeah," Zander says flatly. "Think I'd remember that too."

Henry glowers at them. Then continues, "Doesn't matter. We're all here now. Sustenance for SiDug."

The lights winkle above upon hearing those last words.

"See what I mean?"

"Because of the lights?" Wayne asks.

"Mostly. Sometimes it uses the lights to lead you where it wants you to go, the way you drag a string across the floor to lure a cat. But sometimes, the lights flicker because it's starved. Right now, I think it's the latter. Having taunted you all too much, it has overextended itself. It gets cocky because it's been around a long time. It likes to test its own limits."

"And how do you know all this?" Mike asks.

"How? Because of this?" Henry shakes the cable. "It's essentially a network cable. It's how SiDug gets into your heads, messing with your mind while draining the life out of you. Takes your personal horrors, both past and present, and streams them in your mind as if they were reruns from Hell. Uses those memories like some perverse paint on a canvas. Expanding upon them with a sadistic stroke of its virtual brush. Stretching them beyond reality, beyond their true origins, or at least from what you remembered–as our minds have unreliable recollections–and reimagining those memories for you. Reproducing them into something worse. Something far more malevolent." Henry rises from his seat, voice growing louder as he goes on, "You can't trust your own thoughts. Or what you believe. Or even... well... what year you think it is, because we're somewhere along the lines of its digestive tract." He eyes each one of them. "And some of us are further along than others."

Wayne winces as if he sniffed something foul. Mike shakes his head from side to side. And Zander... there's a snarl on his face, as if he's not buying into Henry's story.

*Clearly, he's in on it,* Zander thinks. *Is he part of the madness? Is this something bigger? Perhaps a top-secret experiment by SiDug that we've inadvertently signed up for?*

*And what's Erik doing here? If that really was him.*

*That snake.*

*My friend? Hardly.*

*Just an opportunistic snake.*

An image of the bloody Santoku knife emerges in his head–

"Ok, that sounds one-hundred percent insane," Wayne announces. "So, is there a way out of here? Or what?"

Henry frowns at the black cord with a somber expression that weighs on his face, making his skin appear to sag. "There is." He feeds the cord back into his nose.

145

"Whoa!" Mike shouts. "What the hell are you doing?"

"If you want to leave, this is the only way."

"Are you crazy?" Wayne demands. Then, with a scoff, admits, "I mean, we already assumed you are."

"I have to reconnect to it," Henry explains flatly. "Put it to you this way: you're all operating on SiDug's Wi-Fi, so to speak. Thoughts and bits of madness are being transmitted back and forth. Some of your mental connections with SiDug are better than others."

Henry winces as he continues feeding the cord up his nose, and the others flinch in response. Wayne turns away for a moment.

Henry issues a grunt. Then continues, "But this is a direct connection to the source. I can see things. Some useful. Some horrific. It's like diving back into the dream—or a nightmare—while you're still somewhat asleep. You get pieces of information." He gestures to Mike's spear. "Now if I act or talk crazy... take me out. Ok?"

Mike looks taken aback. "W-what?"

"Kill me."

"I'm not killing anybody! I just want us to get outta this place," Mike declares.

"I should've passed long ago."

"But if there is a way out—"

"There's nowhere for me to go," Henry growls. "Now promise to kill me if I act up."

Mike trades glances with Wayne and Zander, uncomfortable with the request. Murder under duress and self-defense, while never ideal, is one thing. To voluntarily kill a man is another.

And the accident with Reggie? Well, that was just that... an accident—

"I promise," Zander says, the tone in his response bereft of emotion.

Mike shoots him a look that screams, *What's up with you?*

"Good." Henry closes his eyes. Turns his attention inward—

Gruesome images flood his mind. Sickening scenes from a horror film. An orgy of tangled bodies, slick and blood-soaked, wriggling. Mouths yawning. Oozing fluids from every orifice. Fingers crooked, clawing at the air, grasping at Henry.

*It's screwing with you,* his mind cries. *Don't let it!*

Then another scene unfolds. One of his family, standing before him, holding hands, on a lush field against a coral blue sky. They're smiling. His wife is waving. One of his children holds up a flower.

An unwanted disparate voice inside his head tells him, *Don't fight me, Henry. You can't win. You already know this. Just because they freed you doesn't mean that you're free. I own them too. I own all of you.*

Henry squeezes his eyelids tighter. Fights back the unwelcome thoughts funneling into his mind.

He refocuses on his family and feels a great sadness well within him. His wife and oldest daughter giggle as they swing his younger daughter between them. His wife laughs with that joyfully light, playful laugh of hers. Their faces beam with beauty and innocence.

She waves at him. "Henry, what are you waiting for, silly? Come on over."

Henry feels the sadness overwhelm him. He wants to cry.

Then he does.

Tears force their way through the slits of his eyelids. He sniffles. Sobs. Stammers, "I... I can't!"

Wayne and Mike look at one another, then back at Henry. Zander stares at the weeping man with a stoic, unmoved gaze.

Back in Henry's mind, his wife waves once more. "Come on, babe! Why are you just standing there?"

Henry cries out to them. He should be with them. He wants to join them, but he can't because they died on Flight 1243 from Tampa to Houston. Henry couldn't go. Work called.

Work always called.

Work always came first.

But someone had to make money. Someone had to bring food and mortgage payments to the table. The family had to make a trip last minute. His wife's mother, Candace, was gravely ill. Henry had never cared about the woman. Candace was a judgmental old hag in his eyes, having never approved of their marriage. So, it was only right in Henry's eyes that karma weighed in on this situation. When the "old hag" needed them the most, he evaded the visit. Blamed work. His wife understood, then boarded the flight with their children and crash landed in Louisiana. Somewhere between Lafayette and Lake Charles, to be exact.

Ironically, Candace died while the family was in transit.

"I should have been on that flight!" Henry cries out to them. Tears flood his eyes. "I should have died with you! Hell—I should have talked you out of it!"

In the distance, a commercial plane nosedives, disappearing into the horizon. A resultant boom blares across the field.

Henry's family suddenly catches fire where they stand.

Smiles ceasing, joviality turns to insanity. Laughter turns to screams. Henry covers his ears but can't block out the chorus of their cries. His children are quickly swallowed up by the blaze, but it cannot spare him from the unfolding imagery of his wife's demise as she is consumed. The fire eats at her flesh, and skin gives way to muscle, then muscle to bone. What charred tissue remains flaps in the breeze like the dried leaves of dead brush.

Henry quakes where he stands, body shivering in an undeniable muddle of grief and regret.

*I wish I died with all of you,* Henry thinks. *I'm such a scumbag! It should have been me! I deserve my current fate.*

*You do,* the unwanted voice says. *And now you're with me. Part of me. Forever. Thank you for that.*

*Shut up! I hate you!* Henry thinks. *Whatever you are!*

*You know what I am, Henry. I've already shown you.*

The scene changes once again, returning to the jumble of bodies entangled on the floor. A faceless mass, writhing like a mountain of worms. Some lack eyeballs. Some lack noses. Others have only mouths. The featureless mannequins of a morbid imagination.

It sickens Henry to see this image, but it's what the creature wants him to see.

It's what SiDug wants him to see.

However, emerging from the grotesque contortion of torsos, ambling limbs, and heads, is that of an older woman. She pushes out from between the bodies, forcing herself from their slippery grasp. Her hair is long, gray, and stained with blood. She is not naked like the others, but has on a basic dark gray uniform, like that of the SiDug cleaning crew.

She extends a single arm, reaching out to Henry.

*It's... her,* Henry thinks.

A name comes to him—a name he doesn't immediately recognize, but it comes to him anyway.

*The one I was looking for.*

"R-Rosita!"

The wriggling bodies reach for Rosita, as if to shield her image from Henry's mind, but she fights back. Swatting away at the faceless mass.

Henry catches another glimpse of her uniform and then it clicks. He met Rosita during training. She was going to be the janitorial manager.

*Rosita?* he wonders. *Where are you?*

Henry reaches for her, but feels hands grab him now. He looks down and around to find the bodies, with their snakelike shimmering skin, grasping him like the vines of some alien plant.

Rosita fights against the tide of indiscernible bodies clawing, hissing, and grabbing at her. She's about to speak when a bloody hand shoots up and clamps over her mouth.

"Rosita!"

With the last of her efforts, she fumbles to stretch her other arm out. Raising both hands in the air, she holds up nine fingers.

"Nine," Henry says. "Nine what?"

Before she can respond, she is consumed by a sea of appendages.

Henry is whirled around, coming about-face with more of the faceless, gory creatures, and that unwanted voice in his head shouting, *Don't you dare!*

Henry opens his eyes to find Mike, Wayne, and Zander glaring at him. Not sure what exactly to say following his visions, he says the first thing that comes to his mind, "Rosita."

"Who?" Wayne asks.

"R–R–Rosita."

"Yeah... who's Rosita?"

Before Henry can answer, the cord shoots further inside his nostril. He wails, jerking back in his chair, hands forcefully trying to pull the cursed thing out before it tears a hole in his sinus.

"What the fuck!?" Mike yells.

Henry feels the fresh blood from his nostril spill over his lips and down his chin. He grasps the cord and pulls, but it only burrows deeper into his nasal cavity, shredding his skin of his hands.

"Somebody do something!" Wayne shouts.

Henry hollers out in misery.

"Like what?" Mike yells.

"I don't know! Something!"

Wayne takes a step towards Henry, but Zander throws his arm in front of him and stops him short. "Don't."

"*N–n–nine!*" Henry nearly screams out the word in one agonizing cry.

"What?" Wayne asks.

Black cable clutched in hand, blood oozing from his nose, Henry shouts, "Rosita! Ninth floor!"

Then Henry's eyes go coal black as the cord snakes its way through his mouth on its own. Threading his skull as if it were a needle.

Mike and Wayne recoil in horror.

Zander's knuckles tighten around his staff.

As the cord slithers around Henry's torso, his body jiggles. Then stiffens, straightening up, as if manipulated by an invisible puppeteer. His empty gaze cycles through each of them as he speaks in a gurgling, raspy tone, the way a serpent might speak if it had vocal cords. "I am enjoying playing with you."

No one says a thing.

"All of you."

Wayne shoots Mike a look, but Mike ignores him.

"I love playing with my food."

"Who are you?" Mike asks.

"Me?" Henry's lips stretch unnaturally wide as he answers, "Why, I am the manifestation of eternal starvation. The devourer of madness. The mirror of dark truths."

"Ok, whatever that means," Mike responds. "So, why are you doing this?"

"Because I am hungry. I hunger for the blight of humanity. The corruption of its conscience. The divine delicacies of those dark things denied. I bring them to light, then feast upon them. Savoring them like the maddening morsels they are." He looks to Zander. "Your friend here has some delicious secrets."

Zander flinches.

"I can't remember the last time such a blackened soul has been served upon my plate," Henry says. "I'm not sure I can thank Mr. Gudu enough for recruiting you."

"What the heck is he talking about?" Mike asks.

"Nothing." Zander raises his spear. Gestures to Henry to back off with a threatening flick. "He's fucked in the head, thanks to that cable. That's all."

"Am I?" Henry's unsettling smile grows. "Am I as *fucked* in the head as you? As what you did to poor old Eri–"

Zander drives the spear into Henry's chest.

Wriggling wildly, Henry's gaze meets Zander's. Through gritted teeth and sputtering blood, he burbles, "Déjà... vu...?" His head then slumps forward, lifeless.

Zander unsheathes the staff from Henry's chest as if he were simply removing it from drywall and not a human being who once had dreams, family, and aspirations.

"Jeee-sus!" Wayne gapes. "W-what the hell? What did you do?"

"I didn't *do* anything. SiDug already took him." Without giving Henry a second thought, Zander makes for the door. "Now, let's go."

Mike stares at the blood pooling beneath Henry's corpse. "Go where?"

"To the ninth floor," Zander replies coolly. "To find *Rosita*."

# Chapter 28–Up, Up, Down, Down

The world beneath Kate and Bishop's feet disappears, stomachs sliding to their throats as the elevator drops.

Then it jolts to a stop, sending them spilling onto the floor. Kate shrieks as she is bounced against the floor. Bishop lands painfully onto his palms, a coarse groan escaping him.

*Did you like that, Kate?* an unwanted voice inside Kate's mind asks.

Without responding either mentally or verbally, Kate quickly sits up. Backs herself against the wall.

The voice prods, *Would you like more?*

The word comes out in a shudder from Kate's quaving lips, "No..."

*Are you sure?*

*I could play with you and your friend all night.*

*Every day.*

*For all eternity.*

*Torment you the way Mina did.*

*Speaking of your loving aunt, do you like what I did with the picture of the men?*

*Those deliciously inventive monsters?*

"Stop it," Kate says.

Bishop pushes up from the floor. Turns his head in her direction. "Kate?"

*Mina, Mina, Mina.*

*What a dirty, defiled soul.*

*And you... the precious little crybaby.*

"Stop-it-stop-it-stop-it!" Kate pleads as she clutches her temples.

*Oh, how I wish Mina were here too. I would have fun with her. Pitting the two of you together? She might just like that actually–*

"Shut up!" Kate claws at her hair, grabbing handfuls of it as she begs, "Just leave me alone–"

"Enough!" Bishop locks his hand around her wrist. Leveraging his body weight, he yanks her to her feet. Their eyes meet, and she glares at him, face flush, cheeks a dull red. Her glasses are smudged with sweat and fingerprints.

Her lips move, but no words come out.

"Snap out of it!" Bishop commands as he gives her a hard shake. "We're getting out of here. Ok?" Louder, "OK?"

With trembling hands, Kate cleans her glasses and offers a half-hearted, "Alright."

"I know you're scared. I'm scared too. But we don't have time to waste. We *have* to get out of here. There's got to be an escape hatch above us somewhere. Now," Bishop threads his fingers together, palms up, and gestures to her, "give me your foot."

Kate hesitates.

"Just do it!"

The elevator does a little bounce.

"Come on!" he presses.

"All right. All right."

"I'm going to hoist you up and I need you to grab onto whatever's up there." Bishop indicates with his hands. "You get one shot at this, ok? My back ain't what it used to be."

Kate nods.

Bishop begins, "One..."

Kate places her foot into his palms.

"Two..."

Kate plants her hands on his shoulders as the lower muscles of Bishop's back painfully stiffen like resistance bands tested beyond the threshold of their elasticity.

"Three!" With a grunt, he flings upwards. Arms raised, Kate pushes through a ceiling tile and clutches one of the metal crossbars above them.

Normally these bars, consisting of galvanized steel, are made to only hold about fifteen pounds. Having helped hang suspended ceilings in his day, Bishop knows this. However, given the desperation of the situation, there was nothing to lose.

And somehow, the frame above them was holding.

*Come on, Kate,* Bishop thinks. *Get a move on! This elevator's got a mind of its own.*

*Either you or this elevator is going to drop at any second.*

"Kate?" His body tremors as he fights to hold her steady. "Talk to me."

Kate tries to pull herself up, but her upper arm strength isn't where she had intended it to be. One of her New Year's resolutions was to get fit. Along with getting a bulldog and landing a new job. Regrettably, the one resolution she's achieved is proving to be the *one* she regrets keeping the most.

"Kate!" Bishop doesn't want to yell at her, but his body seems to do the talking, influenced by the duress of the situation. Teeth gnashing, muscles trembling, he growls, "Find... the... hatch."

Kate does. Spies a handle just out of reach. "I see it!"

"Ok. Hurry. Please!" Bishop's muscles shudder. He's going to drop her at any second.

She reaches for the handle. The tips of her fingers are just inches away. "Almost... got... it..."

The handle appears big enough, secure enough, for her to grab onto it and hang from it–if she can reach it.

And if she can pull down on it hard enough.

And if it is not locked.

Bishops body tires. "KATE!"

Kate reaches...

Reaches...

"Got it!" Kate grasps the handle just as the elevator jerks. She screams as the hatch drops open and she spills onto Bishop. While he breaks her fall, he takes the brunt of the impact. He lands on his tailbone, sending an agonizing bullet of pain shooting up his spine.

Kate gets to her feet. Takes Bishop by his hand and puts everything she has into peeling him off the floor. "You ok?"

Bishop grunts breathlessly as he presses a hand to his back. His gaze travels to the hatch swinging above them like a pendulum. "You got it open."

"True, but I let go."

"That's ok, kiddo." Bishop winces at the twinge just below his scapula. "Come on." He weaves his fingers together once more to give her a boost. "Let's try it again." *Because this thing could drop at any minute, kiddo, and you and I will be dead as doornails, and I will not let that happen.*

"You sure?"

The elevator lurches again.

"You want to stay here?"

"No!" Kate shouts.

Bishop pumps his hands. "Well, then let's go!"

Kate feeds her foot into his palms, and Bishop, against the excruciating protests of his entire body, launches her up once more. She snatches the handle, then throws another arm up through the opening, and pulls herself on top of the elevator carriage.

She gets to her feet, looks up, and to her surprise, sees incandescent lights lining the walls of the shaft, disappearing to a dim point above. A single ladder scales the wall, along with the sealed interior elevator doors of the floors above them, numerically marked by red spray paint.

They're on the fifth floor.

"Hey, kiddo," Bishop shouts from below, "you ok?"

"Yeah."

"Good. Is there a ladder near you? One that you can easily get to?"

"Um... yeah." While a curtain of cables and steel flex-conduit stands between her and the ladder, it is otherwise accessible–

The elevator hums as the cables come to life. The carriage ascends.

Kate backs away, surveys her surroundings, unsure of where to go. It's not like she's ever ridden an elevator *from the outside.* "Bishop?"

"I'm here!"

"Did you push one of the buttons?"

"No, not at all."

155

"Ok." The panic in her voice grows as she presses, "So then... w-what do I do?"

"Just..." Bishop frets, then shakes it off. "Just don't move!"

The elevator hums steadily as Kate stares at the doors as they climb.

Sixth floor.

Seventh floor.

Eighth floor–

The elevator comes to a rough stop. Kate yelps and it echoes throughout the shaft, bouncing off the cold concrete walls.

"You ok?" Bishop calls out.

"Uh-huh."

"Good. See anything?" Bishop asks. "The car control panel's still off. Don't know where we've stopped."

"We're on the eighth floor."

The button labeled '8' on the elevator's control panel lights up. Bishop narrows his gaze, suspiciously.

There's the sound of grinding metal as the elevator doors slide open revealing a perfectly normal looking floor–*normal* considering it is amply lit and full of:

"People," Bishop utters.

"What?"

"Kate, there's people here... and they're very much... alive?"

# Chapter 29–Laughter Abound

Zander and Mike move out of the office and make for the exit door with Wayne trailing. He looks back at Henry. The cable dangles limply from his nose. The massive gash in his torso weeps blood. Wayne keels over, vomits.

Zander gives Wayne a cursory glance, then studies the door.

Mike stops short, taking inventory of Wayne's reaction.

Wayne's eyes flush with teardrops, not out of sadness but sickness. A single string of vomit mixed with saliva leads down to the oatmeal-like puddle at his feet. In the absence of a significant other in his life, Wayne has supplanted that void with video games. Over the years, he'd slaughtered armies of knights, soldiers, zombies, and monsters. But those foes, as they expired by bullet or blade, were only pixels. Virtual entities conceptualized from the imaginations of programmers and designers. Their deaths had only enough meaning to advance Wayne to the next level or earn him the next achievement.

This was different.

This was an actual person who Zander just killed. Skewered him as he were a piece of meat at the end of a shish kabob.

Mike puts a hand on Wayne's shoulder. "You ok?"

Wayne wipes away the string of spit, extends a shaky thumbs up.

Zander stares at the exit door. He raises his foot and kicks at the panic bar, which does not engage. He kicks it successively harder, cursing all the while.

"Hey, hey, hey, give it a rest. Clearly it's locked!" Mike moves toward

Zander, but Zander shoves him aside. "Whoa." Mike takes a step back, hands up. "Easy, bud. We're on the same team."

Chest and shoulders heaving from the effort, Zander casts Mike a wary glare that asks, *Are we?*

"Not feeling like it with how you're looking at me."

Zander scowls. Turns to the door, throwing his body against it with the rabid fury of a trapped raccoon ferally trying to break out of its cage.

"Yo, it ain't budging." Mike senses his unease with Zander grow. After having seen how emotionally efficient Zander was at killing Henry, Mike knows the man has become unhinged. This building has gotten to him.

Zander ignores him. Emits a crazed yell, a veritable battle cry as sweat flicks off his body. He heaves his shoulder against the door with such force the wall rattles.

"ZANDER!"

The exit door surrenders with a mechanical pop. A fragment of the door hardware flies off, disappearing into the stairwell with a noisy clatter.

Exasperated and covered in sweat, Zander looks back at Mike and Wayne, who stare on with worried expressions. "Not letting," he wheezes between breaths, "this place... kill me." He leans against the doorframe, shoulders rising and falling, undulating like waves. He rocks his head back and closes his eyes momentarily as he gasps for air.

Mike says nothing but keeps a watchful eye on him as he scoots past. Inside the stairwell, there's an exit door that most likely leads outside. "Ok, so forget the ninth floor." He smiles as he presses the panic bar and it opens. "We're getting out of here—"

He stops in his tracks.

The exit door doesn't lead outside, to the parking lot, or towards anything resembling freedom and not this cursed place. Instead, it's as if borrowed from one of those old cartoons where the characters open the door to find nothing but a shallow room lined in unfinished cinder block on all sides.

Mike's smile evaporates.

"You're kidding," Wayne says. "You are absolutely freaking kidding."

Mike backs away as he drags a hand down his face in disbelief.

Wayne turns to Zander. "Think you can bust through that too?"

Zander, still catching his breath, snarls. "Don't be stupid."

Laughter ricochets off the stairwell walls and the men stiffen.

"Laugh all you want!" Mike shouts. "But we're going to find out who you are and kick your ass!"

The laughter grows louder.

Then stops altogether.

Zander starts for the stairs.

"Where are you going?" Mike catches Zander by the arm and it's an unwelcome gesture based on the murderous look Zander gives him.

"I already told you," he hisses, shaking Mike off, "to the ninth floor."

"Wait-wait-wait," Wayne implores, waving both hands. "You don't seriously believe Henry, do you? I mean, the guy was nuts."

*Not that I'm sure you're not as well*, he thinks.

"So, what if the guy was crazy? I mean, what's you guys' master plan?" Zander asks. "Test every dead end in this maze until we *eventually* find our way out?"

"That's one option, I guess," Wayne admits with a shrug.

Zander scoffs incredulously. "Look, crazy or not, the stiff mentioned the ninth floor, and some chick named Rosita. If she knows a way out, I'm all ears." He makes his way up the stairs. "Now I don't give a rat's ass what you guys do, but that's where I'm headed."

"And what if it's a trap?" Mike asks. "You think about that?"

Zander stops short. Peers down at the two of them. "We're already in a trap." Then continues on.

Mike whispers to Wayne, "Much as don't trust him, he has a point."

Wayne throws his hands in the air as he argues, "But we're already on the first floor. Let's just keep looking."

"I don't think we should split up."

"You're preaching to the choir here, ok. I play Dungeons and Dragons. And that is the cardinal rule. You never split the group, so I agree, but this makes no sense! We're going to locate one person within this endless tower of terror?"

The lights in the office go out, leaving only the stairwell lights on. Both men eye the room, then each other.

"You wanna go through that again?" Mike gestures back into the pitch-black office. "Stumble between cubicles, copiers, and weird stuff moving around? Be my guest." He climbs the stairs. "I'll take my chances that maybe Henry was telling the truth. Something kind of tells me he was."

Wayne mulls this over. Looks back to the office. Stares deep into its darkness.

"Eggie?" Something whispers from the shadows. "Eggie, follow me."

A voice none other than Chet's.

"Follow me and I'll help you escape."

In one swift motion, Wayne reaches for the stairwell door, slams it shut, then races up the stairs after Mike and Zander.

# Chapter 30–The Office People

Bishop stares in awe at the activity before him. The office is bustling with people conducting seemingly routine tasks. Some converse with one another. Others work at their desks, glued to their computers.

"Bishop!" Kate shouts down at him.

"Y-yeah?" he stammers, ogling the office staff.

*Who are these people?* he wonders. *And where'd they come from?*

*Were they always here?*

"Bishop, what did you say about there being people?" Kate cranes her neck but can't see much of anything with her limited field of view from the hatch.

He ignores her, cocking his head as he quickly processes the situation:

*What if these folks are part of this fiasco? What if this is a trap and Kate follows me down here with them and they hurt her? I don't want to separate us, but I can't chance it that these are actual people and not involved with whatever's going on!*

*Then again, they could be regular folks who might actually help us. By leaving her up there, I could risk getting her stuck.*

*It's a fifty-fifty chance.*

Bishop makes a call. He looks up at her as he says firmly, "Get to the ladder and wait for me."

"W-what?" She shakes her head defiantly. "No. No way! I'm not going anywhere without you." She drops onto her butt and feeds her legs through the hatch–

"There's no time to argue and I don't know who these people are! They could be screwed up like everything else in this place."

"Ok, then forget them and follow me up here." She reaches into the elevator with both hands, "I'll just pull you up."

"By that you mean I'll just pull you *down*," he points out. "I'm way too heavy."

"We've got to try–" The elevator hops, threatening to drop.

Bishop points into the elevator shaft, over her shoulder. "Just go! Wait for me! I'll get help."

"No, don't leave me! I'll come with you!"

The elevator bounces again. Kate falls backwards, smacking her head against one of the pulleys. Bishop stumbles. Given the commotion, the office workers finally take notice. Bishop eyes them, then tells Kate, "Go!"

Kate rubs her head as she rolls onto her side. She navigates the mess of wires and the uneven footing the elevator roof provides as she makes her way to the ladder. "I'm here!"

"Good. Stay put! I'll be right back. I promise I will not leave you."

*You better know what you're doing, old man,* he thinks. *You could be sending her alone to a death sentence if you're wrong about these people.*

As if arguing internally with himself, another thought follows, *Well I wouldn't be surprised if the brakes on this elevator don't work. So at least if the damn thing falls, she won't be on it.*

*That's a minor comfort.*

Bishop spurns the noise in his brain and targets the first employee that walks by–a clean-cut man, sporting a violet tie that hugs a button-down shirt with enough starch ironed into it to stop a bullet.

*Ok, good. Maybe Mr. Violet-Tie here will help me out,* Bishop hopes.

Violet Tie stops in place. "Hi." His eyes narrow as he notes Bishops haggard, disheveled appearance. "You alright there?"

Other employees stop what they're doing and begin to check out what's happening, rising from their desks like moles from their nests.

"Not really." Bishop motions to the elevator. "My friend's stuck up there. I need help getting her down."

"O-Ok." Violet Tie turns to the other office workers who start gathering around. "Someone fetch me the stepladder from Hannah's office."

One worker responds with, "On it!"

*So maybe since these people are helping me out,* Bishop thinks. *They're ok after all.*

"I need a chair or something too," Bishop tells them.

Violet Tie responds, "One second!" He wheels over an office chair. "Here."

Bishop takes it and lays it down between the elevator doors, preventing them from shutting. The elevator responds with a persistent chime that degrades into a muted, staticky beep. He then calls up to Kate, "We're bringing a stepladder over and getting you down."

The employee makes his way down the aisle, squeezing between people, saying excuse me. He's a mousy young guy with unusually small eyes and large ears. He was probably picked on a lot at school for his appearance. He hands Bishop the ladder just as the sounds of ropes snapping and the piercing squeals of metal-on-metal fill the air. This unnerving racket is followed by a whoosh as the elevator plummets and a loud boom as it crashes into the pit.

Bishop flings the ladder aside and sticks his head into the shaft. "KATE!"

"I'm ok!" She's hugging the ladder for dear life.

Unfortunately, the ladder is on the *other* side of the elevator shaft.

"Ok, just hang on. We're going to get you down," Bishop assures her, all the while wondering how in the hell he's going to accomplish that. "Just don't look down."

Of course, Kate peers down the shaft, which seems to go on forever. "Oh my God."

"I told you not to look down!"

"What'd you expect me to do?"

"Just... just hang on!" He turns to the others.

*Hang on?* Kate wonders. *For how long?*

Between the worry of losing her grip, the tingling anxiety welling in stomach, and the forthcoming fatigue on her muscles, she questions how long she really can hang on for. Above her, the ladder scales the wall, diminishing beyond what her eyes can see. She feels her heart tank.

*God... please, please help me out of this. Whatever this is!*

She hears Bishop and the office workers debating below about how they are going to get to her. Bishop pummels them with questions: *Where does the ladder lead? Are there building plans? Is there an emergency hatch or call box somewhere?*

"Bishop?" Kate calls out. "Bishop, what's going on?"

"Hold tight, please!" Bishop argues with the staff. They contend they knew nothing was wrong with the elevator, or the building, but Bishop gives them some insight about the madness they've survived.

A horrid grinding sound causes Kate to nearly lose her footing. This is followed up by Bishop shouting, "NO!"

She looks down to see the elevator doors slamming shut, snapping the office chair in half like a toothpick.

"Bishop!" she calls out as a terrifying realization sinks in.

She's on her own now.

# Chapter 31–Concrete Climb

**W**ayne struggles to keep pace with Mike and Zander, who are nearly two floors above him now. "Guys!" He shouts, his breathing taxed. "Guys... slow down!"

Zander marches on, disregarding the pleas.

"Zander!" Mike reaches out, catches him by the shoulder. "Wait for Wayne."

Zander shakes him off, snarling. Lip twitching like a junkyard mutt on the verge of lashing out.

*Don't let his size fool you,* Zander thinks. *You could take him down if he tries to keep you here.*

"Don't like the way you're looking at me right now," Mike admonishes. "All I asked was to let the man catch up."

"Don't tell me what to do."

"I'll say whatever I want to say. If I ask you to slow down, then that's what you do. We're in this together." Mike tucks the spear into the crook of his elbow, then cracks his knuckles. "And if we ain't, then let's straighten this out right now."

Wayne finally catches up, clumsily slides between the men. "Whoa, people! Let's save the testosterone..." he catches his breath, "for outside, ok?"

Zander grinds his teeth. With a snort, he backs down.

*What are you doing?* he thinks. *Don't be a pussy! Don't let Mike intimidate you. You let Erik do that, and where did that get you? Nowhere. It opened the door for him to steal Vicky.*

Zander is unsure if the thoughts are his own or whispered into his head from the belly of this interminable staircase, but either way, one thing is for sure—he agrees with them.

"Whatever." Zander turns, soldiers on up the stairs.

Mike glares at him, then shoots Wayne a look that says, *I ain't so sure about this guy.*

The three of them continue upwards, and as they pass the fifth floor, Wayne groans with exhaustion.

"Hey, man," Mike suggests, "you might want to start hitting the gym once we get out of here."

"Like that'll make a difference." Wayne clutches the railing as he huffs, maintaining contact with it as they progress. "Unlike you, I wasn't born with the metabolic rate of a furnace. I look at a burger the wrong way and gain ten pounds."

"Well, maybe it's time you rethink that attitude? Maybe this whole thing's a blessing in disguise. A chance to check in on the stuff you've been slacking on. I know I'm gonna revisit some goals myself."

"Yeah?" Wayne pauses. Wipes the sweat off his face with his shirt. "Like what?"

"I dunno, like getting an actual degree. Growing up, the streets were my school. But I want a proper education."

"Well, trust my student loans—school is not a silver bullet for financial freedom. It's a bullet point on a resume that converts four years of your life into forty years of debt."

Zander keeps ahead of them, never contributing to the conversation.

"I don't care, it's worth the cost to me. Construction was never my dream job. Earning a degree while I played college football for UCF or USF was. Always loved throwing the ball around. But I never even got to try out for my high school team, because I had to drop out to help pay the bills since my dad was a bum. Hanging drywall paid better than McDonalds and was safer than dealing drugs—"

Several loud *thwack* sounds reverberate through the stairwell.

The men halt.

"W-what was that?" Wayne asks.

They look around, catching the lights illuminating the levels below turning off in succession, stopping at their floor.

"Just more electrical issues, people," Zander says flatly as he peeks down into the pitch dark below. "Let's keep moving."

Mike studies Zander as he continues to climb the steps and thinks, *The heck is up with this dude?*

Zander feels their eyes on him as they round the sixth floor. *These assholes are judging me. Who do they think they are?*

*Maybe you should do something about it when the time is right,* that external voice suggests.

Zander gives his bloodied staff a good squeeze.

*Maybe they are part of this building,* the voice continues. *Part of this place.*

*Maybe they are in your head and don't want you to escape. Keeping you in this nightmare.*

*Or maybe...*

*Just maybe...*

*They're working with Erik.*

The group passes a door marked FLOOR SIX.

*Keep an eye on them, Zander,* the voice warns, *because they don't have your back!*

*They're watching it.*

*Waiting for the moment to stab you!*

Zander closes his eyes for a second. Exhales as he thinks, *Are these thoughts my own? Or are they really coming from somewhere else?*

He opens his eyes, blinks several times as he keeps climbing.

*No. They have to be my own, because that second voice is me, right? And it knows that these assholes behind me are going to screw me over when they get the chance. Somehow, some way, they've got it in for me and they're gonna show it!*

*So, screw them–*

"Holy mother of God!" Wayne exclaims, exasperated. "It's like we're stuck on a StairMaster from Hell."

This time, Mike agrees. It is almost as if the building has expanded. Reaching the sixth floor feels more like the forty-sixth.

They round the seventh floor.

Then Wayne hears something behind him.

A whisper: "Hey."

Every hair on Wayne's body stands up.

"Hey, Eggie."

Terror tears through him. *Keep going,* he tells himself. *Don't turn around.*

Wayne tries to ignore it, but the whispering sounds like it's right behind him. "Hey, Eggie, remember that time when I cornered you in the locker rooms?"

Wayne stiffens. Feels a cold sensation flush his body as the image of a dirty locker room, with school-bus yellow rusted lockers everywhere, invades his mind. It's an image from the past. He had just left the showers, dressed in only a coarse white towel.

"Yeah, remember that?" the whispering voice prods. "It was just you and me, and I chased you with a towel wound tight like a horse's tail and popped you in the face. Square in the eye!"

Yes, Wayne remembers.

The pink, diagonal welt across his eye looked like he had been whipped by a dragon. Blinded him momentarily and caused excruciating pain, but he didn't have time to process because Chet was chasing him. So, he ran out of the locker room screaming for help, dropped his own towel, and headed right into the gymnasium full of his classmates.

Chet got detention for the incident. A whole three days.

But Wayne's sentence was longer. He became a laughingstock for the rest of the year, suffering from a barrage of names: Free Willy Wayne, Wayne the Whale, and Wet Willy. These nicknames persisted into the following school year. He was forced to grin and bear it, as his unsympathetic parents chalked up the taunting to societal tough love.

"Deal with it," his father, a successful programmer, would chide. He was a self-made man who had started his own IT company and took no prisoners. He was not a man who liked to hear excuses. "Make something useful out of the pain. Make something useful out of yourself."

Following graduation, Wayne signed up for Taekwondo. Decided he wanted to take action in the future should he ever be threatened again. But it was too little, too late. While the martial arts bolstered his confidence, aiding him later in his professional life, it didn't help mitigate the damage from Chet's tormenting, which had already been branded in his mind.

What he would have given to deliver a nut-crushing knee to Chet's groin.

"Yeah, you remember that, don't you?" the whispering voice asks.

Wayne finds himself unable to move. Transfixed by the thoughts troubling his mind, he watches Zander and Mike move along without him.

"Look at me," the voice urges.

Wayne grips the handrail so tight, his knuckles bulge.

"Look at me."

*Keep going, Wayne*, he thinks. *What are you doing? Don't stop!*

"I said look at me, Eggie! Or are you still a little wuss? Still afraid of me?"

Anger washes over Wayne as he turns to the voice. "I'm not afraid of you, Chet—"

He comes eyeball to eyeball with Chet. Big, brawny, reeking of armpits and Doritos. He's wearing his trademark fire-engine red Converse, loose fitting Levis, and an aptly inappropriate t-shirt with the words BEAVER FEVER on it.

"Chet?" Wayne ekes out.

Chet still looks like he's in his late teens.

"Wayne!" Mike shouts from above, snapping Wayne out of his stupor. He looks up at Mike, who's about a floor up from him now. "I thought you were right behind me, man. Move your ass!"

Wayne looks back to Chet, and the young bully's eyes are now puffy, pink, and swollen shut. A villainous grin spans his face. "How fast can ya run, fat boy?"

Wayne scrambles up the stairs, footsteps clapping against the concrete in his wake.

The clamor grabs Mike's attention. He tells Zander, "Hold up!"

Zander ignores him and keeps going.

"Asshole," Mike mutters.

Wayne rounds the next bank of stairs and practically crashes into Mike, but the big man stops him short.

"The hell, man?" Mike says.

Wayne's ashen skin is the color of wax. He's drenched in sweat. His breathing stertorous.

"Why you out of breath? I thought you were right behind us?"

"I-I was." Wayne double-checks behind him. No sign of Chet. Just a stairwell fading down into oblivion. "But I saw Chet down there. He's... stalking me again. Just... just like he used to."

Mike brushes past him, edging towards the darkened steps below. Calls out, "Listen up, whoever you are." He raises his spear. "If you want someone to mess with, come on out and mess with me, you punk-ass bitch!"

Mike's words drift into the shadows. Only dead quiet in response.

With a *humph*, he gives Wayne a pat on the shoulder. "Come on. Let's keep moving. If your buddy shows up again, I'll take care of him. Hate bullies. Real or...," he scans the building then continues, "or imaginary."

Wayne nods. "Thanks."

"Just stay in front of me this time, alright?"

"Roger that."

They proceed up the stairs, Wayne leading, Mike in tow with his spear prepped should Chet make another appearance.

"Zander, where you at?" Mike shouts. "Zander!"

No response. Only the sound of a door above slamming shut.

"That dickhead left us behind," Mike says incredulously.

"Are you surprised?"

Mike chuckles. "Nah."

They round the next floor and Zander is standing in front of the door for the eighth floor.

"Hey, why didn't you respond, asshole?" Mike demands, storming towards Zander. "I was shouting out your name."

Zander's brow wrinkles, eyes narrowing with anger. "No, you weren't."

Mike scoffs. "Please. This stairwell is a goddamn sound chamber. I know you heard me."

Zander steps closer to Mike. "No." Leans in. "I didn't."

"I know you did. And I also heard a door slam shut. You trying to leave us?"

"Now *that* I heard. And *no*, that wasn't me."

"I don't know what your beef is," Mike says, "but once we're out, me and you are gonna settle up."

Zander inches even closer. "Fine by me."

Wayne intervenes. "Break it up!" Pushes the two men apart. "We already did this."

Zander angles back. His gaze unwavering. "Déjà vu, right?"

"Well, if you guys would cut the machismo, this wouldn't keep happening!" Wayne complains.

"Not talking about us. I'm talking about this." Zander raps on the stairwell door marked FLOOR EIGHT. "While you two were screwing around down there, I've passed this door like three times."

Mike laughs disbelievingly. "Right."

Zander motions for him to carry on up the next flight. "See for yourself."

Mike gestures with his spear hand. "You first."

Zander pauses. Smirks. "Appreciate the base level of trust." He starts up the stairs.

"Well, clearly I don't trust you," Mike says as he and Wayne follow.

"I know."

They round the next flight and end up in front of a door labeled FLOOR EIGHT. They stare at it as if it were a riddle they were trying to decipher.

"So, maybe the construction crew, in their rush to finish this place, mis-marked it," Mike offers. "Along with all the other things they rushed on."

"Already considered that. But watch this." Zander takes his spear, carves a 'Z' into the door's paint.

"Oh boy. Z for Zander," Wayne mocks. "Cute."

Zander gawks at him scornfully. Then moves up the stairs. "Follow me, assholes."

The three of them ascend the next flight and are met with a door marked

FLOOR EIGHT, and a 'Z' is carved into it.

Wayne stammers. "W-what's going on?"

"What's going on, genius, is that we've gone up this same flight of stairs *several* times."

"Meaning?"

"Meaning, we can't get to the ninth floor!"

# Chapter 32–The Fakes & The Real Dilemma

"Kate?" Bishop smacks his palms against the cold elevator door. "Kate!" He presses his ear against the door seam, listens intently. Hears a distant, muffled, "I'm here."

"Are you alright?" he asks.

"My arms and legs are shaking. I don't know how long I can hold on for."

"Just hang on, kiddo. We're going to get you out of there, ok?"

She responds with a muted, "Ok."

Bishop turns to the workers. "We need to force these doors open. Do you guys have access to an elevator drop key?"

The mousy guy appears dumbfounded. "The what?"

Bishop taps at a small hole near the top of the door. "An elevator drop key. It's used in emergencies and situations like this to force the door open."

The mousy guy exchanges confused looks with the other employees. Some shrug. Some stare vacantly. Bishop feels like he's speaking Chinese to them. "How about a maintenance closet? Is there one on this floor? You know, for tools and stuff."

"We know what a maintenance closet is," Violet Tie says. "And yes, there's one down the hall."

"Show me."

Violet Tie crosses his arms, smirks, and trades smiles with the others.

Bishop's brow furrows as he fumes. "Now!"

"Why?"

"*Why?* What do you mean why?"

"I mean, why?"

"Because my friend needs help, that's why!"

Violet Tie shrugs apathetically. "That's really not our problem." He turns away. "Everyone, get back to your desks. We've got work to do—"

Bishop explodes, snatches the man by his tie, and tightens it against his neck like a noose. He protests, but is yanked sideways and pinned against a wobbly cubicle wall.

"What do you think you're doing?"

Bishop slaps him so hard, the other workers flinch in response. "Now you listen here, you little turd. If you guys don't help me, so help me God, I'm going to beat the ever-living piss out of every one of you. Starting with *you*."

It takes a moment for Violet Tie to digest this. When he does, he opens his mouth...

And then breaks out in laughter.

The cachinnation spreads to the other employees.

Bishop gapes at them, bewildered. As if he somehow missed the punchline. "Don't know what's so funny," Bishop grumbles as he knees Violet Tie in the nuts and the man drops, curling up into a ball, "but forget it. I'll find the closet myself."

"I thought you were going to beat us up," one worker taunts as they form a wall and block his way. "Don't you want our help?"

"Changed my mind." Bishop growls, loads up his right fist. "Now get your asses out of my way, or I'll put you down like I did Hugo Boss there."

The mousy guy cuts in front of the others. Grants Bishop an odious, toothy smile. He shakes his head *no* defiantly. "Make us move—"

Bishop punches him dead in the nose, and he takes a hard tumble onto his backside.

The other employees advance.

Bishop seizes the step ladder and holds it outward as if fending off a pack of wolves. "Anybody else?" He steals a glance at Violet Tie, who rolls onto his side, grimacing from the unyielding pain of his throbbing groin as he tries to stand.

The group seems undisturbed by the violence and undeterred by Bishop's newfound weapon. They help the mousy guy to his feet, laughing as they help him up.

Bishop advances, but the group closes in. "I'm warning you people! Get out of my way!"

"No one's getting out of your way," Violet Tie tells him as he stands. "You want to know what we found so funny? The nonsense you were talking."

Bishop raises an eyebrow, confused.

"You're crazy to think you can leave SiDug."

"You bet your ass the kid and I are leaving!" Bishop raises the step ladder as if it were a great sword. "Now move!"

The group stares blankly for a beat, then lower their heads in unison, as if to pray or commence with some ceremonious cantillation. However, not a plea or chant is articulated. Instead, a black cord slithers out from under their shirts and blouses and wiggles into their nostrils. Their heads jitter as the cords imbed themselves, earning grimaces and grunts from some, bleeding noses from others.

Bishop's jaw drops.

*Do something, old man! These people are screwed up!*

Bishop swings the ladder at the mousy guy and knocks him aside with one satisfying thwack. The group closes in, but Bishop takes another wide swipe with the stepladder and strikes a woman across the jaw. Sends her screeching as she drops like a cinderblock. Bishop feels a split-second of remorse–never one to physically harm a woman–but given the situation, he's forced to defend himself. Kate's wellbeing takes priority since clearly these people don't have their best interests in mind.

A towering man with a salt and pepper beard lunges at Bishop. The ogre wraps his bulky arms around Bishops torso–but having been in enough street brawls in his formative years, Bishop reacts with surprising efficiency. He headbutts the big guy, popping him in his ear. He immediately lets go and lands on his hands, stunned.

Bishop's head spins, lurching from the blow. When you're twenty, fist

175

fights and bar brawls are survivable. Taking on a mob when you're pushing seventy is another. The growing fatigue highlights that fact.

*Kate's counting on you. Keep fighting, old man.*

*You've been through worse–*

Three people grab ahold of him and lock him up. He struggles now to shake them off, as the stepladder is torn from his grip. Something is flung over his eyes in a violet blur and wrapped around his neck. Bishop tries to speak, but the noose around his neck makes it impossible. Only a cackled gurgle escapes him as the veins in his throat engorge with blood.

Violet Tie waltzes in front of Bishop... without his tie.

*I'm being strangled by that dirtbag's tie!*

Hands clasped together, he informs Bishop, "No one leaves."

The mousy guy, sporting a shiner that's soon to be a black eye, sneers as he brings a bristled black cable to Bishop's nose. "We're all food here."

# Chapter 33–The Eighth Floor

Wayne stares dumbstruck at the primitive 'Z' carved on the door by Zander. "How... how is this even possible?" He looks up to the next floor, then back to the door. "Unless you knew this," runs his finger along the 'Z', "was already here and you just replicated it down there for show?" he muses.

"Now why would I do that?" Zander scowls.

"I don't know. Maybe you're working with SiDug? In on this–whatever–to keep us here."

Mike folds his arms. "He's got a point."

"There's a loop, assholes! We've passed this floor already, and I didn't have a thing to do with it. But here's an idea." Zander smacks the door with an open palm. "Why don't you carve something yourself? Then well head up yet... *another* flight of stairs and see."

Wayne looks to Mike, who shrugs, *Why not?*

"Alright." Wayne uses his spear to carve an 'X' into the door.

"X marks the spot," Zander says. "How original."

"What'd you want? My signature?" Wayne asks, as he turns and bolts up the stairs. The two other men follow. They rush towards the door on the next flight and find it clearly marked FLOOR EIGHT along with an 'X' and a 'Z' scored into it.

Zander chuckles. "Sure, you don't want to sign it next?"

"This one big joke to you?" Mike snaps.

"No. It's a loop. We've been hiking up a mountain with no peak–"

A door above them slams.

Followed by laughter.

A child's laughter.

Mike stiffens.

"I wasn't the only one that heard that, right?" Wayne asks.

"No," Mike utters quietly.

"Because I really feel like I'm losing my mind."

*That is the point,* that secondary voice in Zander's head interposes. *To break you. To force you into the basement of your brain. Into the derivative corners of your mind.*

*The area I feed from.*

The child's laughter is playful at first, then devolves into something more minacious.

The giggling makes Mike shudder. He heads for the next set of stairs. "Let's keep going."

"What? Why?" Zander demands, a snarl on his face. "You *still* don't believe me?"

*No. I want to know who's laughing,* Mike thinks. *Because I know that laugh.* "I don't know what to believe, so I'm going with my gut."

Zander rolls his eyes.

Wayne and a reluctant Zander follow. As they make it to the next floor, the laughter abruptly stops. The floors below go dark, the gloom ominously trailing their progress as they ascend. They pass an exit marked FLOOR EIGHT once more.

"Would you look at that?" Zander says, eyeing the door. "We're going in circles."

"Hey, I wanted us to stick together. But if you're dead set on going your own way, help yourself." Mike hurries up the next flight. "Meanwhile, I'm going to figure this motherfucker out."

*And figure out if that's Reggie laughing,* he thinks, *because it sure as hell sounds like him.*

Zander's jaw bulges as he grinds his teeth in frustration. Part of him agrees with Mike, but he doesn't want to acknowledge it.

Wayne sighs. Follows Mike, but glances back to see Zander isn't following suit. "You coming?"

Zander remains quiet as he turns away and stares down into the shadowed abyss below.

"Earth to Zander."

"I heard you, dipshit." Zander's nostrils flare as scowls at Wayne. "Just thinking."

"About what?"

"About what to do next." *Since I don't like the two of you,* he thinks. "I'm fine."

Mike's footfalls thump from above as he proceeds without them. Noting this, Wayne adds, "Yeah, but we really should stick together—"

"I SAID I'M FINE!"

Wayne throws his hands up. "Whatever." He clumsily stomps up the stairs. "Mike, wait up!"

As Zander fumes, a paranoid narrative festers within his brain.

*What's the rush? Where are we going?* he asks himself. *Erik texted Vicky. Our relationship is ruined. It'll take a lot of work to convince her it wasn't me. And even if I can rectify things once I'm out of here, I'll be back at square one looking for work—good paying work that pays well. I'll have to work two jobs just to make ends meet. Which would negatively affect our relationship—and who knows—with all of that time apart, maybe Vicky will get lonely and seek the next partner?*

*She's done it before... with Erik.*

*She'll do it again.*

*And it'll be all my fault.*

*So, what is the point of going through all that heartache? What am I rushing to?*

From several floors above, Zander hears Mike exclaim, "Impossible! You're not real!"

The maniacal laughter of that crazed child responds.

"You ain't real, Reggie!" Mike shouts. "Because you're dead!"

# Chapter 34 – Misery Hike

There are no other sounds in the elevator shaft other than Kate's winded breathing and occasional sniffling as she tries to suppress an intense desire to bawl her eyes out.

*But what good would that do,* she thinks, *except confirm what Mina mocked me for? For being a crybaby.*

Kate clings to the wall, stuck like a stowaway clutching the side of a box car.

*Well, I'm going to prove her wrong,* she tells herself as she squeezes her eyes shut.

But with her arms jittering and legs shaking with fatigue, she questions just how long she really can hold on.

The silence of the shaft is broken by the muffled groans and cries of what sounds like Bishop. He curses, then shouts, "Stick that thing up my nose... and I'll ram my foot up your ass!"

Laughter erupts.

"Bishop!" Eyes open wide now, her glasses fog up as she screams his name. He doesn't respond. Silence falls again but is followed by what vaguely sounds like a tussle. It's hard to make out what really is going on beyond those thick elevator doors. She's surprised she heard as much as she did.

*I got to do something,* she thinks. *I can't hold on like this forever.*

She slowly turns her head, sweat pouring down her brow, her glasses misting with each shallow breath, and eyes the elevator door. From where she's at, it's so ungodly far away. Her heart and stomach sink.

The commotion behind the doors has ceased. The deathly quiet has resumed.

"Bishop, please talk to me!" she begs but receives no reply.

She searches the walls for a ledge she could use to work her way along the wall to the other side, one sideways step after another. Indeed, there is a ledge, but a shallow one, only four to six inches wide. Doable, save that there is nothing for her to hang onto.

There are conduit and pulley cables dangling in the center of the shaft–but as far as what they are connected to, that is another question. Kate can't exactly picture herself making a calculated leap and swinging to the other side like some wild monkey.

Kate's gaze trails the infinitely tall ladder. It just goes on and on, vanishing beyond where the eye can see.

*Maybe I could just keep climbing,* she thinks. *Maybe I'll get to the roof, get out, and get help?*

She closes her eyes, says a brief prayer, and then with her white knuckled grip, climbs, one shaky arm quivering as it takes hold of the next rung. Her wobbly legs follow. With her body shuddering, she presses as close to the ladder as possible, tackling one set of rungs at a time, climbing with the careful diligence of a cautious spider.

*This is going to take forever,* she thinks.

She looks up again.

The view is dismal. The lines of the shaft and ladder extend and seem to come together at a point. It's going to be a miserable hike up. She lets out a quiet, "Oh God."

She finally hears something else within the elevator shaft aside from her own bated breaths.

A hissing sound that stops her mid-step.

She dares to glance down and sees something that causes her to expel a scream from her lungs the likes of which she herself has never heard.

The Beast and Mr. Shimmer are climbing up the ladder too.

# Chapter 35–Who is Rosita?

"What's the rush, grandpa?" The mousy guy brings the cable to Bishop's nose. "We like to eat slow. Don't you? We don't mind our steaks... aged."

Bishop seethes.

"You took this out," the mousy guy chides as he shakes the cable, "when no one asked you to. When you join SiDug, you join for life. That means that there's no leaving. You're part of something bigger now. You're an eternal meal in a web of dedicated employees."

The surrounding office workers make sounds of agreement.

The mousy guy moves in. Bishop tries to fight back, but they've got his arms bound tight. He's twisting his head left and right, trying to avoid getting that cursed thing shoved up his nose again. His nostril aches at the thought. He grunts, "Wait!"

The mousy guy hesitates. Motions for the others to ease up the restraints.

"Before you do that... answer me one question," Bishop insists, eyes scanning the room. "What is SiDug? This some kind of experiment? A cult?"

The employees break into laughter, exchanging bemused looks.

"Not even close." The mousy guy carefully aims the cable at Bishop's nose. "Now hold still–"

Bishop knees mousy guy's groin, sending him skittering backwards. He then throws his head back, connecting the crown of his skull with Violet Tie's nose. The man unleashes a throaty wail and releases him.

"Bishop!" Bishop hears Kate's muffled voice from the elevator shaft.

The other employees tighten the circle. Bishop brings up his hands, guarding his face, and advances, ruthlessly delivering blow after blow with his roughhewn knuckles, knocking these untrained assholes aside. Some go down with one hit. Others take two, with a *pop-pop*—a right to the jaw, a left hook to the nose. Arms flail and fists fly in retaliation, but he bulldozes through the crowd.

"Bishop!" Kate calls out again. Bishop's about to tell her he's coming, when he pivots in time to see Violet Tie swinging the ladder at him. He raises an arm to block, and the ladder connects with his left wrist. The pain is blinding, but Bishop retaliates with a precise jab that sends the man spinning into a graceless pirouette and flopping against the elevator doors.

Bishop examines his hand. His senescent creaking joints and bones aren't what they used to be. Though his hand is swelling up, the adrenaline assuages the pain for now.

The mousy guy wriggles to life at Bishop's feet, and he promptly plants a foot on the squirrelly guy's chest. Bishop takes hold of the black cable anchored to the guy's nose, winds it around his hand, and announces, "This is gonna hurt."

The mousy guy's eyes widen. Bishop leans back, yanks the cable out of from the little man's nose.

*Snap!*

The cord breaks free, and Bishop almost falls backwards. Mousy guy covers his nose with his hands, squealing in agony.

"How do I open the door?" Bishop asks.

His eyes are watering, blood seeping down his chin, obscured by his cupped hands. "Y-you can't on this floor."

"Then how?!"

"You go up!"

"Go up? Where?"

The mousy guy rises, eyes his bloodied, shaking hands. Paralyzed in some sort of post-SiDug disconnected stupor—

"Hey, I'm talking to you!"

183

"You have to get to the ninth floor." The mousy guy slowly looks to Bishop, face half-stained with blood. "Where Rosita is."

"Who's Rosita?"

Behind them, Violet Tie comes to, along with the others.

"Where's the stairwell?" Bishop asks, looking for an exit sign. The tortuous pain from his wrist makes it hard to concentrate.

"Follow me," the mousy guy insists and takes off running with Bishop as the office workers stir behind them. They reach the stairwell exit door and the mousy guy jams on the panic bar. The door budges, opening only slightly. They alternate kicking at it with all their collective might.

In the meantime, the employees are headed their way, shouting things like, "Over there!"

"No one leaves!"

"What are you doing helping him?"

The mousy guy and Bishop work the door until it's open enough to push their way into the poorly lit stairwell. Bishop squeezes through like a rat in a hole that's just slightly wide enough to accommodate its body. The mousy guy follows him, but as he inches halfway through the threshold, several arms shoot out and pull him back in.

"Find..." The mousy guy fumbles, fighting against the hands clawing and dragging him back into a now darkened office. "Find Rosita!" As he's swallowed by the mob, arms wrapping around his body and neck, he throws out a hand and flings something at Bishop which clangs at his feet.

The door slams shut behind him. Bishop tries to reopen it, but it's locked. He reaches down and picks up what the mousy guy tossed his way.

A key.

He stuffs it in his pocket and storms up the stairs as fast as his creaky knees will take him, fueled by two things on his mind: finding Rosita and getting Kate out of here.

# Chapter 36—It Ain't The Sneakers

Mike is transfixed by the adolescent black boy who appears no older than ten or eleven guarding a door marked FLOOR NINE. The boy opens his mouth, and a bizarre cackle bubbles up from the back of his throat, causing every neuron in Mike's nervous system to fire off like a Fourth of July fireworks show.

"So much for the stairwell being a loop," Wayne snaps. "The ninth floor does exist."

The boy makes a face, as if what Wayne said was completely ludicrous. "Course it does, dummy. It's right behind me."

"Uh... Mike," Wayne says from the corner of his mouth. "You know this kid?"

"Oh, he knows me," the boy assures him.

"His name's Reggie," Mike tells Wayne, then gives Reggie a sideways glance. "But that can't be Reggie, cuz Reggie died a long ass time ago."

Reggie maintains a smile that would make a normal person's cheeks hurt, eyes pulsing like warning lights on a dashboard.

"Ain't no way in hell this is you here now," Mike insists.

Reggie pushes up off the ground, back glued to the door as he stares down Mike. His brown eyes deaden, turning a milky, pale blue—the same color they were when Mike found him decades ago.

Reggie lived in a ramshackle roughened bungalow on the east side of Orlando. They had this rotting fence that had been terrorized by termites snaking along their property line. Some parts of it leaned so far out, it almost

185

looked like it was about to topple over, but it didn't.

One blistering hot July day, Mike easily hopped the fence, expecting to find Reggie out back, playing in the yard, either building a makeshift fort or shooting hoops off the sunburned teal laundry basket his mom bought him from Goodwill to use as a hoop. Reggie would often complain to both Mike and his mom that he needed some Air Jordans to up his game. To be as good as the other ballers in the neighborhood.

"It ain't the pretty sneakers that make the athlete," his momma used to tell him in front of Mike. "It's that they work. Every. Single. Day."

"Yeah but—"

"Yeah, but nothing, Reginald. Look at Kobe. He's a superstar, not because of his shoes. It's because he studied other players and practiced his ass off. You wanna be a superstar? Then be happy you even have shoes and get your behind outside and practice."

The memory evaporates from Mike's mind as a sound shakes him back to the moment at hand. There's that telltale *pang-pang-pang* of a ball bouncing around above them. As if guided to them by some other force besides gravity, the ball makes its appearance, hopping down the steps from the flight above. Both he and Wayne watch in awe as the ball comes to a gentle stop at Reggie's feet, bumping against him like a cat wanting attention. As Reggie scoops up the ball, the color on his face drains, turning the color of cardboard.

Reggie's skin was the same hue when Mike found him that day. Face up, body contorted, in the backyard, the basketball just out of reach near his head. He died with what Mike thought at the time was a smile, but later learned it was more of a pained sneer.

"It's me, alright," Reggie says as he dribbles the ball in place, the pang of the ball hitting the floor sounding dull. "I'm a superstar now!" He sticks one foot out, showing off a blazing white hi-top sneaker that's stained with blood. "How you like my kicks?"

Mike wants to say something, but part of him is still trapped in his own head. Transported to that day when he found Reggie dead as a doornail, and rather than informing his parents their baby boy was outside, glossy-eyed, staring up at the limitless blue of the Florida sky, Mike turned tail and ran.

Ran so fast, he lost track of time and space and even where the hell his home was. Instead, he found solace at a retention pond, where he stopped at the water's edge and puked his brains out, later telling his parents that he was ill because he ate something bad at school.

What he never told his parents... was that Reggie died because of him.

Reggie dribbles faster and the steady *pang-pang-pang* unnerves them.

Mike edges toward the door, moving as if he's going to pass Reggie, but Reggie angles his body. Blocks him from getting past.

"Nah-ah," Reggie warns as he dribbles. "You wanna go see Rosita, don't cha?"

"Get out of my way... whoever you are."

"Bitch, you know who I am." Reggie cocks his head to the side. Still dribbling, "If you wanna get past, you tell your fat-ass friend who killed me."

"No."

"Tell him, Mike."

Mike goes to shove Reggie aside. "Move—"

Reggie launches the basketball at Mike's stomach with such force, Mike keels over, dropping his spear. Reggie recovers the ball. As he hammers the basketball against the concrete, he presses Mike with, "Tell him what happened, man. 'Bout how you killed me."

Wayne's eyes dart to Mike. "What's he talking about?"

"Tell him about Captain Cody," Reggie says with a giggle. "Then ya'll can pass."

Mike arches his back as he straightens up, taking his spear with him. "Alright... when I was in middle school, my pop got into a car accident. Jacked up his back. They gave him Codeine for the pain. A.k.a. Captain Cody. I got bored one day. Went snooping. Found the pills. I'd heard they make you feel like you're floating... like a boat on a gentle pond. Something like that."

"Damn right they do," Reggie agrees as he dribbles the ball from one hand to the other.

"So, I tried one. Liked that feeling. Then tried another. Got hooked. Then made the mistake of telling Reggie about it. See, he was stressing about some girl he had a crush on. But she wasn't feeling him—"

"Tonja!" With venom in his tone, Reggie shouts, "Her name was *Tonja*!"

"Yeah, Tonja. Whatever. Well, she broke his heart. He was down, so, I told him I had this stuff that made me feel chill. Like I didn't give a crap about anything. Figured it'd help with the heartbreak. So I gave him some pills. Didn't know he was gonna take them all at the same time."

Reggie bursts out laughing like a lunatic. "Oh, he knew."

"What?" Mike asks.

"Bro, you knew. You told me to take three of them. Four of them if I wanted to sail with old Captain Cody and totally forget about Tonja."

Wayne's gaze shifts between Mike and Reggie. The staff juddering in his hands.

"Yeah, I sailed alright," Reggie says, "Sailed right to sleep. Never woke up."

"I never said to take them all!" But Mike's words are stained with doubt—an uncertainty that floods him with questions. So many years have passed since the incident. How could he remember what he said when he was only eleven or twelve? Did he tell him to take all four at once? Or just one at first? Had he been high himself when he gave them to Reggie?

"I was just a stupid kid trying to help a friend," Mike tells Wayne, as if pleading his case to a jury. "Been living with this guilt since then. Done wrecked my relationships. My job. My life!" To Reggie, "That what you wanna hear? That making you happy?"

Reggie stops dribbling. "Nah. What makes me happy is that you're here. Got my buddy back." Spins the ball on one finger. "I ain't alone anymore. Now you, me, and chubs here can play some ball. Play for the next thousand years. And that totally makes up for you helping me OD."

Mike growls. Takes aim at the kid with the spear.

"Oh, you gonna kill me again?"

"I told him what happened like you wanted," Mike insists. "Now get out of our way."

Reggie pauses, his smile widening.

"Last time you died on accident," Mike warns as he grips the staff, ready

188

to drive it through this... this wicked shadow of Reggie, "but this time I'm gonna end you on purpose if you don't move."

"You can't kill what you don't understand," Reggie says smugly.

"I'm gonna start understanding right now then–"

Reggie hisses as his mouth widens, bearing fangs.

Mike lunges with the spear, but the boy bounds backwards, as if yanked by invisible strings. He shoots the ball at the two of them–missing completely. Then jumps across the stairwell like a flying squirrel, landing clear on the other side. Gripping the railing tightly, he turns his head in their direction, once again exposing fangs and hissing some more.

"Could Reggie do that when you guys were kids?" Wayne asks.

"Told you, that ain't Reggie."

Reggie flips around, as if prepping to jump out of a plane, but he's not going to launch from an aircraft, instead using the railing above them.

Mike motions for Wayne to try the door, while he keeps his staff trained on Reggie.

*Come at me, you little shit,* Mike thinks. *I'm gonna skewer your ass.*

"Of course it's locked!" Wayne blurts out.

Reggie leaps. Sailing towards them with arms out, fingers splayed apart. Both men ready themselves to lance this flying creep–

There's the sound of a door lock being thrown–or several. Followed by an older woman's voice who barks, "Get your asses in here!"

Something seizes ahold of Mike and Wayne and pulls them onto the ninth floor. The door slams shut just as Reggie crashes into it.

# Chapter 37–Where Are You?

**Z**ander hears the ruckus above him cease, as a door is slammed shut followed by a loud thump.

*Those assholes*, he thinks, *they found a way out.*

*Or maybe they're dead?*

Suddenly every light in the entire stairwell goes out.

*Damn. Guess I should've kept up with them.*

"Yeah, you should have," a familiar voice says from the shadows.

"Erik?" Zander calls out.

There are footsteps, slowly and steadily coming down the stairs. He readies his spear.

*I'm going to kill this asshole once and for all.*

"Are you?" Erik asks.

Zander feels his breath quicken, limbs tighten. The muscles of his neck and back shrink and lock up. Fingers grip the life out of the staff.

*Damn right I am*, he thinks.

"You mean just like you did Henry?" Erik asks.

Zander's apprehension transitions into anger as he thinks, *This asshole ruined everything. He stole Vicky in my absence.*

What was once a friend has now become his most hated enemy.

*I didn't have a choice*, Zander reasons. *I had to kill him.*

"Sure," Erik's voice sounds closer as he taunts, "but part of you enjoyed it. Just like you are enjoying the thought of killing me."

"Get out of my head!"

Erik cackles mockingly. He sounds like he's right on top of him. Zander turns toward Erik's voice.

"I don't want to get out of your head," Erik informs him. "I like it too much. I'm having so much fun."

Zander adjusts his footing in the darkness, trying to pinpoint exactly where Erik is based on his babbling.

"It's been forever since I've savored a buried hatred such as yours!"

"Shut up!" Zander is dialed in on the voice. Erik is directly in front of him. Erik laughs, amused with himself.

*Good. Keep on laughing,* he thinks. *Just helps me to figure out exactly where you are.*

"Are you sure about that?" And now Erik sounds like he's behind Zander, who whirls around and lunges, the spear sailing through the shadows with ease.

Zander curses inaudibly.

"I can be anywhere," Erik says. "Because I *am* everywhere. I am God here."

"Stop screwing around. Face me like a man."

Erik cackles again, and it's borderline irritating. "Who says I'm a *man*."

"If you're not a man, then what are you?"

"I am everyone, and no one." Erik has moved once again.

Zander spins in circles, stabbing into thin air as Erik burst into laughter. "What the hell are you?"

The laughter stops, and Erik answers, "I'm hunger."

Zander's eyes dart in the blackness, heart bumping against his chest, fueled by adrenaline, fear and frustration.

*That's it,* he thinks. *I've gone crazy.*

"No, you're not crazy," Erik assures him from somewhere above.

There's a loud thunk as all the stairwell lights flick on. Zander looks for Erik, but there's no sign of him anywhere.

"You're just in love," Erik says from behind him, "with the woman I'm banging."

Zander whips around to find Erik nude and grinning. The massive open wound on the left side of his chest oozes blood.

"Erik!" Zander seethes as he jams the spear into the man's stomach.

# Chapter 38–I'm Going to Savor You

Kate scales the ladder, and while trying her best not to look down, she looks down–

Worst-case scenario has quickly reared its ugly head–or heads, rather. She glimpses the long neck of The Beast, followed by Mr. Shimmer. Both of their heads swerve on vine-like necks, like two serpents alternating from left to right. As they climb, they keep their toothy gazes locked on Kate.

Kate presses on, grabbing each successive rung and yanking herself up as fast as she can. She doesn't exercise. Doesn't really do anything physical, so this is proving to be the most challenging workout of her life.

And she knows she doesn't have a choice. The hissing creatures below are unrelenting in their pursuit of her. She's amazed that with their monstrous knee-high black boots, they can ascend the ladder so quickly.

*Please God*, she thinks as she frantically reaches for rung after rung, *please don't let them get me.*

But the sounds of the two creatures below, from their oily black gloves to their gargantuan boots, continue.

Clink. Clack. Clink. Clack.

"Bishop!" She doesn't know why she screams out his name, but she does. "Bishop!" Unfortunately, the only answer she receives is that of her own voice resonating throughout the shaft. As she continues up, she eyes the never-ending elevation of the shaft above. She's unsure if it's ever going to end, if she'll even make it to the top, and what's even up there.

The creatures hiss and it sounds like they're closing in.

A shock wave of fear stirs within her. This doesn't help with the rapidity of her breathing, the tension in her muscles, and her overall fatigue.

*Dear God,* she thinks, *I can't keep this up.*

Clink.

Clack.

She wants to break down. To press her face to the cold metal bars of the ladder and bawl her eyes out. But she fights the urge.

*You're such a crybaby,* she hears Mina say in her head.

Clink.

Clack.

However, today she's going to prove Mina wrong. She *has* to prove her wrong. She's not a crybaby. She's a fighter. Her glasses fog up and it's like looking through a steamy bathroom window, but still she presses on.

Clink.

Clack.

The hissing draws closer.

Clink.

Clack.

Kate's arms are burning now. Legs turning into jelly. She glances over her shoulder at the other side of the shaft. The door is marked FLOOR ELEVEN.

*How many floors are in this nightmare?* she ponders. *I should have paid more attention when we were in the elevator. Can I even trust what's on those stupid doors?*

"Kaaate..." Mr. Shimmer beckons in a guttural voice.

A knot of dread wriggles within her stomach. She picks up the pace, climbing as fast as her thin arms will go.

But so do her pursuers.

*Clink-clack-clink-clack-clink-clack-clink-clack.*

Kate looks down. The Beast's head swerves to the right. Mr. Shimmer's head is angled to the left. Both grin wickedly at her as they ascend.

They're almost upon her.

Using every iota of energy, she pushes herself to her max, grasping each rung and using the momentum to pull herself to the next, and to the next.

*Clink-clack-clink-clack-clink-clack-clink-clack.*

"Kaaate!"

Kate keeps climbing. The ladder just goes on forever.

"Look at how hungry we are, Kate!" Mr. Shimmer implores with his haggard voice. A voice markedly stertorous, like that of a smoker who's indulged in one too many packs of cigarettes.

She climbs, climbs, climbs–

Until she misses a rung with her left hand and her foot follows suit. She's suddenly hanging on by her right hand and the tippy toes of her right foot. The Beast shoots up a hand and hooks her left foot, catching it as she tries to swing it back.

Kate screams at a pitch that could shatter bulletproof glass as she tears her foot away. She locks eyes with the creature, its sickly smiling face grinning up at her with a sharklike row of teeth–and she kicks it square in the face repeatedly, feeling its skull crunch in with each blow as if it were made of Papier mâché and not bone.

Mr. Shimmer calls out from below, "You're not going to leave us, Kate."

Kate keeps kicking at The Beast's face, crunch, crunch, crunch. As it dimples inwards, it feels to her as if she's attacking a rotten pumpkin with her heel.

"We have a desire–a hunger for you that no other man on this planet could give you."

Kate doesn't let up, pummeling The Beast's skull with her heel until it shatters, unveiling its eerie contents–a mishmash of vines. No blood. No fragments of bone or lumps of tissue. Just a tangled mess of bristling, black vines.

"There's nowhere to go," Mr. Shimmer warns as its elongated neck lengthens, sprouting upwards.

The vines erupt from The Beast's broken skull, spraying all over the ladder and Kate, covering her like some malignant silly string.

"NO!" Kate shouts. "GET OFF ME!"

She tries to break away, to pull herself away from them, but the aggressive creepers attack her. Consuming her. As she screams and fights against the unexplainable onslaught, her body is enveloped in a cocoon of vile vines, tethering her to the ladder. Only her head is left exposed.

Mr. Shimmer's neck rises above the flaccid remains of The Beast, and with its sparkling, clinquant star-emblazoned eyes, comes face to face with her.

"Let me go!"

"Why? You're a precious dessert, Kate," Mr. Shimmer says with breath that smacks of decay, "and I'm going to savor you."

# Chapter 39–The Fiery One

Rosita shoves Mike and Wayne aside as she locks several deadbolts, and a bulky slide bolt which slams into place with a satisfying click. She spins around, planting her back flat against the door as she exclaims, "Odio a ese cabrón!"

Wayne and Mike stare at Rosita, not sure what to make of her. Is she real? Is she going to freak out and attack them?

Rosita sizes them up with her prominent hazel eyes. She's in her sixties, Hispanic, with salt-and-cocoa hair that stops short just below her shoulders. Her features are gaunt. The wrinkled flesh hugs her eyes. Her cheeks sunken. She's wearing a janitorial gray uniform outfitted with front pockets, from which she fishes out a cigar. Her hands are bony, with knots for knuckles and skin stained with shades of amber. As she strikes a match, eyes drifting up to the sprinklers above, she assures them, "No se preocupe. Los aspersores no funcionan. Como todo lo demás aquí."

She exhales smoke which spirals upwards, dissipating as it caresses the ceiling tiles and flares out. Flakes of what seem like snow fall from the ceiling. Creeping along the ceiling tiles are white vines with yellow flowers, branching out like a spiderweb.

"I'm sorry. No *comprendo*." Wayne talks to her as if she's hearing-impaired. "No speak Spanish."

Rosita folds her arms.

"No. Hablo. Espanol," Wayne tells her.

Rosita scowls as she takes a drag of the cigar. The end turning a blistering shade of orange. She blows a gray stream in Wayne's face. "I no like you."

As he waves it off and coughs, "I have that effect on people."

"And I was saying not to worry about the sprinklers." She tokes on the cigar as she speaks. "Nothing in this place works right, anyway."

"So, you *do* speak English?" Wayne asks.

"Yes. I'm bilingual, not deaf."

"Noted."

Rosita takes a moment to study both of them. "If you two *pendejos* are wondering if I'm part of this crazy place, I am not."

"Oh, really? And how do we know that?" Wayne asks.

"How do I know *you're* not part of this crazy place?"

"Well... I'm... we're not."

Rosita takes a puff. "I already know that. Seen enough *gente loca* here to recognize crazy when I see it." She waves a finger at Wayne. "You... you're not crazy. You're just stupid and talk too much."

Wayne makes a face. "You've known me all of five minutes, lady."

With a shrug, "I know what I know. But even though you're just a *pendejo*, I still take my precautions." She motions to the deadbolts. "That includes those. I do my best, but I'm old, so sometimes I forget to lock up. Lots of doors in this place, you know?"

"Oh, we know," Mike says.

"So, you know *my* name. But I don't know yours. Who are you people?"

Wayne opens his mouth, but Mike cuts in, "I'm Mike. And this is Wayne."

Rosita clamps the cigar between her teeth as she takes a step closer to Mike. With a scrutinizing gaze, asks, "How did you find me?"

"A guy named Henry told us," Mike answers.

"Hmm. What did he say exactly?" she asks.

"He told us your name and mentioned the ninth floor. We asked him if there was a way out, and he directed us to you," he replies.

Rosita tests her cigar. It's dead. "*Mierda.*" She cuts between the two men and calls out to them, "Ok, pendejos. Come with me."

"Where are you going?" Wayne asks.

"To my office. To get my lighter."

Wayne asks Mike, "What does *pendejo* mean?"

"It means asshole," Rosita answers, her voice trailing off as she walks away. "Now follow me, and we'll talk about getting you out of here."

# Chapter 40–A Squeaky Wheel

**B**ishop makes his way up the stairs without incident until he hears the telltale chirp of Larissa's wheels.

"Bishop," Larissa's raspy voice calls out to him.

Bishop shakes it off. *It's in your head, Bishop. Ignore the noise,* he thinks. *Besides... how the hell could her wheelchair climb stairs?*

"You? Ignoring me?" Larissa snickers. "Wouldn't be the first time."

Bishop rounds the next flight, coming to a door labeled FLOOR NINE, which appears to be secured by several deadbolts. He tries it to open it anyway but discovers that it is indeed locked. He takes the key mousy guy gave him out of his pocket.

*Here goes nothing,* he thinks. *If there is a God, I hope he's got my back. If not mine... I hope he's at least got Kate's.*

He puts the key into the first lock–

"Bishop, what are you doing?" she demands. "You're just going to leave me again, aren't you? Just like before, you selfish asshole."

Without looking back, he unlocks the first deadbolt and exhales a sigh of relief.

"ANSWER ME, DAMMIT!" He hears what sounds like her wheels squeaking closer.

"You're not real. You're not Larissa!"

"Oh, I'm very real." She sounds like she's right behind him, but he doesn't turn around. Instead, he proceeds to unlock the other deadbolts. Pain from his injured wrist travels down his arm. He winces and drops the key, swearing between his teeth.

"I'm more real than you could ever imagine."

"No. Larissa died." He bends over, secures the key and several vines attempt to wrap around his feet.

"I'm very much alive. Been alive longer than you know."

Panicked now, he kicks at the vines as they lunge at him. One of them grapples his foot and loops around his ankle.

"You loved me once," Larissa reminds him with a hiss as Bishop struggles. "You can love me again."

Bishop fumbles with the key as the vines loop up his leg.

"Stop running from me," Larissa's voice darkens as she rages, "for once in your pathetic life! Show me the love you owe me."

Bishop pushes the door open, but it grinds against the floor, squealing in protest as if there's something blocking it.

"You're going to stay with me and love me. You owe me that after what you let happen to me."

Bishop ignores her, throws his back into it as he leans into the door with his shoulder.

"I can give you more than you'll ever find out in that miserable world you call a home."

"You've given me enough. Now get away from me!" Bishop pushes with all his might as the vines travel up to his waist now.

*Come on, old man!* he roars inwardly. *You can do this. Push, dammit! Don't let Kate down!*

Bishop drives his body weight into the door, and it skids open another few inches.

The vines tighten around torso like a garter belt from Hell, but Bishop throws his body into the door, hammering it with his shoulder. It groans as the metal of the bottom of the door grinds against the concrete, opening a bit more but still not enough for him to squeeze past. He catches a glimpse of what's inside: blindingly bright white lighting, a stark contrast to the bleak and blackened ambiance that is pervasive throughout this building. He squints at first, as if stepping out onto a snow-covered field in the dead of winter.

Something else catches his eyes—white vines everywhere, dotted with yellow flowers. They scale the ceiling, branching out in countless directions. And... snowflakes of some sort. Or pollen lazily drifting downwards. The vines rapidly wind up his back like the straps of a knapsack crisscrossing his neck.

Larissa snickers. "You don't get to leave me this time. No one leaves me."

Bishop wrestles with the suffocating net weaving itself around his body—

"Qué en el nombre de Dios?" a woman calls out from the other side of the door. Her voice hushed but audible.

Footsteps follow.

Then fingers appear from around the door frame. The door groans, then is yanked open. Mike, Wayne, and an old woman are standing there.

"Ayudalo!" The old woman orders. "Help him!"

Mike and Wayne grab Bishop, pull him into the ninth-floor office, and the black vines attached to Bishop's body crumble.

Larissa squeals. Ogles the old woman with her one good eye. "You! You are my poison."

"Déjanos, monstruo!" The old woman replies as she slams the door in Larissa's face.

# Chapter 41 – That's Not Snow

"Who are you?" Rosita is all business.

Bishop stands there. He's still in shock from the crisscrossed vines that almost enveloped him in their black death.

"Is your friend deaf?" Rosita asks Mike and Wayne as she strikes a match, relights the blackened stub of her cigar, and puffs at it as if it were an inhaler.

Mike pats Bishop's shoulder. "You alright?"

"Yes." Bishop takes a moment, blinking emptily. "But Kate's not."

"Kate?" Wayne's forehead wrinkles as he recalls her name. "You mean the girl with the glasses that are way too big for her face?"

"Yeah... I've got to get to her. She's in stuck in an elevator shaft–"

"Who's Kate?" Rosita asks, puffing smoke in their direction.

"My friend. Who are you?" Bishop asks.

"I asked you first, viejito."

"Bishop."

"I'm Rosita."

Bishop feels the room shrink. An image of the mousy guy pops into his brain. He narrows his gaze as he reveals, "Rosita. I was told to look for you."

"Yeah, join the club," Mike says.

"Congratulations. You found me. Now come." Rosita signals everyone to follow her to her office. Inside is a beat-up desk, an old CRT monitor and two plastic cushioned chairs. Behind her, a golf club leans against the wall.

Mike and Bishop take a seat. Wayne throws his hands up in surrender. "K, guess I'll stand."

Mike turns in his chair and glares at Wayne as if he wants to slap him, because he does.

Rosita plops down in her seat. In front of her is a large, onyx black ashtray. She gently lays down what little remains of her cigar, retrieves a new one from a drawer, gives it a loving glance, removes it from its cellophane wrapper, cuts it and then fires it up.

"Your desk double as a humidor?" Bishop asks.

"I raided Mr. Gudu's stash several times before buckling down here. He's the one with the humidor."

Wayne notes the golf club. "So you smoke cigars... and play golf?"

Rosita glares. "You judging me?"

"Not at all. It's just... interesting," he replies.

"*Interesting?*" she asks as she adjusts her seat. "Por qué? Because an old lady smokes stogies and keeps a golf club handy? I come from a cigar-rolling family from West Tampa that also used to grow tobacco in Cuba." She hikes a thumb at the golf club. "And *that* was supposed to be a gift to Mr. Gudu from one of the employees I started with. Now I keep it for self-defense in case some maricón gets stupid." She adjusts her seat and hunches forward, focused on her massive monitor while furiously typing at her keyboard.

"And how about that relic?" Wayne asks, motioning to the screen with his hand.

Rosita pauses, eyes rising from the monitor to meet his, as if to ask, *What about it?*

"Thing's like twenty-something years old."

Rosita stares at him as if he's the dumbest person alive. "Impossible. I bought it from Best Buy last year."

"Last year? What year do you think it is? 1998? They don't sell those anymore. Everything is flatscreen," Wayne informs her.

"Last I checked, it was 1999, gordito, and I know nothing about flat-screens."

Mike and Bishop share a look.

Wayne's eyebrows arch, perplexed. *1999?*

As Rosita resumes typing, Bishop studies her. Asks, "Are you really

Rosita?"

"I am." She raises an eyebrow. "Are you really Bishop? Mike?" Scowls at Wayne. "Or gordito?"

"It's Wayne, not gordito."

Rosita leans back in her chair. Takes a long drag. "I know you're all who you say you are, because if you guys were part of that cabrón, that cursed vine out there, you would have crumbled like ashes the moment you walked in here."

"Vine?" Wayne repeats with a scoff. "What do you mean, vine?"

The end of Rosita's cigar burns bright as the sun, then she exhales the words, "It's exactly what I said. A vine. You know, like where grapes come from? Pero, the buzz this cabrón gives you is worse for your health than chardonnay."

"Wait, lady," Mike begins, "you're telling us that thing out there is a fucking plant?"

"*Mas o menos.*" With a shrug. "It grows everywhere throughout the building. It's the veins of this place."

"It's the veins? A *vine*?" Wayne asks, stifling a laugh. "So, what is it? Kudzu?"

"Qué es Kudzu?"

"An invasive vine from Asia," Wayne answers. "Kudzu was originally planted back in the 1800s to control soil erosion. Since it practically grows a foot a day, it spread like cancer across the southeast, choking out other plants and smothering trees like a green blanket of death along the way. Nothing seems to stop it... except goats. I heard goats will eat 'em."

Mike shakes his head in awe. "Man, you're like an encyclopedia of random crap."

"Not all of us played sports as kids," Wayne offers with a glib grin.

"Look, I know nothing about all that," Rosita bites on her cigar, throws her hands up in the air. Her wrinkly skin wobbles like the sagging wings of a flying squirrel as she answers, "But what I do know is that this vine is an evil thing. And it's been here a long time."

Wayne gapes, trying to process what she just said. "Are you one of those crazy vegans?"

"This is not a joke, pendejo!" Rosita bolts up from her chair. "You think I'm making this up?"

"I don't know, lady." Wayne recoils, thrown by her outburst.

"I've been here a long time. Seen many people come and go through this place. And while it *should* be 1999, I'm well aware it is not. But one thing I know... the one *thing* that keeps me grounded, is the thought that someday someone who stumbles into this trap will get away. And maybe, if we are all lucky, they can kill this cabrón on the way out." Rosita takes a drag, the end igniting like a fireball. She then points at each one of them. "If you guys want to survive and want to save your friend—that's if she's still alive—then you better believe what I am telling you. Coo-coo as it sounds, ok?"

"Alright," Bishop says with a cautionary glance at Wayne, who responds by rolling his eyes, "we believe you. Please go on."

Rosita taps the ash accumulated on her cigar. Looks at Wayne as she explains, "When I was first trapped here, back in 1998, I was hired to be the janitorial manager. Mr. Gudu was younger. Very fired up. Excited. Charming. Tenia mucho carisma. He sold Henry and I on SiDug's promises and possibilities with his cariño."

"His what?" Wayne asks.

"His *cariño*. His passion." Rosita continues, "But within our first day of training, things started happening. The other trainees got transferred to different departments right away or suddenly quit. At least that's what I assumed. I remember little of the actual training. Everything was foggy and now I know why. Henry and I went to our different departments. I ended up on the ninth floor with a crew of about eighteen people—kids, mostly. Fresh out of high school. I didn't get to work with them very long. It was all a blur. By the end of the first day, most everyone on my floor disappeared."

"What happened to them?" Bishop asks.

Rosita pauses mid- drag. She rests her cigar on the notch of her ashtray. With a wave of her crooked index finger, she tells them, "This place got to them." Her eyes gloss over. "Some vanished. Others went loco."

"You mean crazy?" Wayne asks, leaning in.

"*Si. Loco, pendejo.*"

"Crazy like what?" Wayne prods.

"Like what?!" Rosita scowls. "Like they were driven mad to the point of tearing their own eyes out. Stabbing themselves repeatedly with whatever they could find to end the pain. Jumping down elevator shafts to their deaths. Whatever they could do to avoid the tormented images this cabrón brought them. Only to still be condemned to this place."

"Look, I'm sorry to hear about what happened to them," Bishop assures her, "but our friend's still stuck in that elevator shaft. Literally clinging to a ladder as we speak. Now how do we get to her?"

Rosita sets the cigar down. Sighs. "You don't. Either she climbs all the way up or all the way down. That's assuming the vines haven't gotten to her already."

Bishop wipes the newly forming beads of sweat with his hand. He can't sit here and listen to this. He promised that he'd be back, and dammit, he's going to keep that promise–

"You're not the first one to come to me, *viejito*, trying to help someone. This thing, the vine, it likes to play with its food sometimes," she informs him.

"What food?" Wayne asks. "You mean us?"

Rosita nods. "This place is one gigantic trap."

"Hold on a sec," Mike says. "Lemme get this straight. You're telling us that whole place is run by that vine, weed, or whatever the hell it is. Then it lures people inside with hopes of employment and then feeds off them?"

"Si. Exactamente." Rosita peels off the cigar label and rolls it up between her fingers. "And it's been doing so forever. *Mira*, do you even know what SiDug means?"

The men stare at her. Unsure.

"It means *trap*. Pitfall. It's from the Sumerians–the oldest known civilization." Upon acknowledging their shaken, stupefied stares, she continues, "Yes, this cabrón has been around that long. You fell into its trap just like many others. Hundreds, maybe thousands, of others. Their screams echo throughout this place–but the echoes originate from the vines itself." Rosita pulls out a pen, writes the word *Muššagana* on a sticky note, then slides it over to them. "Seen that before?"

It takes Mike a moment. "Yeah. I have. On some kid's drawing."

"Means ravenous hunger," Rosita explains with a nod. "That is what SiDug is."

"Ok, lady," Wayne says, "how do you know all of this?"

Rosita taps her nose. "Because I went through the training too."

Mike waves this off. "Not me. It never got me like that."

Rosita does a slow shrug. "Si, pero, how are you so sure?"

"Because I'd remember if I had a goddamn zip tie up my nose, that's how."

"Ok, well then why don't you put your finger up each nostril. Tell us if it hurts."

Mike hesitates. Then puts the tip of his index finger up his left nostril... then his right—a sharp pain draws a wince and a curse out of him.

Mike's eyes widen and feels his color drain at the realization that maybe he had the same black cord up his nose. Was it today? Last week? Last year?

"No..." he mutters. "No way."

"Listen, if you have seen or heard something from your past, something that troubles or had traumatized you, then it has connected with you. Peeked inside your brain." She points to Bishop. "And your brain." Then Wayne. "And even your brain, gordito."

Wayne's retort is quickly extinguished by the thought of some vinous plant reading his mind via his nasal cavity.

"That's what it feeds off of." Rosita taps at her temple again. "The things you fogged but never forgot. It haunts you with yourselves. And as it drains you, as it makes you crazy, it weakens you. Then it reconnects whenever it wants and controls you like a puppet or bleeds you dry like a mosquito."

"What about you, Rosita?" Bishop asks. "What's so special about you? Why won't it come in here? Why did it fall off from me when you guys pulled me in?"

"Yeah, I was wondering the same thing!" Wayne gestures up to the ceiling, the sprawling white vines with their poignant yellow flowers. "And what's with these vines? And the creepy snow?"

"That's not snow. It's mold." Rosita smiles, showing off her checkered, burnished teeth. "I used to work in blueberry farms just north of Tampa. Worked them for so long, that my hands stunk like compost, and even the color of my skin changed. Maybe it was the soil. Maybe the fertilizer. I don't know. But the most curious thing was that the mold off the blueberries stuck to me. I came here right after working the fields. I was strapped for money. Always have been. Didn't have time to shower. I just wiped myself down with paper towels, rinsed off my face, put on perfume and bam! I was starting the new job. What I didn't realize was that me not taking a shower, was the best thing I could've done."

"I guess I'm not following," Bishop says. *Make your point, sister. I've got to get to Kate!*

"Turns out, this wicked vine," Rosita reveals as she waves her hand towards the stairwell, "isn't as godlike as it likes to think it is."

"Meaning?" Wayne asks curtly.

"Meaning, pendejo, that whatever I brought from the blueberry fields, whatever mold that afflicted those plants, affected this cabrón as well," Rosita explains. "This cabrón is over two thousand years old–older than the son of God himself, yet a little exposure to mildew, and it's screaming for the hills."

"If it's as old as you say," Wayne asks, "then why the heck hasn't it encountered mold like this before?"

Rosita throws her hands up. "You think I'm a scientist? I don't know. Why don't you go ask it yourself?" She pauses, pondering her next words. "Whatever I brought with me, saved me. I found refuge here. But at the same time, I've been stuck here."

"So, what have you been eating all of this time?" Wayne asks.

"What have *you* been eating, gordito?"

"Stop calling me gordito!"

"Ok, then I call you *little fat boy*."

"I'm not fat!" Wayne argues.

Rosita chuckles. "Claro. So, since we are talking about food, let me ask you... when *was* the last time *you* ate? Any of you?" She watches the men take personal inventory of their nutritional intake since starting with SiDug.

No one recalls when they last ate.

"Ah. Can't remember?" she asks. "That's because you all don't know how long you have been here. The vine plays with time. Messes with our metabolism. Feeds us through our," she makes finger quotes, "connection with it. Or at least, that's what I figure. I mean, they diagnosed me with cancer. Gave me six to eight months. I *should* be dead by now, depending when *now* is."

A heavy hush falls over the room.

"That's one reason, aside from money, that I took this cursed job," she continues. "The benefits. However, I didn't realize that the benefit of me maintaining my health would involve that cabrón sticking itself up my nose. I think it halted my cancer–or it's at least keeping it at bay. Once I leave, there's a possibility that it could come right back. So really, why should I go?"

"Because you shouldn't be a prisoner to this... thing," Bishop answers.

"Nah," she responds with the dismissive wave. "Cancer aside, there's no one to go home to. Nothing for me out there. Besides... I'm old, tired, and not up for some crazy escape plan. I just want this cabrón dead." She leans forward. "Even if it means I die along with it."

"I'm game for killing it too. But how do we do that?" Bishop asks.

Rosita spins the old monitor around. There's a pixilated, yet discernable image of the very building they are in. The photo is an aerial shot. The men lean in close as Rosita taps at the screen, noting the top floor.

"This is where this place wants you to go. To the top," Rosita explains as she relights her cigar. "The vine takes a special pleasure in people leaping to their deaths. But the people never hit the ground." She splays out her fingers and grasps at invisible objects in the air, as if snatching at flies or something the others cannot see. "The vines shoot out from the building, through open windows or splinters in the facade, grabbing the people, and yanking them back inside."

"And no other buildings, no one else sees this?" Mike asks.

Rosita shakes her head, no.

"How's that possible?"

Rosita carves a circle with her finger around the ashtray to represent what she is saying. "The vine creates this sort of fog around itself–the building–masking itself like a chameleon. Blending in. Shadowed from the rest of the world, *como un lagartija o pulpo.*"

"Uh... come again?" Wayne says, one eyebrow raised, puzzled.

Rosita shakes her head. "Like a lizard or octopus. This place... this bastard... it modifies itself, remodels to change with the times where it wants to. It modernizes whatever hallways and offices it needs to, to play the role, to lure the new food–the new employees. The rest of the building remains dated, so it can conserve energy. This place is like a Hollywood from Hell. Showing you only what it wants. The behind-the-scenes is the real horror. And that's how it has survived for so long. It's here, out in the open, but no one sees it–like a billboard you've passed a hundred times but never read–only it doesn't want to be read. It just wants to exist along the highway, *como un opportunista.* Putting out the message... the promise of employment. Advertising the perfect job." She opens her hand and then draws her first closed tight to emulate a trap. "But it's nothing more than a flame, capturing every moth that is drawn to it."

"And we're the moths," Bishop mutters.

"Speak for yourself, grandpa," Wayne says. "I'm no moth. Just a dude who took an awful job at a bad time and ended up in this insane asylum with Ms. Loco Lady here, you two unfortunates, and psycho-boy outside–"

Wayne barely finishes his sentence when Mike leaps out of his chair and slaps the shit out of him. With a thundering whack, Wayne's head is knocked to one side. A trickle of blood seeps from the corner of his mouth. He touches it with his finger in shock. Trying to process what just happened.

"Unfortunates, huh?" Mike admonishes him. "Bitch, you better check yourself. We're all in this together. You wanna take your chances out there because you got it all figured out? Well then," he points to the door and commands, "go for it. Me and Bishop? We're gonna get Kate and then split. So, you either secure that attitude or leave." Mike gets in his face. "*Tu comprende, amigo?*"

Wayne nods. "I-I understand."

"Hope so."

The men settle down.

"I like you," Rosita tells Mike with a wry grin. "Now..." She returns her attention to the old monitor, typing away at the keyboard. A series of blueprints show up on the screen. She clicks through them until she finds the one she wants.

"Wow, you're really good at computers," Wayne says, then cautiously adds, "for your age, I mean."

Without looking up from her keyboard, she threatens, "Want me to slap that other cheek, gordito?"

Wayne shrinks.

Rosita finds the plans she's looking for, ending her search with an exuberant, "Aqui! Here is where you need to go."

On the screen, it shows a complex network of air conditioning ducts that crisscross and empty into:

"The basement?" Bishop asks.

Rosita nods. "Si. *El Gran Raiz.*"

Wayne shoots her a puzzled look.

"The grand root, gordito. When it is done with a building, or wants to move, it's like a snail. It pulls itself from its former home, enters the ground, and moves to a new structure, altering it both physically and mentally for its guests. It is a powerful, sentient cabrón." She waves a crooked finger in the air as she goes on, "Pero, there is a catch. In everything it does, from moving the walls around, to manifesting your nightmares, all of that takes energy. And I truly believe it is running out of energy. It's played with its food for so long."

"And how do you know that?" Bishop asks.

Rosita leans forward, dead seriousness in her eyes. "Because I can feel it. Cabrón and I have a weird connection. It probably rues the day it invited me into its nest. Perhaps the mold I've inhaled over the years contaminated me. I'm the rotten fruit it can't get rid of. But I know most of its secrets, just as it knows mine. So, if you boys can get to the grand root, the source, and kill that puta, all the vines will die. Perhaps your friend might be freed along with it."

"How do we kill it?" Bishop asks. "And how do we get down there?"

"Here." Rosita digs out an actual set of the blueprints and lays them on table with a hard thwap. Something goes skidding off the table. Bishop leans over to grab it. It's a pair of gold scissors.

"To answer your second question, this is how you get there. It's a straight shot down." She points out several access points leading from her floor down to the basement. They connect to a service stairwell that leads directly to the basement. "I've been feeding my strain, my moldy version of the vine down there. The cabrón knows that, so it's avoided having any of you all find that stairwell because it's a hall pass taking you up and down this building. But the cabrón is smart. It uses your nightmares, your unwanted memories, to guide you where it wants you to go... in circles."

Bishop gestures with the scissors. "You dropped these."

"Feliz Navidad. Keep them," she replies. "They were a gift from mi mama. Brought me good luck, all my life."

"Define good luck," Wayne comments.

Rosita shoots him a stony gaze. "Well, I'm still alive, pendejo."

Wayne huffs, looks away.

"They're beautiful," Bishop says as he smiles and pockets them.

"Gracias. An antique like you and me, tu sabes?"

Bishop nods. "So, back to this grand root. How do we kill it?"

"Oh yes." Rosita climbs onto her chair and reaches up to the white vines scaling the tiles above. She coils one creeper around her hand, pulling until it snaps and causes a chalky cloud of white dust to flare up into the air. She hops down and angles the vine in his direction as its tiny flowers go limp. "With this."

"Seriously?" Wayne stares, incredulous. "What are we supposed to do? Whip it to death?"

"Mira, pendejo, I've been stuck here longer than you, and I know it works, because I've tested it, ok?" Rosita tosses the vine on the desk, exchanging it for her now unlit cigar–which she shoves in Wayne's face. His nose crinkles at the stink. "I've had my share of growing tobacco, blueberries, and now this variant of the cabrón." She flings the cigar aside as if it were a cigarette butt and grabs the white vine, giving it a fervent shake as she insists, "I've cut pieces of it off. Thrown it at the cabrón, and it doesn't like it." She points at Bishop. "How do you think I saved your friend? He came in here, unharmed, because of what I've grown here. Now listen, if you want to sit here for the next eternity talking about this, we can." Rosita gestures towards her door. "But if you prefer to get out of here, trust me when I say, por la gracia de Dios, I got this moldy strain to grow. Now..." She fishes under her desk and retrieves a backpack which she promptly slides over to Bishop.

"What's this?" he asks.

"Inside is a Ziploc bag full of spores."

Bishop unzips the backpack to find a sealed plastic bag inside filled to the brim with white powder.

"I know it probably looks like baking soda, or cocaine," Rosita says, "but I assure you... it's the new strain. It's the mold. And the cabrón won't like it." She shakes her head. "Not one bit."

Mike and Wayne peek into the bag too.

"Sprinkle just a little of that onto the black vines when they come at you, and it will shrivel away like an estupido ex-husband pressured to pay child support." Rosita laughs at herself. "Trust me, I say this from experience, on both accounts." She promptly rises, pushes aside a small bookshelf behind her, and slides open a false wall–a thin slab of drywall that moves away easily.

The three of them look on in awe.

Once the wall is moved aside, an air conditioning duct is revealed, just big enough for them to crawl through.

"Here," Rosita explains as she points to the opening. "This is where you go. Follow this all the way to the end. You'll come to grate. Kick it open, and the stairwell is a straight shot down to the basement. Don't look back. Don't pay attention to anything you hear within the walls. The cabrón won't come at you unless you get off the path–the stairwell."

"Um..." Wayne can't help but ask, "what do you mean exactly by *get off the path?*"

"Ay, gordito." Rosita puts a palm to her forehead. "Have you ever seen Wizard of Oz?"

"Of course. Ha. Who hasn't?"

"Ok. Well... you know... the yellow brick road?"

Wayne nods.

Rosita taps at the entrance to the air duct. "This is your yellow brick road. The cabrón might mess with your head since it won't go into the stairwell. So, whatever you do, don't listen to it. Stay on the path."

"If it can mess with our heads in the stairwell, what's stopping it from doing it now?" Bishop asks.

Rosita smiles. "There's something about this moldy viejita here that blocks the cabrón. It's either me or these beautiful creatures above you that have something to do with it. Yo no se." She taps the air duct entrance, and it makes a rattling sound. "Now... mueve tus colitos! Your friend needs you!"

"Hold up. I'm a little confused." Mike puts his hands up in surrender. "What the heck do we do with this powder once we find the root?"

"You shower it with that and pray it dies. If it doesn't, then I guess you'll be stuck with me and every other pobrecito that it's taken alive."

The three men share a look, then enter the air duct without looking back. Bishop is the last one in–

"Oh, one more thing." Rosita hands Bishop a flashlight. "You'll need this... but only for a bit."

Bishop nods. "Thank you... for everything."

"Thank me after you dust that cabrón. Now cuidate." She winks. "That means, take care."

And the sound of Rosita sliding the slab of drywall into place secures their next adventure into this accursed building.

# Chapter 42–Heartache Like A Perfume

Zander's spear runs clean through Erik, and he trembles with the furtive twitches of a dying animal.

"How... does that feel?" Erik asks, blood dripping from his lips.

Zander releases the spear and backs away, watching Erik jiggle. He turns to run—but Erik is suddenly in front of him. "Feels good, right?"

Zander pushes him away, races off in the other direction.

Erik is there. Laughing. Adam's apple bobbing up and down. He rips the spear from his stomach. "Feels natural, doesn't it?"

Fear overtakes Zander, he darts back around, desperate to get out of this stairwell and away from Erik—or whoever he is.

But no matter which way he turns, he comes face to face with Erik, who whispers, "I know that feeling."

"Get the fuck away from me!" Zander yells, giving the bloodied Erik another shove backwards and bolts, heading up the next flight of stairs.

Erik laughs this off. Watches Zander race around one flight, then the next flight and then the next. It isn't long before Zander has traveled up another five floors, though each one of them looks exactly the same to Zander as the last.

The lights cut off again while Zander is midway up the next set of stairs. He stumbles and trips onto whatever floor he may be at. He pushes himself to his feet. And as the lights pop back on, Erik stands in front of the door to the ninth floor, which is blocked by this lunatic. The gash in his stomach and the yawning wound on his chest steadily weep blood.

Zander stares at the door with a moment of confusion. *I've climbed several flights and still arrived at floor nine? How?*

Upon reading his thoughts, Erik says, "I know. Crazy, right?"

Zander glares at him.

"You feel you've gone in circles." Erik winks. "Because you have. Though it takes much of my energy to manipulate this structure the way I have, the resultant suffering you and your friends have endured has proven worth the cost."

"They're not my friends," Zander snaps as he searches the floor with his eyes. The spear is gone.

"Of course. You know," Erik muses with lips trembling, as if delighting in some sort of invisible delicacy, "I can't remember the last time that someone came to me as heartbroken and angry as you."

Zander squeezes his fists into balls, ready to beat the crap out of Erik.

Erik lowers his gaze like a crazed man, that wide, joker-like smile plastered on his face. "You radiate hatred, and it is utterly divine."

Zander snarls.

"You want to leave?" Erik asks.

Zander says nothing.

"What? To get back to... *her?*" Erik closes his eyes on the word her, relishing it like a sip of the finest Cabernet. "You exude heartache like a perfume. A perfume I have not inspired in a century."

"What do you want?"

Erik licks his lips. "To eat."

"Eat what?"

Erik takes a step closer to Zander. "The dark bits of the human mind. Their fears. Their worries. Their pain. Their...," he eyes Zander squarely and continues, "secrets. The things they tuck away under the carpet of their ego." A black, briary vine snakes up Erik's leg from the floor and curls around his body.

Zander backs away.

"But those things can't be hidden from me," Erik reveals. "I know how to extract them. Feed on them. Just like I've been feeding on you."

"Bullshit. How?"

"How?" Erik taps his own nose.

*That black cord,* Zander thinks. *But I never woke up with one up my nose.*

"How do you know this," a black cord sprouts from Erik's hand as he outstretches it and murmurs, "wasn't tucked into your brain?"

"Because it was at my feet, not my nose."

Erik scoffs. "You sure?"

Zander feels his stomach drop. *Was he sure? Was he always awake?*

"Don't try to understand," Erik warns. "Your feeble brains are not designed to distinguish reality from the subconscious. And if you wish to understand why that is, that's a whole other conversation."

"So, do you want to kill me then?"

"I don't want to *kill* anyone. Just want to eat. To survive like all living things."

Zander glances again at the door to the ninth floor.

"And I know you want out." The black cords wrap around Erik's neck and slink inside his nose. The wounds on his body, both bloodied gashes, heal miraculously, closing themselves up, as if the injuries had never happened.

Zander looks on in awe.

"Here is my proposal. Kill your friends and that old Betty in there." Erik gestures towards the door. "And I let you go."

Zander mulls this over. "Thought you don't want to kill anybody?"

"I'd rather not murder my food, but your friends are out to get *me.* I can sense it," he says. "Just do it and you can walk right out of here and go home to Vicky."

"But there's no point." Zander spits the words out as he laments, "The texts you sent her ruined that."

"I never sent her anything." Erik throws his head back, laughs. "I was just having fun."

Zander moves to punch Erik and a barbed cable whips across his face, lashing him. He flinches, touches his cheek. Drops of blood dangle on his fingertips. "Cute," Zander says as he licks the blood. "Why don't you kill them yourself?"

"Your friends I can handle. It's Rosita I can't get to."

"Why not?"

"You ask too many questions." Several vines flare out from behind Erik, forming a veritable pair of black wings. "I want that old hag dead because she's an aberration. She's contaminating me!"

Zander shrugs off Erik's anger. His show of emotions humanizes him on some level, giving Zander a bit of comfort, sensing it as a weakness. "So then, just let her out."

"She doesn't want to leave!" Erik shouts, the black tendrils of his floating mass of wings stiffening, electrified with rage.

*Ha! This thing needs me,* Zander thinks. *I have leverage–*

"Don't get cocky, Zander Lyle." Erik's black cords reach for Zander and he shrinks. "If you don't kill them, then I'll keep you here with me, forever. Just like everyone else. And then I'll set your friends free, but first, I'll be sure," he taps his nose, "to infuse a dash of influence over them. Send them off with a wanton desire to have their way with Vicky. Has she ever been with two men at once?"

"Fuck you!"

"Then do what I ask! Either you kill them and go free. Or I free them. I will eat, either way. And just as I've found you all, I can fish humanity for more, sadness, hatred, anxiety – renewable resources that I've been harvesting for eons."

Zander mulls this. The thought of killing Mike and Wayne brings hesitation, but that is overshadowed by images of them taking turns straddling Vicky. Fists tightening to the point of cramping, Zander glares at the floor, then Erik. "Fine. I'll kill them. But you'd better keep your promise and let me go."

"Of course." Erik steps back, fingers darkening as if scorched by an unseen flame, they lengthen, thinning into vines that worm into the door seam of the ninth floor. He grunts as his body twitches, mutters, "Rosita knows how to hurt me."

Before Zander can ask what Erik means, several locks slide open from the other side, along with the heavy clunk of a slide bolt coming undone. When Erik's fingers retract, they're noticeably sallow and crumbling like the ashen edges of a clump of charcoal. He quickly hides his hand behind his back and nods to the door. "It's open. Now, the next time I see you, I want to see fresh blood on that spear." With an expectant smile, he adds, "Rosita's blood."

# Chapter 43- Déjà Vu?

Rosita secures the drywall with a few crooked nails as she hears the men crawl off into the depths of the building. She presses a palm flat against the drywall, kneels and bows her head as she signs the cross. "Dios, por favor protégelos." She looks up to the ceiling as if looking to God. "Protect them—"

A grinding sound makes her jump. She snaps her head in the disturbance's direction. Listens intently. Her ears are met with soft footsteps. Bated, yet audible. Having been on this floor for so long, she knows every creak, every noise. While her hearing isn't what it used to be, it's enough for her to detect that something or someone is there with her. Rosita spies the golf club. Her mind drifts as she clutches it in her wrinkled, bony hands.

*Mr. Gudu. The avid golfer,* she thinks. *Mierda!*

The only thing that snake was avid at was recruiting people for the cabrón. He worked the way of a familiar to a vampire. Free to wander the world and do the deeds of his master. Posting job ads. Holding interviews. Being the face of SiDug, but without having to be physically tied to it.

Mr. Gudu brought the cabrón lunch, and the cabrón made him practically immortal. Allowing him to stay the same age by regularly letting it infest his mind, worming its way inside his head, repairing any hints of disease, slowing the aging process, and like a drug—inducing a rewarding euphoria that could numb any pain.

SiDug let Mr. Gudu come and go as he pleased with only with one caveat: That he would have to return to the office every forty-eight hours, lest the disease and aging it had suppressed manifest all at once. So, like a dog on a short leash, Mr. Gudu traded immortality for eternal imprisonment.

Rosita knew all of this, because the cabrón knew all of this.

But there were limits to what Rosita could glean from the wicked weed. She knew enough to know this thing needed to be destroyed, and that she wasn't strong enough to do it on her own. Perhaps this new batch of recruits was going to be its death knell once and for all.

Rosita snaps out of her thoughts as the sound of footsteps draws closer. She tucks herself behind her office door and waits. The footsteps creep close, then stop altogether just on the other side of the door. Foul body odor laced with blood wafts into her nose and she withholds a gag.

*Come on in, pendejo,* she thinks as she squeezes the club's handle. *I'm ready for you.*

The figure steps into the office, spear in hand, and Rosita jumps out and swings with a satisfying thud. Hits Zander on his shoulder. "That hurt, you stupid old bitch!"

Rosita wheels around for round two. "Stupid old bitch? I'll show you what a stupid old bitch I can be!"

Rosita explodes, swinging wildly, forcing Zander backwards. He throws up his free arm up, clumsily deflecting the blows as he tries to put space between them.

"You think I'm going to let you kill me without a fight?" Rosita demands as she pummels him with the golf club, as though he were a mouse scurrying away from her sandal. "I'm not stupid. I know that cabrón sent you to do what it can't." Given the shortened striking distance, most of her swings lack enough momentum to do significant damage—

Zander trips over something and lands on his back. Rosita is on him in a flash. She raises the club for a finishing blow, but he kicks her squarely in the stomach. She releases a pained gasp and buckles over. With the wind knocked out of her, the golf club clatters onto the floor with a *klang*. Zander rolls onto his feet and kicks the club aside. He charges her, clutches her by her throat, and slams her painfully against the wall. She lets out a strangled gasp as the soft folds of her skin give in to his vice-like grip.

Zander pauses. His world freezing. Mind locking up.

This all feels too familiar: this irascibility. Striking a woman. Pinning her. Déjà vu?

Is this place playing with his mind?

He breaks his mind from the distractions. He brings the spear up with his other hand as he asks, "Where did they go?"

Rosita grimaces, tries to speak, but his grip is too tight. He lets off, and she replies, "¡Vete al infierno!"

"English, abuela!" Zander rattles her body with a rough shake. "WHERE DID THEY GO?"

Rosita spits in his face.

Zander snarls as he wipes the spit off with his shoulder. "Look... I'm just trying to get out of here and get back to my girl."

Rosita squeezes the choked words from her throat with a pained smile, "You're not... going anywhere. You're going to die... *here*... like the maricón you are!"

"Wrong answer!" Zander roars as he takes the spear and jams it up into her ribcage, piercing her heart. Her eyes go wide, mouth frozen open in pain, a single haggard gasp escaping her lips as she shudders violently. Then her head slumps to one side.

Zander retrieves the broomstick and backs away. Her frail body slides down to the floor as a bloodstain traces her path along the wall. She lands with an empty plop.

Zander's hands are shaking. He stares at the blood on the staff. On him. On the wall. All over Rosita. He's killed two people already, yet all of this, while surreal and somewhat unnerving, still feels vaguely familiar.

*Keep moving, Zander,* he thinks. *You didn't know the old fart, anyway. She means nothing.*

Zander leans over and grabs the golf club. With a cursory glance to Rosita, he says, "Worthless." He steps out of her office and eyes the rest of the floor. Scans for exits. There's one at the other end of the room. He rushes over and tries that door, but it's locked–

Someone sneezes from somewhere within the space–a stifled sneeze.

Followed by several mumbled voices. Indistinct chatter that is quickly fading.

Zander moves towards the wall, towards the voices. He hears several men talking, muffled and indiscernible, but audible.

*It's them,* he thinks.

Zander backs up, studies the wall. It cuts clear across a path of cubicles and butts up against Rosita's office. He hurries into her office and the first thing to catch his attention are the blueprints sprawled across the table.

*Guess I caught the old bag by surprise before she could clean this up.*

Zander pours over the top page on the stack. He quickly gathers it's the very room he's in, as Rosita marked it as *Mi Oficina* in red ink. Then traces a shaft outlined in dashes that goes from this office to a stairwell that is marked *Secreto* in red ink as well.

Zander makes quick work of the room, tearing away the white sprawling vines, which yield clouds of particles in protest. He rips pictures off the walls, tosses the old monitor aside and moves furnishings out of the way until he finds the slab of drywall secured by a few nails. He lays down his golf club and uses the spear to pry the flimsy piece off the wall.

The drywall gives way with little fuss, revealing the shimmering aluminum skin of a large AC duct that only goes in one direction–towards where the stairwells are on the blueprints.

Zander kneels down and peers inside, listens intently. The slight scuffing of shoes against metal and hushed whispers travel toward him. He rises, searches Rosita's desk, and spies a flashlight. He flicks it on to make sure it works. He sheaths the spear under his shirt, securing it between his shoulder blades. Then, with his golf club, climbs into the AC duct–

"Hey, puta!"

Zander turns to see Rosita on all fours, glaring at him. Blood seeping from her lips and gushing from her chest. He stares at her, shocked that she's still *alive.*

Rosita holds up a shaky, clenched fist, as if to hand him something. Her fingers unfurl, she exhales, and a cloud of white dust masks his face.

He coughs violently. Waving off dust, he shouts, "What the fuck!"

When the cloud dissipates, he finds her face first on the floor in a pool of her own blood.

"Twisted old fart."

*Whatever,* he thinks as he dusts himself off. *No more distractions.*

*One down.*

*Three to go.*

*Vicky, I'll be seeing you soon, baby.*

# Chapter 44 – Eternal Duct

Bishop leads with the flashlight as Mike and Wayne trail close behind, crawling at a steady pace through the duct. There are white vines all along the inside of the duct, and occasionally they crunch their knees against them as they pass or have to maneuver over a carpet of rambling creepers.

After a lengthy time crawling, Wayne asks, "How much farther until we reach the stairwell?"

"No clue. We keep going until we hit the grating," Bishop says.

"Well, what do you see ahead?" Wayne asks, grimacing as his shin clips a twisted knot along the floor of the duct.

"More ductwork," Bishop replies.

Beads of sweat gather along their foreheads as they traverse the narrow conduit.

Wayne swipes a forearm across his face, wiping away the sweat as he says, "You're a funny guy, Bishop."

A sharp spasm stabs at Bishop's wrist where he was hit with the stepladder. Crawling like this is only exacerbating the nagging ache. "And you're a pain in the ass."

"So, I've been told."

As they continue through the narrow duct, Wayne snorts. Then sneezes several times in a row.

Mike pauses, looks back. "Yo, you alright?"

"Yep," Wayne answers as he rubs his nose. "I'm just peachy."

"Peachy?" Bishop scoffs. "You've been sneezing since we climbed in here."

"I guess it's your cologne," Wayne retorts, laughing at himself. "I thought Drakkar Noir died with the Eighties?"

Behind them, Wayne hears something clatter. He freezes in place.

"W-what was that?" Wayne asks.

"What was what, man?" Mike asks, with a frustrated groan in his voice.

Bishop flips the flashlight back in their direction. "Yeah, now what?"

"You guys didn't hear that?"

"No, Wayne," Mike replies, gritting his teeth. "Bro, all we hear is you."

"No, I heard something." Wayne glances over his shoulder at the enveloping black behind them. "Behind me. I swear."

Mike seizes the flashlight from Bishop, barks at Wayne, "Get out of the way!" He shines the beam of light into the belly of the duct. "Ain't nothing there, bro, so stop trippin'." He hands the flashlight back to Bishop. "Now keep moving. Let's get the hell up out of here and finish this."

They crawl on for what seems like an eternity, but really isn't. The white vines follow them along the way. They finally reach a grate which is weaved through with white vines, allowing light to spill in from the stairwell on the other side.

"We made it." Bishop tests the grate. Despite the invasive foliage, it's still held securely in place. "Back up!"

Mike and Wayne comply.

Bishop pushes back against the duct wall, brings up his leg, and with one solid kick, sends the grate flying outward. It rattles around on the stairwell like a fallen coin as the three of them file out from the duct, grateful to no longer be confined to such a claustrophobic space.

As they make their way out, they pause and marvel at the stairwell. It is well lit, walls teeming with Rosita's white vines, climbing in both directions. Just as on the ninth floor, these vines are dotted with the tiny yellow flowers. Flakes of mold spores float in zigzag patterns, falling gracefully like minuscule leaves.

Wayne sneezes hard.

"Jeez, what is going on with you?" Mike asks.

"I don't know!" Wayne wipes the snot from his nose using his forearm. A bloody, phlegmy streak trails from his wrist to his elbow. "This crap is tearing me up!"

"Well, this *crap*'s keeping us alive," Mike snaps as he heads down the stairs. "Now come on! Let's get to the first floor, then the basement."

Bishop follows.

Wayne lags. He peers down at the spiraling repetition of flights below, watching as Mike and Bishop circle down to the eighth floor.

Mike glances back up at him. "The heck?" Mike waves him on. "Come on."

Wayne groans. "I'm sick of stairs. My knee's killing me."

"I don't want to hear it, bub," Bishop calls back. "For chrissakes, I got scars older than you."

"Yeah, move it, man." Mike shakes his head and keeps going, calling after him, his voice trailing as he descends, "We ain't gonna hold your hand."

Wayne closes his eyes. Tries not to dwell on how exhausted and achy his body is feeling right now. Mike and Bishop's footsteps echo throughout the stairwell.

"Wayne!" Bishop shouts from further below. "Come on! Get your ass down here!"

*The old geezer's right,* Wayne thinks. *Get my fat ass moving, so I can get back to porn and pizza and my pretend future Colombian girlfriend.*

Wayne jogs down the stairs to catch up with the guys. His feet moving in a sort of quickened one-two-one-two cadence, when he is suddenly pushed from behind. He loses his footing, at first slipping down the first few steps, then tripping and tumbling onto the flight below.

Mike and Bishop stop. Their shoes screeching as they halt. "Hold up," Mike tells Bishop. "Wayne? Hey Wayne, you good?"

Wayne wobbles to his feet, grimacing, with a hand to his lower back, he straightens up to find Zander standing before him, blood stains all over his clothes.

"Zander?" Wayne shivers as he stammers, "Wh-what the heck happened to you?"

Zander stares him down with a caliginosity in his eyes, as if they were black holes incapable of reflecting light. He's holding a golf club in one hand, the bloodied spear in the other.

Wayne's gaze falls to the weapons, then back at the crazed Zander at the top of the stairs. His back against the wall, he now wishes he had stuck with the guys. "Y-you don't look so hot."

Zander steps down the stairs toward Wayne. Then another.

Very. Deliberate. Steps.

Wayne jumps up and sprints, gunning for the next floor down as he cries, "Guys! Zander is here!" Without looking back, the hairs along the skin of his neck prickle with panicked anticipation as he jogs as fast as he can, winding around the seventh-floor stairwell onto the sixth-floor landing.

"Hang on!" Mike calls up. "We're coming!"

But Wayne doesn't hear them.

He's busy evading Zander. Practically tripping down the stairs, propelled by the impending thundering of Zanders footsteps right behind him.

Wayne rounds the next flight, glaring down at a wide-eyed Mike and Bishop, just a single floor below him as they both shout up to him, "WATCH OUT!"

"BEHIND YOU!"

Too late.

Wayne screams out as the bloodied end of a spear erupts from his stomach.

# Chapter 45–Be Useful

F or a moment, all time seems to stop, allowing Wayne to stare in shock at the bloodied end of the makeshift spear protruding from his gut.

*Oh my god,* Wayne thinks. *He stabbed me! He really stabbed–*

The blood-tipped spear disappears from Wayne's abdomen as it is pulled in reverse. He places a futile hand to the gaping, gushing wound on his stomach and U-turns into a stone-faced Zander.

*He stabbed me.*

The pain is like nothing Wayne has ever experienced.

"I never liked you, fatso," Zander says.

*Eggie,* a voice whispers in Zander's head. *Call him Eggie.*

"Or should I say, Eggie?" Zander prods and readies the spear for another go.

Eggie–that blasphemous moniker goes off like a tactical nuke inside Wayne's head.

*Eggie?* Wayne mentally chews on the word as the flush that comes with losing blood seems temporarily superseded by the rush of adrenaline that has flooded his system.

Zander lunges at Wayne with the spear but misses as he slides out of the way, then throws a shin kick that earns a strained grunt out of Zander.

"Wayne!" Mike shouts from below, but Wayne can't hear them because something has just exploded inside his mind, blotting out the peripheral noise and distractions save for this crazed asshole in front of him.

Zander.

Just another bully.

Zander uttering that hateful name ignited a repressed ball of fulgent anger that has been festering inside Wayne since he was a teenager. The butt of so many jokes, so much bullying. So many days he cried, alone, hidden from the harsh eyes of his hypercritical parents. The haunting taunts of Chet. His father's stern, stoic voice, telling him to deal with the pain.

To make something useful of himself.

Zander recovers, spins on his heels and swings wildly, first with the spear and then the club, but Wayne's keeps his distance. His feet act on autopilot, pre-programmed by years of training to avoid attacks. To deal with Chet. But no, Chet wasn't here. Zander took his place. Another bully in his godforsaken life.

*I'm going to make something of myself,* he thinks.

Zander roars as he whips around, taking the golf club with him. But Wayne leans back, and the club sails uselessly through the air. With one hand clutching his gut, he brings his other hand up and punches Zander in the ribs. Zander wheezes, loses his grip on the spear.

*I'm going to make something of myself.*

*Going to rid this world of one more asshole.*

Zander brings the club around, countering clumsily, but Wayne has already closed the distance. He throws all of his body weight against Zander, pinning him against the railing.

"Get off me, Eggie!" Zander protests as he tries to break free.

The mention of that heinous nickname condenses within Wayne's mind like a laser beam, propelling him to ignore the mortal wound that will soon steal his life...

And to deliver one solid, Taekwondo inspired knee to Zander's groin.

Zander buckles with an unearthly growl.

Mike and Bishop charge up the stairs in time to see Wayne wrapping Zander in a great bear hug. As Wayne takes the two of them over the railing, with Zander screaming in his ear, he thinks,

*I'm finally doing something useful, Dad.*

*I'm finally useful.*

*I've made something of myself.*

"Wayne!" Mike calls out as he and Bishop race to the railing, only to watch the two men plunge to obscurity below.

# Chapter 46–Organic Matters

Both Mike and Bishop stare over the railing, speechless.

"What... what on Earth just happened?" Bishop stammers, gazing blankly below. Trying to process Wayne's sacrifice.

"Wayne saved our asses. *That's* what happened." Mike grabs Bishop by the shoulder. "Don't wanna sound cold, but we'll grieve later. Let's go kill this thing!"

Bishop breaks away from the railing and they proceed down the stairs, keeping an eye out for Zander or any other surprises. Nothing so far. But they notice the vines are thinning out as they reach fifth, fourth, and third floors. Even the moldy flecks, floating about, are less abundant.

Conversely, the further down they go, the less light there is, and the walls become suffocated by black vines–those belonging to the *cabrón*, as Rosita would put it–gripping the wall like soiled fingers.

Bishop states breathlessly, "You're seeing what I'm seeing, right?"

"That things are getting dark?" Mike answers, equally taxed. "Yes, sir."

As they descend to the third floor, then the second, they discover black vines are everywhere. Choking out the light fixtures, adding to the obscurity. Coiling around the railing. Crisscrossing from one side of the stairwell to the other. Weaving through the madness proves challenging, but they manage.

Then they finally reach the poorly lit first floor. What little ambient light from above that strains to reach them is a welcome gift. At their feet is a ribbed carpet of bemired, fibrous vines, smothering the concrete floor. Along the walls, a gnarled webwork of the putrid plant's spindly appendages are splattered against those surfaces like inky paint. The vines are everywhere and there's not a sign of Wayne or Zander. Where they expected to find two corpses, wrenched in a morbid embrace, skulls shattered, blood everywhere...

There are only more vines, thick ones, thin ones, knotted ones, spiky ones, all shrouding the floor.

"What?" Mike surveys the room, then searches Bishop's face for an answer. "Where'd they go? Where are the bodies?"

Bishop shakes his head, equally stumped.

To make matters worse, the men realize they can't find the access point to the basement since the walls are masked by the invasive foliage. Mike regrets not ripping off the top page of blueprints, giving them at least some idea of where to look within this clustered, mangled mess for a door. Rosita ushered them out and, in their haste, they failed to grab it. Armed with only a spear, a backpack of mold, and the waning glow of a flashlight, it's hard to tell which wall is which. Still, Bishop tries. He aims the beam from left to right, up and down, until finally something catches their attention–a bundle of vines moving. They unravel, releasing something:

Wayne's slumped body.

Several ends of vines protrude from his belly like horns. A circle of blood outlines each of the exit wounds. His body spills aside as another curtain of vines behind him parts, unveiling Zander who leaps out, swinging wildly with the golf club.

Mike dodges, but trips on a vine, dropping his spear. He crashes onto his side. Several barbs tear into the skin on his arm as he bumps his head on an unforgiving black knot, blurring his vision.

With Mike down, Zander goes for Bishop. Swings again. Bishop tries to block the attack, but the face of the golf club strikes him just below the left elbow. He howls as the pain drops him to his knees.

Zander's shoulders rise and fall as he says breathlessly, "You're probably wondering how I'm still alive?"

Bishop grinds his teeth together, cradling his arm, trying to suppress the agony.

"The vines. They stopped our fall." Zander chuckles, amused, and adds,

234

"But only one of us had a lucky landing."

*Keep going, old man,* Bishop thinks. *This hurts like a bastard, but you can't let this sonofabitch get away.*

The pain is brutal, to the point of nearly stealing Bishop's breath. Still, he asks, "Wh-who's blood is that?"

"Oh, that annoying old fart, Rose. Rosie—"

"It's Rosita, you asshole!" Bishop wobbles to his feet. "You killed her?"

"Sorry, but I'm doing what I have to do to get back to my life. To my Vicky. And *you people*," he seethes as he points at them with the club, "are the only things standing in my way."

"You're a sociopath."

"Sorry about your fat friend too." Zander winds up the golf club. "But he was annoying as fu—"

Bishop flings the flashlight at Zander, who flinches, distracting him just long enough to allow Bishop to leap from the ground. He throws a right hook, clipping Zander's chin, sending him hobbling backward.

Mike pushes himself up, spins on his heels, and charges. With arms outstretched, he tackles Zander. Takes him down with such force, blood spurts from Zander's lips as he's driven to the floor. Mike doesn't let up. Straddles and pins him against the uneven bed of vines beneath his back.

"You're gonna pay, asshole!" Mike punches Zander, knocking his head to one side. "Gonna pay for what you did to Wayne!" Another punch. Zander's head is popped the other way. "You hear me?"

Zander accidentally releases the golf club. Bishop seizes it. Tells Mike, "Move." Mike climbs off Zander as Bishop raises the golf club high above. He brings it down—several vines shoot out from the wall and grab ahold of the club, stopping it midair and tearing it from his hands. It disappears into a dense heap of vines splayed across the wall—but in its efforts to capture the weapon, the heap has thinned out, and it inadvertently reveals what it was hiding:

The exit door.

Bishop and Mike turn to stare at the basement entrance—

Mike is struck in the back of the head by Zander's fist, right at the base of the skull. The dizzying blow sends Mike stumbling to the ground.

Zander goes after Bishop. Throws several haymakers in Bishop's direction, but lacking the fighting experience that Bishop has, he misses every time as Bishop sidesteps the sloppy punches. He counters, delivers a sold jab to Zander's nose with his right hand.

Zander moans. Instinctively cups his face.

Bishop closes the gap. Like an enraged bull, he follows up with a left-right-left-right combo that flattens Zander, putting the asshole on his back. Bishop's left arm is ablaze with pain from the assault, but he ignores it, adrenaline assisting in the distraction. He sticks a hand out and helps Mike back up.

"Bastard got me good," Mike admits as he rubs the back of his head. "Sucker punched me!"

"Forget him. Come on." Bishop gestures towards the exit door. "That's the way out." He points at the vines masking the door. "Get the powder. Toss it at those vines."

Like some indestructible robot from Hell, Zander is already getting back up. "You're not touching Vicky!" he shouts as the vines writhe under him, making him float onto his feet as if coming off a crowd-surfing adventure. "You hear me?"

"I hear you, dickhead!" Mike moves toward Zander–

Bishop stops him and says, "I'll handle nut job. You clear the door."

Mike nods. Goes to the exit door, reaches into the backpack, and nabs a handful of white powder. The barbed vines wriggle to life, as if sensing his intent, and one of those vines whips at Mike. But he leans back, avoids the flogging, and flings the white powder back at the vines.

The result is immediate.

The vines go white, shriveling on contact with the substance. There's even an accompanying screech that reverberates throughout the stairwell.

Bishop grimaces. While the pain from his wrist and elbow is blinding, the newfound rage he has towards this psycho, multiplied by the amount of adrenaline in his veins, mutes the discomfort. He brings up his one good fist, eye level, and gestures for Zander to come at him.

Zander lowers his gaze, narrows his eyes, and rushes Bishop. He roars as the vines fan out behind him like the feathers of a peacock.

Bishop flicks his wrist, exposing something gold and shiny–the antique scissors. As Zander and his viny appendages crash down onto Bishop with the force of a tidal wave, he jams them straight into Zander's neck.

"Bishop!" Mike shouts and breaks away from the door.

The curtain of vines blankets the two men, but Mike flings a handful of the powder at it. The vines crumble, revealing a gasping, bleeding Zander on top of Bishop. Mike kicks Zander's body aside and gets the old man to his feet.

"You ok?" Mike asks.

"Yeah..."

The two of them gaze down at Zander. Flat on his back. Glaring up at them with hate-filled eyes, burbling a mouthful of blood. His quivering hands grasp at the golden shears impaling his neck as blood pools from behind his head.

"That's a gift from Rosita," Bishop says with a snarl. "Feliz Navidad, asshole."

Zander stares up at them, gurgling, choking on his own blood.

Mike snatches up his spear, then pats Bishop's shoulder, urging him along. Bishop picks up his flashlight, along with Zander's spear, and they make for the door which is now completely clear of vines.

"The dust worked!" Mike exclaims.

But as they throw open the exit door that leads into the basement–they find that their journey into the belly of the beast is much more than they expected.

# Chapter 47–The Slick & Sentient

M ike and Bishop step into the darkened basement. The miasma of muck and manure dominates the air, forcing both men to cover their noses with their shirts. They descend a short flight of stairs but stop halfway as the bated beams of flashlights dance along the glinting surface of what appears to be water below.

The two men share a look, then seeing as it's the only way to go, they take a step into the water and feel their feet and lower legs go cold and wet.

"The heck is this?" Mike exclaims as he shines the light down at the murky water, which goes up to their shins. "It's like a God-blessed sewer, man." The water is full of detritus and floating, fleshy chunks, like some biotic soup. One chunk drifts up against Mike's leg and he casts his flashlight on it, revealing that it's a spongy, waterlogged half of a human hand.

Mike instantly turns and heaves.

Bishop recoils at the site. He lays a hand on Mike's shoulder. "Ok there, boss?"

A string of drool dribbles down from Mike's chin and he wipes it furiously. "I'm alright."

*Be better when we're outta here,* he thinks.

They scan the room with the feeble glow from their flashlights. The walls are oozing, glossy as the insides of the mouth of a whale. Color is hard to discern. The ribbed black vines extend everywhere. There's an opening straight ahead–or what looks like the only way to go.

They slog through the muddy, shallow water, enduring the effluvium, certain they are trudging through the sewers of this building. As they progress, they hear movement behind them. Mike whips his flashlight around, sees several dozen vines dangling down.

The vines suddenly retract and disappear upwards with a hiss.

"Damn things are everywhere," Mike complains as he combs the room with his flashlight.

Bishop nods, though Mike probably doesn't see it in the dark.

They press on, one disgustingly wet step at a time. Bishop keeps his light aimed straight ahead. Mike continues to survey the walls and the ceiling, and anytime the pale swath of his light lands on a blanket of vines, they shrink away, as if the light itself hurts them.

"You're seeing this, right?" Mike asks.

Bishop nearly loses his footing on whatever is under his feet. Recovering, asks, "Seeing what?"

"Anytime I shine the light on them, they disappear. You think these things fear light?"

"No." Bishop squints, straining to see. Ahead is a set of steps that lead to a door. "It fears us."

Mike asks, "Think so?"

"Clearly it's sentient. And it's been in our heads. It has also physically seen that we have something that can kill it. So, it's trying to get the jump on us."

"Well, that ain't going to happen." Mike shines his light on every angle, every surface of the room. Sometimes he finds vines, sometimes he finds just the great trunks of the plant, thick and smooth with moisture.

*God only knows what that liquid is. Water? Or blood?* Mike shivers at the thought.

They climb up the steps, get to the door and, to Bishop's surprise... it's open. "So, this door is unlocked? Of all the doors in this building?" He looks back at Mike. "Why? Why let us just walk right in?"

"Maybe it wants us to come in." Mike pauses. "Maybe it's a trap."

The door into the next room opens with an unnerving screak, and both Bishop's and Mike's eyes widen at what they see next.

# Chapter 48–Bathed In Blood

**M**ike and Bishop enter the basement and are immediately struck by the foul, meaty funk of the previous room, coupled with a distinctive coppery, metallic scent. Aside from the stench, the air is thick and damp, weighed down by the humidity of a steam room.

"Blood," Bishop says, and Mike shoots him an incredulous look. "It smells like blood."

They cover their noses with their forearms as they move in. To their surprise, the basement boasts better lighting than the stairwell, illuminating just how rampant these vines' infestation is. The walls are teeming with brambly black shoots, some as thick as telephone poles. A myriad of wild shoots claw at the ceiling like the spindly fingers of a giant. Other vines dive into the concrete floor, rendering entire sections of the subfloor swollen and broken by the aggressive weaving rootstock.

"This shit really is everywhere," Mike marvels.

They approach a railing perched above a walkway that encircles a large pool of the same nebulous water they trudged through in the hallway. Unfortunately, under the improved lighting, Bishop's assessment is confirmed.

The pool is indeed filled with blood. A veritable crimson lake is liver-red, a shade darker and deeper than rosewood. Littering this blood pool are indiscernible, pale yellow objects, wafting about like the scattered remains of a recent shipwreck. At the center of the pool is an imposing trunk that towers above them like the grandiose centerpiece of a macabre fountain. Covering its shaft are oval bumps, roughly the size of footballs. Mike aims his flashlight at the trunk and it becomes clear these are not footballs—but faces.

Everywhere.

Frozen mid-scream. Mouths gaping, teeth bared, tongues dangling. An organic sculpture of gore adorned with the reliefs of those ill-fated souls trapped within it.

"Dear God," Bishop mutters.

They shine their lights on the drifting debris in the water for a second look, gasping as they realize these are not indiscernible objects. They're heads.

Human heads.

Bobbing up and down like driftwood, drenched in crimson streaks that glimmer along their sodden skin.

Mike directs his light at one head—one that he recognizes.

*No way. No freaking way! That's the kid who left,* he thinks. *That's Kyle.*

Only Kyle never left SiDug. Instead, he somehow ended up here, becoming just another ingredient in this broth of body parts.

"This..." Bishop glares at the horrendous sight. "This is what Rosita was talking about," he says as looks to Mike. "The grand root."

Mike flings the backpack around so that he can easily get to the powdered mold inside. "Well, I'm gonna put some weedkiller on this bitch right now—"

"Not so fast!" A familiar voice booms from the other side of the room.

Mike and Bishop catch Mr. Gudu appearing from behind the root. He approaches with a casual gait, wearing a perfectly pressed suit free of blemishes and blood.

"I wouldn't do that if I were you. Not if you want to see your friend..." Mr. Gudu pauses, recalling her name, "Kate. It's Kate, correct?"

"You should know," Bishop reminds him. "You hired her."

"I've hired many people." Mr. Gudu stops short. Chuckles. "If you do this long enough, all of your employees blend together like one long sentence with no commas."

"This ain't English class, asshole," Mike says, shaking his spear in Mr. Gudu's direction.

"Indeed. Based on your usage of our shared vernacular, we are not within

241

the confines of an educational institution." Mr. Gudu places a hand to his heart and exhales, feigning offense. "I have heard the English language develop throughout the centuries. From the dark ages, to the texting ages. What a shame the language has deteriorated to its current derivative state of informality, corrupted by the laziness of contemporary speech. Losing context in lieu of convenience. It's all so harrowing."

Mike turns to Bishop. "Is it just me, or did this jerk get a whole new personality since we first met him?"

Mr. Gudu waltzes slowly their way. "I have absorbed many personalities. Unfortunately, humans are so banal that it is rare when I have found something that is not a copy of a copy from centuries past."

"Whatever," Mike says. "Now where's Kate, Gudu-boy?"

"Gudu-boy?" He stops short and lowers his gaze at them, eyes shimmering with insult. "Do you even know what my name means?"

"That you're psycho," Mike replies.

"Not hardly, Michael."

"Don't call me Michael. Bitch, you don't know me."

"Oh, I know plenty," Mr. Gudu assures them as he gestures towards a bundle of vines. They wriggle to life, parting like a black curtain, revealing Reggie. He sneers at Mike.

Mike snarls. Shoulders heaving, fists balled up, he looks like he wants to knock Mr. Gudu out. "Like I said before, he ain't real. Reggie died."

Mr. Gudu nods. "Yes, yes. And that is thanks to you. Real or not, you killed him."

"You weren't there!" Mike takes a step forward, spear raised, but Bishop throws his good arm in front of him.

"Don't," Bishop warns calmly under his breath.

"No. Sadly, I wasn't." Mr. Gudu sighs, then clears his throat, continuing, "Anyway, as I was saying, my name is Sumerian–which is the oldest known language to man. And in English, *Gudu* translates to Divinely Anointed. The priest of the temple. This temple. I am the one who feeds my god."

"Your god is a damn weed," Bishop tells him.

"Says the agnostic." Mr. Gudu folds his hands together in mock prayer.

"You are hardly one to judge."

"We're standing in a room of blood, corpses, and vines, and you want me to suddenly believe in the divine?" Bishop argues.

"I want you *two* to think bigger." Mr. Gudu moves along the walkway, getting ever so close. "What if I could guarantee you both eternal life? No disease. No death. To live forever as I have. All thanks to the Source."

"The Source?" Mike points at the towering root. "You mean the shit-stack?"

Mr. Gudu's eyes blacken. "Don't you dare refer to the Source as that!"

"I'll call it whatever I want."

"The Source has been alive longer than you. Longer than your civilization. You were nothing but a figment in your mother's vagina, and her great-great-great grandmother's whore vagina before that!"

Mike boils with outrage. "What'd you say?"

Reggie laughs tauntingly. "He said your momma, grandma, and her great grandma were all whores."

Mike tightens his grip around his spear and marches toward Mr. Gudu—but Bishop steps in front of him.

"Mike, stop!" Bishop tells him. "They're trying to get us more worked up than we already are."

"You plebes just don't understand." Mr. Gudu rests his hands on the railing surrounding the blood pool and the grand root. "The Source can make you more than you ever would be on your own. It can give you eternal life—what more could you want? There's nothing out there in that bleak world you call life but the inevitable disease, depression, and death that awaits you. What sort of existence is that?"

"Real life," Bishop says.

"Hardly. You act as if the Source has nothing but vile things to offer. The Source has peeked into man's mind for many a millennium. The corruption in humanity's hearts and minds never came from the Source, but was already there," Mr. Gudu explains and motions toward the root. "But if you'll just allow it, the Source will show you what I have learned. That there is more meaning to life than what it can give you. The Source can give you more."

"No thanks. You want to stay tied to the strings of your puppet master," Bishop says, "you go right ahead."

"I can come and go as I please."

"That's why you're here talking to us. Because of your own free will, right? Or did this thing phone you in," Bishop taps his temple to make his point, "so that you can come reason with us because it's afraid? Because it's growing weak?"

Mr. Gudu takes a measured pause, repressing an urge to respond in a much harsher tone. His words are tempered, dancing on losing his cool. He declares sternly, "It's not growing weak."

Mike digs out a handful of the dust and a dash of it sprinkles onto the ground. The vines under his feet siss and shrivel.

Mr. Gudu eyes Mike's backpack.

"Let's keep this simple," Mike suggests, holding up the white powder. "Give us Kate and let us go. Or I dust both you motherfuckers. You and your plant-god."

Mr. Gudu waves his hand in the manner of a gameshow host at the grand root. It unravels, whirling in place like a tornado, to reveal Kate, restrained by a jumble of vines. Some crawlers feed into her mouth, into her nose. Some wrap around her waist and her limbs, trussing her.

"You can do that, but if you kill the root, you kill her too." With a smug laugh, Mr. Gudu adds, "Wasn't planning on that one, were you... *motherfuckers?*"

# Chapter 49 – Just A Pinch

"Here's the deal," Mr. Gudu tells Mike. "Give Reggie the backpack, and Kate goes free."

"And if I don't?" Mike asks.

"Then I will summon the four monsters she reviles, and with their jaggy tongues, they'll savor her like a fine aperitif. Imbibing upon her essence and her fears. Drinking in her intoxicating misery as she is bled dry and rendered a worthless scrap of desiccated meat." Mr. Gudu waves his hands in the air as if conducting a ghastly symphony, practically singing, "And you'll bear witness to every exquisite moment."

Several vines sneak up from the floor, attempting to grab them.

"Then you simps will be next," Mr. Gudu informs them. "The Source has delicious plans to torture you both for the next century."

Mike flings the mold at their feet, and the sibilating crawlers wither away.

"Tell me," Mr. Gudu asks as he studies the vines as they wilt, "just how much of Rosita's mold do you have in that pack of yours?" He spreads his arms wide, asks, "Enough to keep all of this at bay?"

"Yeah, Mikey," Reggie echoes with that unnerving giggle. "How much you got?"

Mike looks to Bishop, searching the old man's expression about what to do—

"Now, now, now. Don't overthink your decision." Mr. Gudu wags a finger in the air. "The Source loves to read minds regardless of how much energy it might take to do so."

Bishop scowls at Mr. Gudu and Reggie. "Then we won't think. We'll just act." And he shoves his hand into Mike's backpack, takes out a pinch of the mold, and eats it. He looks to Mike with an expression that says, *Do the same.*

Mike does. Takes some power and pops it in his mouth.

"What..." The confidence in Mr. Gudu's tone melts away. "What the hell are you doing?"

Bishop presses his hands to his temples, throws his head back, and hollers uncontrollably as if someone had just shoved an icepick into his brain.

His reaction is followed by Mike's. Eyes squeezed tight, hands clutching the sides of his head, it's brain-freeze on steroids.

Bishop recovers, catching his breath. "What are we doing?" he answers. "We're clearing our heads."

Mike feels an undeniable sense of relief and clarity wash over him. It's as if the fog and the veiled dread have been lifted from his mind.

"You both think you're so clever?" Mr. Gudu's smug demeanor evaporates like a puddle in the desert. "You can't outsmart something that has been here before Christ!" He shouts, "YOU CAN'T OUTSMART A GOD!"

Everything goes to hell:

Reggie rushes straight for Mike.

Several vines fire out from the grand root towards Bishop.

Kate's eyes flutter open. Her vision is blurry. Her glasses are missing. She tries to move and suddenly finds that she's immobile. She looks down to find vines coiled around her body, pinning her to this monstrous, black plant covered in fleshy ovals.

Faces.

Horrified, Kate tries to scream, but her cries are gagged by the crawlers in her throat.

The vines grab a hold of Bishop. One of them wraps around his bad arm and hand and squeezes so tight, he yells out. Another vine locks onto his leg.

As Reggie closes in, Mike lunges with the spear, but the childlike creature is agile. He giggles as he dances around Mike's attacks with ease.

"You little shit!" Mike makes another stab at Reggie, but the boy ducks, cuts behind him and hops onto his back, seizing the backpack's straps as if they were reins and Mike his horse. "Get off me!" He spins in circles as he attempts to grab hold of Reggie, but the kid doesn't let go.

Kate gathers herself as best she can. She squints, sees movement. Makes out Mike and Bishop and a kid. She utters a gagged, "Bishop!" but it comes out more like, "Bif-hopf!"

Bishop is yanked forward by the volley of vines, pulling him toward the grand root. He crashes against the railing encircling the blood pool. The vines draw tight, but Bishop wraps his good arm around the railing, digs in. A tug of war ensues and the circulation in his limbs cuts off.

Reggie cups his hand, smacks Mike's ear. The blow feels like an explosion in his ear. He staggers to one side, loses his balance and lands on his hands and knees. His spear rolls out of his hand.

Kate squirms, trying desperately to wriggle free, but can only get her left hand loose from the barbed vines keeping her tied to the cold, wet mass. She grabs the vine in her nose with her free hand, and once again, pulls with all her might—reinjuring the fresh wound in her nostril. She cries out in agony, squeezing her eyes shut as she tugs. The jagged cord bites into the soft skin of her inner palm, earning fresh blood from her grip. With a final pop, the cord breaks, and she wails in exasperation.

Bishop's grip falters. Muscles trembling, he is moments away from being jerked over the railing.

As Kate works at the vines in her throat, she powers through the ungodly pain, pulling until they snap free. She coughs up a bit of blood, gasping for air. She throws her head back against the grand root, eyes tearing up from the pain.

Reggie attempts to wrestle the bag from Mike's shoulders. The kid gets one strap loose, but Mike hooks his arm around the other strap, stopping Reggie from tearing the bag off his back completely. He throws a kick at Reggie; it's clumsy, but the foot hits its target. Reggie's head snaps to one side, and his neck tears open, exposing a network of vines. They swirl up from within his torso and pull the boy's head back onto his frame. Reggie then jumps onto Mike's back once more. Several vines emerge from the skin along Reggie's legs and dive into the fissures along the concrete. In one swift motion, the vines tighten, and Reggie and Mike are pinned together, anchored to the floor.

"Gonna get you back, chump," Reggie threatens. "Gonna suck the life out of you."

"You... ain't... Reggie." The side of Mike's face is glued against the concrete.

Bishop's arm twitches uncontrollably as he fights not to let go, but the vines drag him up onto his tippy toes. He glances over his shoulder, frustrated he can't help Mike. Then looks to Kate as she battles her restraints. Their eyes lock and he feels the weight of disappointment sink inside him.

*No! I will not let you down, kiddo,* he thinks as his shivering muscles are on the brink of failure.

Mr. Gudu casually walks over, squats next to Mike's head. Folds his hands as he says calmly, "The Source sometimes enjoys playing with its food too much. Isn't that right, Reggie?"

Reggie nods.

"We've learned this valuable lesson from you and your friends during this training session, and all good managers know that training is a two-way street." Mr. Gudu gives Mike a pat on the back and Mike grunts in protest. "So, thank you both for your contributions to SiDug. The Source and I will study your mold sample." He breaks the strap from Mike's shoulder, then snags the backpack. "Then we'll kill it off. Just like we did that pain in our ass, Rosita."

Mike practically spits out the words, "Fuck you and your shit-stack!"

Mr. Gudu is just about to zip the backpack shut when the door into the basement is thrown open with a loud thud.

Everyone turns to see—

A blood-soaked Wayne stumbling in.

# Chapter 50–The Resignation Club

Wayne waddles like a penguin toward Mr. Gudu and Mike.

Reggie hisses at the sight of him.

"You just don't want to die," Mr. Gudu laments as he rises.

Wayne mumbles something to himself. Blood spills from both his lips and from the gaping holes in his torso. He looks like he's been riddled with an automatic weapon, yet somehow survived. His gait is limp. His expression is vacant, staring beyond the grand root, as if staring off into the horizon. His hands are tucked behind his back, as if trying to prop himself up as he shuffles their way.

Mr. Gudu narrows his gaze.

Wayne mumbles again, and this time his slurred words are more audible. "Make... somefin..."

"What are you doing?" Mr. Gudu demands as he takes a step towards Wayne. "You should be dead!"

"Make... somefin... of..."

Still clutching the railing and grimacing, Bishop now hovers above the ground, about to go flying into the viny arms of the grand root to join Kate.

"What are you doing?" Mr. Gudu shouts at Wayne.

"Make... somefin... of..." Wayne stumbles closer.

Mr. Gudu's eyes widen, reading Wayne's shrouded intentions. He snaps his finger at Reggie, gesturing for the boy to attack.

"Make... somefin... of... yourself..." Wayne is almost upon the men.

Reggie tears away from floor, and the anchoring vines fall aside as he leaps from Mike–

But Wayne reveals what was behind his back. He swings the golf club at Reggie–connecting with the creature's head. Reggie goes sailing off, but being blessed with the dexterity of a cat, rolls onto all fours. He springs at Wayne and both of them tumble to the ground.

Mike jumps to his feet, rushes Mr. Gudu, and tackles him. The two scramble for the backpack, but Mike wrestles it free from Mr. Gudu's grip.

"You want something to study?" Mike asks as he scoops out a handful of the dust and flings it in Mr. Gudu's face.

Mr. Gudu goes berserk, clawing at his face as if it were on fire.

"Study that, asshole!"

"Mike!" Bishop shouts.

Mike spins around to see Bishop just about to go over.

"The bag!" Bishop yells, as he's seconds from being torn from the railing. "Give it to me!"

Suddenly Mike is at the end zone at UCF. This is the Hail Mary play that will make the entire game. This is the shot on the field that he never asked for. Pack in hand, he winds his arm back and launches it.

Bishop throws his hand in the air, catching the backpack just as the vines draw him right into the trunk of the vine–right into the awaiting, sharpened end of a spur. Bishop shouts in pain as the spur's jagged tip erupts from his chest, impaling him.

"BISHOP!" Kate calls out as she stares down at him from above.

Bishop gasps, then insists without looking up at her, "I'm good." As the blood gushes from his chest, he shakily stares down the spur protruding from his torso.

*Good* couldn't be further from the truth.

"Bishop, please!" Kate tries desperately to pry herself free but can't. "Bishop, you can't die on me!"

"It's ok, kiddo." As his trembling hands fall to his side, he flips the backpack upside down, dumping its powdery contents all over the base of the trunk. "I think your God... brought me here," he gasps as he clumsily gives the backpack one last shake, ensuring it's completely empty, "to kill some weeds."

The white mold goes everywhere, expanding like a sandstorm. Looks as if he's unloaded a sack of flour onto the root.

Bishop goes limp.

"Bishop!" Mike hops over the railing but is immediately thrown to the ground as the entire room shudders and shakes. The vines everywhere sizzle and shrink.

Kate's restraints weaken and she drops, sliding down the length of the rapidly crumbling trunk, joining Bishop at the murky foot of the root—she suddenly grabs at her head, struck by the same stabbing sensation that Mike and Bishop experienced earlier. As the remnants inside her brain from the Source fade away, she feels overwhelmed with an inexplicable sense of calm.

Reggie darts around the room screaming, as if consumed in flames, then bursts into a dense mass of dust.

The walls wobble, and the vines covering them turn gray, crumpling like singed paper. Streaks of white spread up the trunk of the grand root. It splinters and pops, distributing more of the mold as it does so.

Mike gets to his feet. Notices Wayne sprawled out on the floor, eyes open, staring emptily at the crumbling ceiling above. He runs to Kate, the blood water splashing all around him, as he takes her hand and pulls her to her feet.

"You ok?" he asks.

She nods.

They turn to Bishop, who's head is slumped forward. His skin is colorless. The spur in his chest quickly turns white and then disintegrates. Mike kneels and gives him a shake, but the old man is gone.

The room quakes violently. The grand root hisses like a huffing steam engine. The white dust expands into a niveous, snowy chaos that engulfs the room.

"We gotta go," Mike tells Kate—who quickly leans over and hugs the old man. "Come on!" He insists as he yanks her away from the banshee cries of the trunk.

As they climb over the railing, Mike scoops up the golf club that is lying near Wayne's body and they break for the door—

"Don't leave me!" a voice pleads.

Mike looks back to see Mr. Gudu wandering aimlessly about, arms outstretched. Hands clawing at the air before him. "Please, don't leave me!" His face is pockmarked with chalk-white sizzling holes, eyes sunken in like two bleached craters. "You can't just leave me here to die."

"Yes, we can!" Kate takes the club from Mike and swings with all her might. Lands a hit that sends Mr. Gudu spiraling down to the floor. "We quit, asshole!"

"Hell yeah, girl!" Mike exclaims with an approving nod. He eyes the grand root. It's engulfed in white flames. He takes Kate by her free hand and leads her out into the stairwell.

Out towards freedom from this nightmare.

# Chapter 51–Narcissism For Dessert

The sound of keys jangling pulls Vicky out of a deep sleep. She shoots up in bed, her voluminous auburn hair spilling across her forehead in a golden-brown wave as she tugs the satin sheets close to her naked body. She fumbles in the dark as she reaches for the lamp on her nightstand, then flicks on the light. As her eyes survey the room, all looks normal. The windows are shut. Their bedroom door is closed. Erik is nestled close, with his back to her, and his face buried in his pillow. Mouth slung open, he is snoring, though it's barely above a whisper.

*Ok. So, I was just dreaming*, she thinks dismissively.

On her nightstand, tucked between two empty bottles of Chateau Ste. Michelle, is her cell phone. She gives it a quick tap and the screen displays it is four in the morning–

Another rustle of keys turns her body to stone.

*Oh. My. God.*

The jingling keys give way to another sound–the distinctive click of a doorknob being turned. Vicky feels her insides ice over. She shivers uncontrollably as a thought, a smidgen of regret, invades her mind: *Why did I put off changing the locks?*

However, the procrastination wasn't wholly her own. Erik, in his limitless confidence, assured her that Zander didn't have the "balls to break in," and that he would change out the locks later this month, claiming that it was just a "five-minute job."

*Five-minutes,* she broods. *Should've changed the goddamn lock! Would've taken all of five minutes!*

"Erik." Without taking her eyes off the bedroom door, she throws a hand on his shoulder and shakes him. "Erik!"

The bedroom door creaks open and a figure stands at the threshold.

Erik snorts as he stirs, "Wha-wha-what?" As he rolls over, he rubs the back of his hand along his mouth to wipe away a bit of drool.

She can feel the stranger's eyes on her.

"Erik!"

The intruder steps in and the amber light from the lamp throws a swath of yellow across his face and the seven-inch Santoku knife he's wielding.

At the sight of the shimmering blade, she inhales deeply as if bracing for impact. She blurts out, "ERIK!"

"What, Vic! Jesus!" Then Erik sees Zander. Stiffens. Then goes from zero-to-sixty, shifting from dazed to disturbed, throwing the sheets aside and launching out of bed in a hysteric fury.

Zander lowers his head, glowering at the pair. His eyes are as dark as a moonless, starless night. Vast and void of any twinkle of humanity.

Upon seeing the weapon, Erik throws his hands up, palms forward. "Look buddy, I don't know what you want, but you need to leave."

Zander doesn't move. Doesn't even blink.

Erik takes a cautious step forward, hands still up. "Seriously, man. Leave or I'm calling the cops–"

Zander lashes out. The blade whips through the air, cutting a perfect invisible horizontal line across Erik's palms. He yelps and backs away, but Zander advances, carving X's in the air, slicing away at Erik. Blood spraying everywhere. Vicky cowers in the bed, screaming for him to stop.

But Zander doesn't.

Erik walks backwards, attempting to avoid the assault, but trips over an ottoman, landing him onto his back. Before he can even process the fact that he's in a compromised position, Zander is already on him. Straddling him.

"Stop this!" Erik pleads as he brings his arms to shield his face. "The hell is wrong with you?!"

Zander is a machine. A human blender. He swings the knife left and right, littering Erik's bony forearms with cut after cut.

"Zander, stop!" Vicky screams as she leaps off the bed and wraps herself around Zander's back like a knapsack, but that doesn't deter him. He backhands her, popping her in the nose. She flinches and slides onto her butt—

Erik shoots his hands up, grips Zander's throat and squeezes with every ounce of strength in him. He digs his fingers into Zander's windpipe, grimacing as he watches Zander squirm and try to break free from his grip. Zander goes cherry red, veins bulging, face swelling, but never releases the knife. Bypassing Erik's death grip, he wraps his free arm around Erik's arms, clearing just enough room for him to jam the knife into Erik's heart.

Erik's eyes grow as big as moons. As his grip falters, Zander easily swats his arms away. Tells him, "She's mine." He leans forward. "You understand me, you snake?"

"ZANDER, NO!" Vicky climbs over Zander, goes for the knife, but it's too late. Zander drags it across Erik's chest, sliding it between his ribs, slicing through organs, muscle, and flesh in its wake.

The lights in Erik's eyes dim.

Vicky goes hysterical. She jumps to her feet and punches and kicks Zander with abandon. But in his psychotic stupor, the ineffective blows do nothing to him. He rises as Vicky has already vaulted across the bed, diving for her cell phone. She tumbles onto the floor, crashing with the phone clutched against her. Hands shaking, she desperately dials 9-1-1 then brings the phone to her ear with one hand and points at him with the other. "YOU STAY AWAY FROM ME!"

Zander rounds the bed in a flash, and he's upon her. He pins her against the wall, snatches the phone from her hand, and hangs up—but not before she knees him in the groin. He winces, bows forward, gasping. She breaks free, cutting past him. Arms out, reaching for the door as if it were a lifeboat—

Vicky feels a sharp, maddening pain unlike anything she's ever felt before in her back. This is followed by an inexplicable, unnerving warmth. Something hot and wet spreading down her backside. The pain catches her off guard—she tries to breathe but finds she can't. She's spun around to face

Zander, with his hollowed expression, eyes vacuous and bereft of mercy.

Then she observes that vacant look on his face melting away as he gazes upon the end of the knife protruding from just above her left breast. His eyes well with tears and the corners of his lips drag down into a frown.

"Oh my god, baby, what did Erik make me do?" he asks as he covers his mouth with a bloodied hand. He drags his palm down his face, leaving behind streaks of red as he watches her collapse in his arms. She slumps to the floor, and he goes down with her. Cradling her in his arms, he rocks back and forth as he mutters, "No-no-no-no-no."

Her skin is still warm. The faint trails of her perfume still dance along her neck.

"Erik did this!" He squeezes his eyes shut and sobs into her shoulder. Between cries, me tells her, "Oh, baby, I'm so sorry. This is all Erik's fault!"

When Zander's eyes flutter open, his ears are greeted by the clamoring collapse of the surrounding stairwell. While the scissors in his windpipe keep him immobilized and just a die roll of heartbeats away from death, he is coherent enough to observe the chaos unfolding.

Whatever transpired in the other room, whatever Bishop and Mike did, Zander knows it has affected this place. Aside from the unexplainable prickle of pain he felt in his head earlier, followed by the inexplicable clarity, his assessment of the two men's actions is substantiated by the surrounding devastation. From the shuddering walls to the grumbling ground to the aggressive pale fire consuming the black vines, SiDug is falling apart.

As he lays wheezing and on the cusp of expiration, he watches the shadowy world around him transform into an etiolated mess of dying vines, going from a sooty black to a pallid grayish white as they wither.

But the destruction of the room is not the only thing he sees.

Two columns composed of vines arise from the floor. Like plants sped up in double-time by a high-speed camera, these vines loop upwards, weaving within themselves, changing colors, and becoming human figures.

Becoming Vicky and Erik.

Stark naked, hands clasping one another's, the couple approaches with funereal countenances.

Zander opens his mouth to speak, but with a mouth full of blood and a pair of scissor blades lodged in his throat, only a stifled gurgle comes out.

As the stairwell groans and twists, the lights flicker. And with each flash, the figures blink closer and closer, until he can see the gaping wounds on their bodies–the ever-present gouge on Erik's chest. And a similar laceration on Vicky's torso, perched above her left breast. Pink and glistening with gore.

Zander glares at her in horror. *Did Erik do this to you? Did he–*

"Stab me in the back with a knife?" Vicky finishes for him upon reading that bewildered look on his face. "No. You did, baby. Right after we broke up."

With a quivering hand, Zander reaches out to her, as if to protest, to say something meaningful, but all that comes out is an incoherent jumble, a dribbling of blood from his lips, and a distant moan.

The couple peers down on him now as if he were six feet in the ground, resting within his casket.

Vicky releases Erik's hand. With a beaming grin on her face that appears more contrived than genuine, she explains, "You tucked my murder away within the bowels of your brain. Hid what you did to me from yourself." She kneels next to Zander. He's still trying to say something, but she ignores his incoherent speech and taps his forehead with her index finger. "You see... denial is part of the grieving process. Part of the human experience." Her smile breaks. "But so is anger. And that's your wheelhouse, baby."

The stairwell thunders, threatening to collapse, but the couple is unphased, zeroed in on Zander despite the impending destruction.

"You blocked out that you killed us *both*." Vicky takes his hand. Vines slink out from her fingers and wrap around his, biting into his skin. "Then you drove out to the middle of an orange grove, burned our bodies and took my ashes with you... to *our* new place." She laughs. "Your car. Where you've been living all this time. And then you signed on with my dearly devout, Mr. Gudu."

Zander attempts to protest, yet only a labored gasp is drawn from his throat. The one thing keeping him alive at this point is whatever dark energy

Vicky is sustaining him with via her vines.

"You told me how excited you were about the opportunity. About how our lives were going to change. And boy, did they!"

The floor roars as the slabs of concrete shift like tectonic plates, bucking and breaking under the strain.

"Fueled by your fervent jealousy, you saw only what you wanted to see." She squeezes his hand until the bones in his fingers snap. "And I thank you for that. You have been the most delectable madness I've gorged upon in an eternity." Through clenched teeth, she hisses, "I love me a good narcissist. They make the best victims."

Zander tries to move, but given the severity of his injuries, his health is failing as rapidly as the surrounding structure. As his body goes cold and muscles go limp, he watches Vicky's face hover above his, eclipsing the dwindling lights from high above.

"I know this because *you* know this, Zander. I am only a reflection of what is in your head." She smiles back at Erik as she says, "We are the ghosts of your sins. And this time, you're dying *with* us."

A trail of white ripples up the two figures and they burst into a towering cloud that smothers Zander like the deluge of embers following a volcanic eruption.

# Chapter 52—The Exit Interview

The stairwell LEDs coruscate like the sodium lights of a fevered disco. Vines siss and slough off the walls. Mike and Kate catch sight of what appears to be a Zander's body blanketed in white dust. Part of his face is exposed, eyes glued above.

"Come on!" Mike shouts.

They rush up the stairs to the first floor, kick open the exit door, and press on.

"This way!" Mike commands as they burst into the room with a jungle of cubicles on either side of them. It's snowing mold everywhere, making it almost impossible to see. Up ahead, a sputtering red exit sign marks their way out. "There!"

As they hurry for the door, the destruction behind them rumbles up through the stairwell and booms behind them.

"Don't look back!" Mike yells to Kate, as they sprint side-by-side.

But Kate does, glancing over her shoulder to see vines springing up from behind cubicle walls. Albeit blurry, she can tell that some of those vines have people attached to them, suspended from their noses like fish on hooks. Squirming, arms flailing, these people cry out as their respective vines crack and break under the pervasive mold—

"Dammit, Kate!" He barks between breaths. "I said, don't look back!"

They are almost to the exit door when Mr. Shimmer jumps in front of them. Decked in his impossibly massive boots and menacing armor, he takes a wide stance, unfurls his tongue, and bellows as if performing some bizarre haka.

Mike throws an arm across Kate's chest, halting her mid-stride. Their shoes squeak against the floor. Even without glasses, Kate makes out the monster's striking white face.

*You!* Kate thinks. *Thoughts of you tortured me my entire life!*

*MY WHOLE LIFE!*

*Screw you!*

Kate goes ballistic. Takes the golf club, charges at him, and swats him in the face with such force, she knocks his head to one side, almost parallel with the floor. He lets loose an unearthly screech as his neck is torn open, exposing the squiggling vines inside his torso to the moldy snowfall. As the flakes gather on the creature, he snarls at her through gritted fangs.

Without hesitation, Kate continues the assault, swinging wildly from side to side, breaking off chunks of his head as if he were made of plaster. Sending pieces of him flying outward with each whack.

"Kate!" Mike tries to stop her, but she shakes him off.

"Get off me!"

Mr. Shimmer falls to his knees and his broken skull flops sideways, scantily dangling by the wilting tendrils of his neck. Still, Kate does not let up. She brings the golf club over her head and hammers the creature.

The entire first floor quakes, and Mike nearly loses his footing. "Kate, we gotta get out of here!"

"NO!" she screams.

The ground beneath them balloons and breaks with a thundering clap. Mike is tossed against one of the cubicle walls.

Kate miraculously maintains her footing. She raises the golf club, and the creature sticks a trembling hand up to shield itself. With one violent stroke, she snaps his arm in half like a twig.

A vine reaches over the cubicle wall, lashes at Mike, but he darts away in time.

"Kate!"

Kate's rage knows no bounds as she pummels Mr. Shimmer with relentless blow after blow, as if to reduce his body to mush.

"Fuck you! Fuck you! Fuck you!" Kate chants as she bashes his skull in, revealing not bones, but more of SiDug's rancid vines, bundled intricately to create this vile illusion from her childhood–

"Enough!" Mike snatches the club midair.

She looks to him, huffing, exhausted. Eyes drunk with hate.

"We're leaving!" He releases the club and pulls her along.

They bust through the exit door and come to the main hallway. At the far end are several sets of glass doors leading out to the street. The thundering behind them intensifies. Cracks branch across the tiled floor as if it were made of ice. From these fissures, white dust gushes upward, spewing more mold into the air.

"Go-go-go-go-go!" Mike takes Kate by the hand. They push through the double doors and jog out into the middle of the street. The fresh, late night air fills their lungs as they gulp it down in big breaths.

The ground around them vibrates and the shuddering building booms loud enough to shatter the windows of neighboring offices. Car alarms go off. Stray dogs bark. But amid the cacophony of chaos, neither Kate nor Mike looks back. Sprinting as fast as they can while the explosive sounds of SiDug's implosion saturates the air. As the crumbling structure folds in on itself, a discharge of dust billows out and in the wake of its collapse, the power goes out for several nearby blocks.

Still, Mike and Kate do not stop.

They haul ass, hurrying away from the commotion, until their legs burn with lactic acid and their hearts throttle within their chests. Running until they find themselves in a city park where they collapse onto the welcoming, damp grass, crashing flat on their backs, gasping for air.

As they lay panting, they gaze up at the gold fog of the city's streetlights that breaks away to the sparse, scattered stars that wink back at them.

"We... made it..." Mike says breathlessly with an enthusiastic laugh. "We freaking made it!"

"Yeah... we did."

"You..." Mike begins, still catching his breath, "you ok?"

"Yeah, I'm... good."

Mike sits up. Kate follows, resting Rosita's club next to her with the reverence due a Japanese sword that brought them through their last battle.

Sirens blare from all around as downtown Tampa bustles with the clamoring of first responders.

Mike winces, taking inventory of his wounds. His head is throbbing from the repeated blows. "You think anyone else survived?"

"Aside from us?" Kate asks with a grim expression on her face. "No. Everyone we left behind was probably too far gone for saving from that thing." She wipes the sheen of sweat off her face, then looks at him. "We were the new batch of food, Mike."

The staccato blasts from a firetruck's horn slice through the air, stealing their attention. They both stare blankly in the distance, blocks away where the debris, dust, and smoke swirls up in a great, expansive cloud, dissipating above the cluttered skyline. They look on as the glimmering lights of a parade of emergency vehicles draws close, splashing between the gaps of SiDug's neighboring buildings.

"What year is it?" Kate asks without abandoning her attention on the clamor ahead.

Mike takes a deep breath. "Last I checked, it was 2021. But for all we know, could be 2031?"

"Let's find out." Kate feels her pockets. Her expression sours as she searches her body frantically. "Oh, crap!"

"What?"

"My cell phone's gone." Kate pauses, recalls the last place she saw it. "I must've lost it back there."

"Hang on," Mike says as he fishes inside his pocket to find to his surprise that his cell phone *is* still with him. However, the screen is shattered, and the power button is mashed in. He tries to turn it on, but the button does not engage, and the phone never comes to life. "'Bout what I figured. So much for the simple way–" Mike looks up from his phone to see Kate stomping back towards SiDug. "Hey, where are you going?"

"To go get my car!"

Mike puts a palm to his face, totally forgetting about his vehicle amid their escape from the mayhem. *Shit*, he thinks. *My car! If the garage fell with the building, which it probably did, my ride's a pancake now.*

The sirens have died down as the area is swarmed with emergency personnel.

"Kate," Mike says as he catches up with Kate, who's beelining for the building, "I'm pretty sure SiDug's garage went down with the building. I mean it *was* attached."

Kate stops short. "Who said I parked in the garage?"

Mike raises an eyebrow.

"I hate parking garages. Too many dark places for creeps to hide in," she says as she hurries toward the pandemonium ahead. "I actually parked in the street. Just paid the toll for a full day."

"Must've been a lot of quarters."

"I used my phone to pay." Kate shoots him a look from the corner of her eye. "You sure it's 2021 in your world?"

"It was a joke."

Kate's expression is flat. "Well, let's pray that my car is there. If is it, then it *is* 2021."

"And if it ain't?" Mike asks, as he keeps pace with her.

"Then our life's about to get a lot more challenging," she says, quickening her steps.

*Please, God,* she thinks. *Please let my car be there!*

*Because if it isn't, then depending on what year it is, our lives will be completely different. Who knows if I still have a car? A bank account? An apartment? What about my family? What if it's been more than a few years? What if it's been, like Mike said, a decade? What then? Do they still even exist on this timeline?*

These thoughts plague her mind, and she breaks into a run. Mike does the same next to her.

They cut down a narrow street that runs right into the felled remains of SiDug's tower. Both it and the adjoining parking garage have been reduced to a mountain of rubble, consisting of dirt, cement, rebar, splintered wood, and fragmented slabs of marble. Above the heap of destruction, ripples of bone-gray soot, floodlit by the spotlights of police cars, cascade through the humid Florida breeze with an eerie gracefulness. The chalky stench of concrete chokes the air. Police tape off the area, EMTs bustle about, and firefighters assemble–all assessing the damage as they begin the unenviable task of searching for survivors, or worse, bodies of SiDug's victims.

They both pause at the site. Gawking like rubberneckers at a traffic accident. Other pedestrians and onlookers gather. The occasional passing car slows to a halt to gaze upon the wreckage, but the police officers along the road are quick to move them along.

Based on what Rosita revealed to Mike regarding SiDug's history on this earth, the authorities may unearth the remains of people who went missing, decades, generations, or perhaps even centuries ago. If perhaps these victims perished in possession of their driver's licenses or other organic material, such as DNA or dental records, their identities may be recovered.

"Come on," Kate says, breaking away from the site. "I parked over here." She leads Mike, and they round the corner. "I have to know what year it is. I have to know what's become of my life–our lives–since we've been stuck in that nightmare."

*Please, let it be there, God,* she thinks. *Please!*

Down a side street they go. The flashing red and blue emergency lights twinkle far behind them now.

"Where did you park? Alaska?" Mike jokes.

But no sooner do the words leave his mouth when Kate dashes towards her forest-green Nissan hatchback. She literally hugs it, pressing her face against the driver's side window, arms clutching the vehicle as if it were her beloved horse.

*Thank you, God!* she thinks as she shouts, "Amy's here!" Kate turns to Mike as she gives her car a pat. "She didn't leave me. That means it is 2021!"

"You named your car Amy?" Mike says with a chuckle.

"Yes, after my childhood cat–now did you hear me? It's 2021!" She then checks for parking tickets or a wheel lock clamp. Neither are present. Then studies the time on the parking meter and it reads EXPIRED. Under neath that is a label that reads, PARKING ENFORCED FROM 7 A.M. to 7 P.M.

Mike points at the meter. "Guess you got lucky they didn't tow you."

"Guess we got lucky we didn't die."

"Yeah," Mike says as his gaze falls to the ground. "Thanks to Rosita, Wayne, and Bishop."

Kate nods. Tears up thinking about Bishop but fights back the urge. Shifting mental gears, she exhales a deep breath then pats down her pockets. "Great. I left my keys back at SiDug with my stupid phone. But it's all good." Along the door handle is a five-digit keypad. She punches in a code and it unlocks, earning an exhale of elation from her. The car's door unlocks with a soft click. She hops in and feels under the driver's seat for her key fob. Once she retrieves it, she leans back in her chair with a grateful sigh.

"You keep a spare key *in* your car?" Mike asks.

"I've lost my other set more times than I care to admit." She extends her hand toward him, keys jangling. "Care to drive? I mean, it's difficult for me to see without my glasses. And since your car is... well..."

Mike gives a final glance back in the chaos's direction, then back to her. "Yeah. Sure."

Kate climbs into the passenger seat, and as Mike slips into the driver's side with his hulking stature, the hatchback does a little bounce. To Kate, he looks like a giant inside of a clown car and she chuckles at the sight of him.

"Definitely the tiniest car I've been in," he admits, grunting slightly as he digs under the chair, lifts the latch, and adjusts the seat back as far as it will go. With a deep sigh he says, "Can I just say how good it feels to sit down?"

"Can I just say how good it feels to get out of there?"

"Amen to that," Mike agrees as he starts the car.

They leave the carnage of SiDug behind them and cruise through downtown, headed for Kate's apartment just west of Tampa. Both reek of blood, muck, and the sludge of decayed matter, so he opens all four windows, keeping the stench at bay. Neither speaks. The only accompanying sounds are the whoosh of the salt-tinged bay air whipping against their ears and the distinct metal hum of the Kennedy Boulevard drawbridge vibrating beneath them as they cross the Hillsborough River.

Ten minutes pass and when they hop onto I-275, Mike finally speaks. "You know, the cops might snag video from SiDug's neighbors. Video showing us leaving before the place collapsed." He glances at her from the corner of his eye. Catches her staring blankly ahead. "Might make us look suspicious."

"I know, but I'm not afraid." From his peripheral, he notices that she's looking at him now. "Are you?"

Mike shakes his head *no*.

"Good, because we did nothing wrong," Kate tells him. "I'm fine with talking to the authorities and explaining this whole nightmare the best way I know how."

"And when you do," Mike laughs to himself, "they're gonna think we're crazy."

"I don't care." And with those three words, the steadfast way she declares them without a second thought, Mike senses he's speaking to a different Kate.

A Kate who is now a veteran of her fears.

"Talking to the police is the last thing I'm afraid of," Kate tells him. "After the hell we went through, do you want to know what I'm more afraid of?"

"What's that?"

"Wasting a single moment more of our lives," Kate says. "We owe it to ourselves and to the people we just lost, to live out our best life possible. No fear. No regrets."

"I'm totally tracking what you're preaching," Mike agrees with an affirmative nod.

They pull off at the next exit, taking a hard right onto one of Tampa's main veins, but given the late hour, it is devoid of traffic. Only a sparse number of cars populate the road. All the lights are green as far as his eyes can see.

"When you're ready to reach out to the cops," Mike says as he casts a quick glance in her direction, noting the exhaustion in her eyes–the same exhaustion he's feeling–before continuing, "Hit me up. I'll be right by your side."

"Thanks, but before I talk to anyone, I want to shower and, if I can... sleep."

*Sleep*, Mike thinks. *Lord help me if I can fall asleep myself given the things I've seen.*

The road seems to stretch like a rubber band, and Mike fights back the fatigue. Last thing he wants to do after surviving SiDug is fall asleep at the wheel.

Kate guides him to take a left at the next light, where they arrive at her apartment minutes later. They exit the car, and Kate asks him to wait outside while she runs in to get something. A few moments pass and when she finally emerges, she's holding a white cable, which she promptly hands him.

"What's this?" he asks.

"What's it look like?"

"A power cord for my cell phone?"

"Bingo," she says. "Also, I called you an Uber." Her eyes dart around, noting the hour. "Not exactly prime-time for car sharing, so they should be here in a few minutes to pick you up."

Mike winces. "They probably won't like how bad I smell."

"Guess you might have to tip them extra," she says. Then adds, "By the way, if I didn't already say it... thanks."

"For what?"

"For not leaving me behind back there."

"Of course," he says with a humble grin.

They exchange numbers, then the crunch of tires grinding on gravel steals Mike's attention as the Uber driver pulls up in a black Nissan Sentra. He marvels at how quickly they arrived. When he turns back to Kate, she's almost to her front door.

"Hey, Kate!" he calls out, and she looks back. "Thank you."

"For what?"

"For what you said. 'Bout wasting our lives." He gives her a thumbs up as he reiterates, "No fear. No regrets."

She smiles to herself, then bids him goodnight.

"Night," he says as he reaches for the Sentra's car door.

*Tomorrow starts a new chapter in our lives*, he thinks as he climbs into the backseat. *Actually... tomorrow's going to start a whole new book.*

*Hopefully, one that doesn't involve vines.*

# About the Author

Jonathan Chateau grew up reading books by Stephen King, Dean Koontz, and Michael Crichton. However, it was Fight Club—both the 1996 novel by Chuck Palahniuk and the 1999 film by David Fincher—that inspired him to pursue writing. He has also had a love of movies since he was five and was even named after James Caan's character, Jonathan E, from the 1975 cult classic, Rollerball.

He has completed five novels, Nightmares in Analog, The Death Wish Game, Faith Against the Wolves, Faith Against the Angels, and The Sprawling.

When Jonathan's not writing, he's working out, hiking, painting table-top miniatures like those from Warhammer or the Walking Dead, playing video games, eating spicy food, jamming out to Emo & EDM, or spending time with his family, friends and his spoiled cat, Boo.

He resides in the mountains of Gatlinburg, Tennessee.

To find out more about him, visit https://jchateau.com/

**You can connect with me on:**

🌐 https://jchateau.com

f https://www.facebook.com/JonathanChateauAuthor

**Subscribe to my newsletter:**

✉ https://landing.mailerlite.com/webforms/landing/z4g3x1

# Also by Jonathan Chateau

### Nightmares in Analog: Three Supernatural Tales
### Video is Dead

The fading memories Jacob has of his deceased mother are buried on a few VHS home movies. Recently haunted by recurring dreams of her, he sets out to pick up a used VCR and finds one at a local yard sale.

However, this is no ordinary VCR. According to the owner, this particular model not only plays movies, but it allows one to communicate with the dead.

Fueled by curiosity, Jacob takes it home and soon discovers that what he possesses opens a doorway to darkness, death, and lust.

### Energy Drink

Miller is frustrated. Hours at the gym and nothing to show for it. But once a coworker introduces him to RECRÜT, a sports energy drink that guarantees results, the gains come quick.

It isn't long before Miller attains the godlike physique he's always wanted. Unfortunately, these twelve little ounces come with a side effect – a high price he never expected to pay.

And the more RECRÜT he drinks, the more his world begins to unravel, uncovering a sinister side of himself he never knew existed.

### The Saltwater Marathon

For the past six months, Bryan Combs has been consumed with guilt. He cheated on his wife, Sirena, and fell for the seductive charms of his boss, Carmela. The adultery proved too great for Sirena to handle, so she hopped in her car and drove it into the ocean. Her body was never recovered.

While the fling may have ended, the remorse remains, and now Bryan buries himself at work, opting for late night shifts at the mall, often drinking himself to sleep in the back office of his once beloved job.

But everything changes the morning they show up...

Strangers at his office door... screaming, pleading and begging him to open the door because they're being pursued and desperately need somewhere to hide. As he awakens from his drunken stupor, he begins to wonder if this some sick joke put on by Carmela? Retribution against him for ending their torrid affair?

Bryan wouldn't be sure until he let these strangers inside. However, once he does, he soon witnesses for himself what has these people so afraid, so panicked, that he finds it impossible to stay caught in his spiral of self-loathing.

### The Death Wish Game

A one-way bus ticket to Florida offers Rodney the chance at a fresh start from his dead-end life in South Carolina. Unfortunately, somewhere along the ten-hour trek to Miami, the passengers are drugged, awakening to find themselves duct-taped to their seats and stranded in the middle of nowhere.

Their captor reveals himself, informing them they're participants in a game of survival. "The rules are simple," he tells them. "Follow the flares to reach the safe zone. Make it there, and you live. Stay, and they will come tear you apart."

Chaos ensues, and one-by-one the passengers are picked off in their seats. Dying within their restraints. It's a race against time, and those lucky enough to escape are forced to play the game, uncovering an impossible secret that has brought them together to face an ancient evil unlike anything they have ever known.

**Faith Against the Wolves (Travis Rail Series Book 1)**

Meet Travis Rail, transporter of supernatural goods. Aside from his martial arts proficiency, skill behind the wheel and solid track record of deliveries, what makes him qualified to do what he does is that he doesn't believe in the supernatural claims of his clients, keeping him objective, honest and detached.

Or so he thought.

When his latest client has him transport a chest containing something touched by Jesus, his world gets rocked. Not twenty minutes into the delivery the Rift show up – an underground cult hell-bent on collecting all the treasures of God. However, it turns out that not only were they after the chest; they were after Travis.

*Who are the Rift? Why do they want him dead? And is what he's transporting of Jesus?*

In his quest for answers, Travis is thrust into another delivery, carrying yet another one of God's treasures. And the closer he gets to completing this delivery, the more he learns that what he's delivering might just be bigger than the package itself.

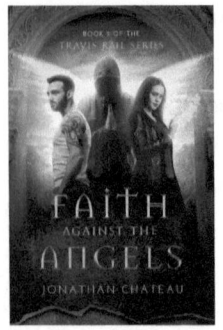

**Faith Against the Angels (Travis Rail Series Book 2)**

Following his last delivery, Travis retires to the mountains of Tennessee. Unfortunately, hiding from his new life as the Rift's most wanted, the Covenant's last transporter, and an angelic aberration proves impossible.

However, for Simon Lajudas, a wealthy and ruthless collector, Travis is an integral part in bringing his recently deceased wife back from the afterlife. He recruits a band of rogue angels known as the Amissa in pursuit of their mutually coveted treasure – the keys to Heaven.

But as Simon and the Amissa tear a path through the Rift's storehouses in search of these keys, war breaks out, angels clash, and the promise of the afterlife reveals something darker than they ever anticipated.